The VACATION Shift

The VACATION Shift

LILY CHU

Quill Tree Books
An Imprint of HarperCollinsPublishers

HarperCollins Children's Books,
a division of HarperCollins Publishers,
195 Broadway, New York, NY 10007

HarperCollins Publishers,
Macken House, 39/40 Mayor Street Upper,
Dublin 1, D01 C9W8, Ireland

Quill Tree Books is an imprint of HarperCollins Publishers.

The Vacation Shift

harpercollins.com

Library of Congress Control Number: 2025948582
ISBN 978-0-06-343062-4

Typography by Alison Klapthor

Printed and bound in the UK using 100% Renewable
Electricity at CPI Group (UK) Ltd

2 CPI 26

FIRST EDITION

MIX
Paper | Supporting responsible forestry
FSC™ C013604

To Nyla

Chapter 1

Since I turned sixteen, I've been living under a curse. Not a real one—or maybe it is, how could I know?—but it feels like it.

Six months ago, my parents separated and Dad packed his bags. I went from seeing him every day to only on weekends. Less than that, if he has a business trip.

Four months ago, they sold the house and Mom moved us into an apartment that meant an extra twenty minutes on the bus to school. Forty minutes a day. Two hundred minutes a week when I could be doing anything besides cringing away from men who keep spreading into my space.

Last month, I failed my first test ever. Literally ever. I'm good in school, although it's been getting harder to focus. I got 49 percent—so close, but Mr. Magon won't round up marks because that's the kind of teacher he is. Once he refused to let Shamira in because she was three minutes late. She had to go to the office for a pass and missed half the quiz, but he didn't care. He loves a good power trip.

Anyway, that grade should have been a knife to my guts, but I could barely bring myself to care. What bothered me most was having to listen to Mom's lecture about working hard, and how she expected better of me, then Dad telling me I would have to do more to get into a good university, and how he expected better of me. You'd think I was a complete failure instead of someone who forgot the impact of Vimy Ridge on the Canadian identity for an hour.

So, when the email arrives from Granite Lake Camp's human resources office, I stare at the subject line, which only reads Important information regarding your application. It has to be good news. The universe *owes* me. My first instinct is to text Connor, since he's the reason I applied to Granite Lake as a counselor in the first place, but I hold back. It's better to confirm it's positive, so I can be the bestest, bubbliest version of myself. Connor won't want to deal with me if I'm upset, and it's tough enough on good days to fake being the kind of cool, fun girl I know he likes.

After a deep breath that makes stars swim in front of my eyes, I tap the screen to check the email.

Dear Ivy, it reads. We're pleased to welcome you as one of Granite Lake's summer staff!

For the first time in ages, a jolt of energy pierces the veil that's been wrapped around me. Sometimes it's heavy enough to make breathing a chore, and sometimes I barely notice the weight, but either way, it's always there. I don't even remember when it arrived to cover me in its folds. Was it when I started high school? Maybe, but I'd been more excited-stressed than scared-stressed. When Mom and Dad's fights turned from loud and hot to quiet and cold? That makes sense. I suppose it doesn't matter, since it's so familiar now I notice it more when it's not there than when it is.

There's no point getting happy, though, since this is only step one. My entire plan to get Connor falling head-over-heels in love with me before he leaves for university in September hinges on *both* of us working at Granite Lake.

It takes forever for the PDF schedule to load, and I tap my feet impatiently on the bed. There, it's up, and my eyes immediately go to the first line. Connor Arnold. He's in. My heart gives a gigantic whump. I scan the rest of the rows. Addison Dare. We're more acquaintances than friends, but she's okay, and there are a few others I know. My own name, Ivy Yu, is at the end as usual. It's safe to text Connor, but I put the phone down. I thought I'd be thrilled about my plan working, but instead I feel a bit sick. I need to chill out.

Flopping on the bed, I close my eyes to think about Connor. He started at Granite Lake two summers ago. The second I saw him, I could barely bring myself to talk, let alone look at him straight. Connor was—is—tall, with sandy brown hair that flopped over his forehead and blue eyes that made me go red and giggly if he was around. Or more accurately, I went red and giggly if I wasn't embarrassing myself in the hope of impressing him. The expression on my best friend Hazel's face told me I was.

Embarrassing, that is. Not impressive.

When we came back to camp last summer, it took exactly one day to realize I was going to have to do more to charm a guy like Connor. I made a point of being super enthusiastic around him, and laughing at his jokes, and doing my makeup to perfection. The smile I got when I brought his favorite muffins (I lied and said I wasn't hungry) was enough to make me crumble.

Still, nothing happened last summer either.

We go to different schools, and although I fantasized about him getting my number off the Granite Lake group chat and asking me out, the silence dimmed my crush to a manageable level. Then, a few weeks ago, I finally gave in to Hazel's nagging that I go out with her. We arrived at her cousin's friend's party to see people spilling out to the backyard, cups and bottles in hand. It was loud and overwhelming, and I was searching for an excuse to go home when I caught sight of Connor walking through the kitchen wearing a black shirt and jeans, with a big smile that made my heart hammer so hard I could barely breathe.

It took some maneuvering, but I managed to casually bump into him in a dark hall and pretended not to recognize him at first, the same as he was doing to me. He'd been drinking, but he wasn't messy. I don't drink at all because I don't like losing control, but when he insisted on giving me some vodka, I decided why not, although it tasted disgusting and made me feel like choking. He leaned against the wall and asked me how I was doing before he said, "Damn, Ivy, were you always this cute?"

Then he kissed me until I couldn't breathe. It was my first real kiss. We had a connection. I *knew* it. When his friend came by, Connor grinned at me and shook his hair into his eyes before he left.

"See you," he said.

Connor Arnold's lips had been on mine. Connor Arnold's hands had been on me. I ran to find Hazel. I was dead.

Not really, though, and a good thing, because then I wouldn't have been able to replay his kiss in my mind every second for the next week, my stomach flipping up and down every time I did.

When Connor texted to ask me to a party the next Saturday, I made Hazel come. While she was talking to some people from her after-school acting class, I found Connor in the backyard. Before long, we were making out against a tree, his mouth wet and crushing on mine. I didn't complain about the branch digging into my back, not wanting to ruin the moment, although it hurt and later I found a bruise. I had stubble burn for two days, and Hazel made me splash my face in cold water before we left because it was so red.

"Do you know what you're doing?" she asked worriedly.

"It's good." I tried not to sound as jittery as I felt. "It's fun, that's all."

"Is it?" She cocked her head to the side. "You actually like

Connor. Do you know how he feels?"

I hadn't answered. I did like him, but didn't all this mean he liked me too? It must, and for the first time in months and *months,* I felt something instead of nothing. He messaged later that week to ask me over while his parents were out, but I'd been grounded after failing that test and couldn't go. Part of me was relieved to have the excuse, to be honest. Hazel had gotten in my head a bit. At least he usually replied when I messaged him.

I grab my phone and text Connor the news about Granite Lake. Twenty minutes later, I text him again, then decide to tell Hazel to get my mind off his delay. He probably hasn't had a chance to check his email yet. Or his messages.

Plan Connor is a go. Hazel's going to be working at her auntie's food truck this summer instead of Granite Lake.

Unlike Connor, she calls me immediately. "You got the camp job?" she demands. "I'm glad your sacrifice to the gods was successful. Is he working there, too?"

"He's on the schedule. I just messaged him."

"Wow, before me."

"Shut up."

"What did he say?"

"He hasn't replied yet."

She doesn't say anything.

"I'm sure he will soon." I'm not sure if I'm reassuring her or myself.

"I don't know why you have such a thing for that guy." A bag crinkles, probably Cool Ranch Doritos, the only chips she eats. "His hair looks like a bird's nest."

This makes me defensive. "We don't judge people on their appearance."

"Fine, I'll judge him on his actions. Connor ghosted you after that party."

"He didn't! He asked me out, and I couldn't go."

"Right, sorry, the second you said no, he ghosted you. Plus he didn't ask if he could kiss you the first time." The vomiting noise she makes is gross enough that I push the phone away.

"I wanted him to kiss me," I remind her.

"He's older and knows you have a thing for him."

"Age gaps are hot." I'm kidding because Connor is only eighteen to my sixteen, which is no big deal. When you factor in when our birthdays are, it's barely two years. Really, more like a year. We're basically the same age.

"You're in grade ten."

"Almost grade eleven!" I correct her indignantly. "Anyway, there's only three weeks left of school, and no one cares what grade you're in during the summer."

"He's leaving for university."

"I *know*." That's why this summer is so important. I won't have a chance against all those smart older girls he's going to meet in the fall. Not girls, but women. Probably with tattoos or piercings, unlike me with my regular undyed dark hair and zero nose rings.

I'm getting ahead of myself. First up is being able to flirt without stumbling over my words or feet. I look in the mirror and try to wrap my short ponytail into a bun, wondering if he prefers girls with pixie cuts or long hair, before getting frustrated when it falls out of the elastic as usual.

"Hey, do you have any more of your amigurumi for sale?" Hazel asks. "My aunt wants a few to hang in her food truck."

"I'm all out." I used to have a steady business selling small crocheted animals at local craft fairs.

"Are you making more? They're so cute."

"Maybe once school's done. I'm too busy." That's a lie, because I don't know why I stopped. One day I looked at the amigurumi I was working on and just . . . That was it. I hated it. The half-done bird was lopsided and ugly, but I couldn't figure out how to fix it and I couldn't summon the energy to take the photos and write the caption needed to get advice from my usual online amigurumi forum. Instead, I shoved it in a drawer I haven't opened for months.

Hazel has to go, and I look at my laptop without opening it. I know how to get a good mark—school is all about figuring out what teachers want and making sure to tell them exactly those things—but I don't want to bother. What's the point of it all, anyway?

Shoving away the laptop, I crawl into bed. Mom will be

furious if she sees I'm wearing my outside clothes under the covers, but I don't care. I shut my eyes, thinking about the summer. As usual, the initial excitement has melted into a sort of dull expectation that something will go wrong, like how hooking up with Connor has turned into this constant pressure of whether I should text him and what I would say. Or why he didn't text me, or ask me out for a movie or food or anything. Or why I was so scared to ask him. At least here in my bed, things are calm. Mom says I need to get out of my comfort zone, but she doesn't get that my comfort zone is comforting.

I pinch my arm to try to snap out of this mood. *This is good news.* I make myself smile, although the expression feels almost unfamiliar.

The front door opens, and I wait for the usual sounds of my mother's entrance to fill the apartment. Her keys clatter in the dish first. Then comes the heavy thump as her bag, stuffed with groceries, books, a laptop, and things she forgot to take out from yesterday, drops on the floor. A sigh of relief as she takes off her shoes, followed by the thump-thump of her tossing them into the closet as if she wants them as far away as possible.

Today none of that happens, and she calls to me from down the hall. "Ivy, are you home?"

This is strange, and I get tense as I throw off the covers. "What's wrong?" I ask as I come out of my room. "Did something bad happen?"

She laughs. "Of course not. Why would you think that?"

Luckily she doesn't expect an actual answer.

"I do have news, though." Mom pulls off her sweater. "I'm starving, so I'll tell you over dinner."

"Over dinner?" I can't believe this. She might not know how bad I've been feeling, but she knows how much I hate being left in the dark. "Mom, what is it? Tell me now."

"Soon."

"At least tell me how good it is." Could it be about Dad moving home? No, it would be cruel to put off news like that.

"It's good," she assures me, walking into the kitchen. "Very good, but you have to wait. I want to have your complete attention."

"You have it now."

"Except I'm hungry."

Two can play that game, and I know how to drive her nuts. "I have news too."

She perks up. "What? What is it?"

"I'll tell you at dinner."

Her lips thin, but she knows she can't be a hypocrite. If I hate not knowing things, my mother hates waiting. Her lack of patience is legendary, and she once took what ended up being an hour's detour to avoid sitting in a few minutes of traffic because she'd rather keep moving than be stuck. "Ivy, tell me."

"You tell me."

She gives me a hug. "Fine, we'll both have to wait. Dinner will be ready in ten minutes."

I go back to my room and stare at my phone, trying to resist messaging Connor one more time.

I can't.

He still doesn't reply.

Chapter 2

"Ivy, dinner!"

Ten minutes wasn't an exaggeration, because we're having ramen, which, in a concession to good health, Mom's jazzed up with spinach and tofu. Dad is the cook in the family. He would dish up spaghetti with sauce made from garden tomatoes, and curries rich with coconut milk, and the best chocolate chip cookies in the world, thanks to his secret ingredient. He refused to tell us what it was "because then it's not a secret," something that always drove Mom nuts.

We sit down in the tiny dark blue kitchen, barely big enough for the table Mom brought from home. She'll be pleased about me working at the nature camp. She thinks I don't see enough green since we moved into the apartment. At least our old house had a garden. I do my best not to think about that, otherwise that gray veil thickens.

"Is something wrong, Ivy?" Mom stares at me, so I bend my face to my bowl, buying a few seconds to get my smile going. The separation has been tough for her too, and I can't make it worse.

"Nope." I take a bite to show everything is fine. She made

the spicy ramen she likes best, which burns my lips.

"Good," she says. "Okay, who goes first?"

"You go."

Mom dips her spoon into the soup. "The last few months have been . . ." She trails off and shakes her head. "The stuff with your father has been rough." That's the only way she refers to their separation. The stuff.

"I know."

She reaches over to touch my hand, and I let her before I turn back to my food.

"It's been a lot, but it's time to cheer up instead of being depressed about something that's over and done with," she says. "We need a change to get us out of this rut."

"We had a change," I say, jamming my chopsticks into my noodles. She's overcooked them as usual, but I eat without comment. When Dad complained about her burning the frozen oven pizza once, she'd stopped cooking for him completely. "A lot of changes."

"A good one this time. Remember what your pohpoh used to say about the winds of change?"

"When the winds of change blow, some build walls and some build windmills," I repeat obediently.

"That's right, so I'm building a windmill."

"For real?" Honestly, I don't put anything past Mom. Dad used to be the voice of reason, but that seems to have become my job.

She rolls her eyes. "No, Ivy, not for real. It's a metaphor.

Do you remember when we saw the cherry blossoms in High Park and talked about how fun it would be to go to Japan?"

I nod. That day had stood out to me, with its cloudless blue sky and rich spring smells. Mom had been happy and the sun warm enough that I could wear a T-shirt.

"Good, because we're going! It won't be for sakura season, since that's done, but there's lots to see."

I'm so surprised I spill the noodles from my spoon. "Japan? All of us?"

We've never gone on a trip without Dad, so I assume he's coming. I knew their split wasn't permanent. I *knew* it. It's only a matter of time before they get back together.

She looks confused. "You and me, yes."

"What about Dad?"

Her look of pity is almost too much to bear. "Oh no. No, sweetie. Not your dad."

"He doesn't want to come?" A rehydrated fish cake floats in my ramen broth, with its pink and white swirl. I watch intently as it bumps into the side of the bowl. There's nothing in my field of vision but that single disc until I pluck it out. I don't eat fish.

"Ivy, your dad and I are separated." She keeps her voice gentle, but the frustration underneath is clear.

"I know that!" Like I could forget. "I was confused, that's all." I do my best to rally so Mom will stop being sorry for me. "What's the plan?"

She looks relieved. "You know I'm not great at planning."

It's true. Mom is terrible at planning, thanks to a firm belief that things will eventually work out. From the fights I overheard, it was one of the reasons Dad left.

Mom piles noodles in her large soup spoon patterned with flowers. "After I decided Japan would be fun, I looked online and booked us a tour with the Adventure Group. All we have to do is show up, and they take care of everything—the itinerary, transportation, meals."

A group trip. I won't have any quiet time, but it will reduce my stress from keeping an eye on Mom and figuring out logistics like bus schedules and flight departures when she inevitably messes it up. "When do we go?"

"July, for two weeks." She digs into her ramen, telling me about the cities we're going to visit.

I stare at her for a moment before I interrupt. "July?" I want to cry. This trip will ruin my Granite Lake plan. I would think it was totally malicious if I didn't know Mom. It wouldn't have dawned on her to wait and ask me what a good time was—she does what she wants without thinking twice. Her smiling face beams into mine, but it's hard to be happy in the way I know she expects. Part of me feels bad for ruining her joy, but the rest of me can only think about Connor. It was the one thing that was finally going to make me happy. It was going to *change* things for me, but my last chance is drifting away like the dried leaves Hazel and I dropped in a stream last fall.

She frowns. "Is something wrong?"

From her tone, I can tell there better not be, so I answer as steadily as possible. "The schedule came from Granite Lake Camp. I got a summer counselor job."

"I thought you weren't going to do it this year."

"I changed my mind." Once I found out Connor was going to be working, anyway.

"Ivy." Her voice carries a warning. "I'm sorry, but you should have told me you were applying. I can't cancel this trip."

Untrue, because she *won't* cancel, not she *can't* cancel. It's always me who has to give in, me who has to compromise. I'm the one who has to withdraw from her summer job. I'm the one who had her life turned upside down because two adults couldn't get along and thought it would be a great idea to flake on their promise—not even a promise, their *actual legal vows*—to stay together. I'm the one with that extra two hundred minutes a week on the bus. I stare at the reddish soup in my bowl.

Still, there might be a chance to save my summer. "Couldn't we maybe change the trip date?"

"No, we can't." She sounds hurt and upset, which means I feel guilty. "I just wanted to do something nice for us."

I can't stand it when Mom's like this, her face set but eyes reddening. We're going to Japan no matter what, so it's easier to give in instead of making a fuss. "I'll tell them I can't take the job."

Mom smiles. "That's my good Ivy. It's too bad, but this is important for us, and you can work there next year, or even in August. We're going to have an incredible time."

"Sure." I stand up from the table with my bowl. I'm . . . ugh. I'm not mad, because that's too spiky and hot an emotion for me right now. It's more like I should have known it wasn't going to work out with Connor. Disappointed, I guess, but more. I wish I had the right word for it.

She holds out her hand. "Is that all you're eating?"

"I had something when I got home." A lie, since I'm hardly hungry these days, but it satisfies her.

"I want you to eat an orange before you go to bed. You're not getting enough vitamin C."

Mom thinks I'm not getting enough vitamin C, D, B_{12}, or iron, protein, magnesium, and a bunch of other stuff. Usually what some social media post has told her is lacking in her own diet and she decides is the same for me. "I will. I need to study."

"Right. Keep those grades up. It's good you haven't been going out so much lately. You need to focus."

Like focusing is easy, the way I've been feeling. But if I say anything, I'll get a lecture on food equaling energy, or the power of positive thinking, or how I need to put down my phone. Maybe that's right, but I don't care right now. I don't feel like eating, I can barely think, let alone think positively, and my phone is easy. Mom won't understand. She doesn't have a lot of patience for feelings. If she could see how messy mine are, she'd probably disown me.

I empty my bowl and put it in the dishwasher, making sure to nod and smile as Mom tells me a few more details about the trip. In my room, I immediately go to the Adventure Group website and skim the colorful photos of laughing people before clicking on their refund page. Only death gets a full reimbursement, although you get half your payment back in case of dismemberment.

I'm screwed. Goodbye, hot summer nights hanging out with Connor. Hello, two weeks with Mom and a bunch of strangers. I'd been thinking about texting Connor again, something cute but not desperate, but that's useless now.

I pick up a book, and when it slips out of my hand to drop on the floor, I want to cry, curl up in a ball, and die. At least in the privacy of my room I can let my face relax and the smile fade. My phone lights up with a notification. Addison has texted the Granite Lake Camp group chat. **Omg, can't wait to see y'all in Julyyyy! I miss you Connor.**

I climb back into bed as the sun sets behind the thin blue curtain. I'll study later. Right now, I need quiet.

Chapter 3

"How's the packing coming along?" Mom pokes her head around the door and flicks on the bright ceiling light, making me flinch. "We're leaving for the airport early tomorrow."

"Almost done." Or I will be once I get off the bed and start putting things in my bag. I sit up and pretend to fold a shirt. "I was taking a quick break."

"I'll tell you when the food's here." She eyes the empty suitcase and leaves.

I jump up to turn the light off. She never does, and it drives me nuts.

While I'm up, I pack some clothes, then open my drawer to look for an old charger and knock my last half-finished amigurumi project in my bag. The hook is still in the ball of blue yarn. I'm about to snatch it out when I see my turquoise Granite Lake volunteer shirt from last year. I send a photo of it with me making a sad face to Hazel.

She calls and appears on the screen dressed in her work apron with her hair in two cute high buns. "You've had weeks to come to grips with this. Reminder. You are going to Japan. I work in a kimchi taco truck. Do you know what my hair smells like?"

"This was my summer of Connor."

Hazel's groan of disgust could power a fleet of food trucks. "I know Connor too. Trust me when I say Japan is better."

"Your taste in men can't be trusted. Vanny from geography?" He's her latest crush.

She gets dreamy. "The way he ran his hand through his hair when he couldn't get an answer right. So cute."

"I will never understand you."

"Same, so shut it about Vanny. You got my list?"

She sent me her present list last night. "Jelly mascara and matcha. By the way, you can get matcha here."

"Not the same, and you know it. Sailor Moon stuff if you can find it."

"I think there might be some."

"And handmade paper from that gorgeous store in Kyoto, the one I sent you. I'm so jealous you get to go there. They supplied the shoguns."

"That's cool." I lie back on the bed in the dim twilight of my room and watch as she tests out how close her eye can get to the camera. She had her lashes done yesterday and they brush the lens. "What do I get in exchange?"

The eye disappears, replaced by a handful of reddish sticks. "I've got six gochujang french fries in my front pocket I was saving for a snack. All yours."

"Gross, you were not."

"No, I was cleaning the counter and they fell in." She tosses them aside into what I hope is the garbage.

The front doorbell rings, and I hear Mom chatting with the delivery guy. Unlike me, she's a total extrovert. It's like she gets antsy if there are no people around. She says she was shy when she was younger, too, and I'll grow out of it like she did. I don't see any chance of that.

"Food's here," I say to Hazel's other eye.

She pulls away from the phone to send me some exaggerated kisses. "Have a good time in Japan." She pauses. "This might be what you need."

"Need for what?"

"To get back to normal. You know, after your parents' split." She spreads her hands apart.

I told her about the separation, and she's been good about not bugging me to talk about it. I didn't want to trauma-dump all over her, and it was easier to not think about it in the first place. Now I shrug, feeling itchy. "I'll get you some rice face masks."

We hang up, and a second later she sends me a lucky cat gently waving its white paw.

"Ivy! Dinner!"

I can't resist one more check to see if Connor has texted me, just in case. He hasn't, so I re-read his message from when I told him I wouldn't be working at Granite Lake.

Damn, we could have had fun.

I'd read it over a dozen times before deciding on a reply.

We can when I get back.

If I don't have anything else on.

I want to believe it means he'll be busy getting ready for university, but I have a bad feeling it means another girl. I didn't bother getting Hazel's opinion. She's already put Connor in the fuckboy category, and I have to admit this doesn't make him look great. Well, you can't help who you like. I'm sure he would have been different if only I'd been with him this summer.

Camp started this week. I went by to say hello, but Addison, who knows about my crush, told me Connor was busy with the campers near the pond and promised to keep an eye on him for me. I waited until it started to feel awkward, then left. My skin prickled with shame all the way home.

"Ivy! Did you hear me?"

"Coming!"

I give in and take an artistically posed photo of my open suitcase after checking to make sure there's nothing embarrassing showing. Then I agonize over the caption. *Wish I could pack you?* Too much. I pick my nails as Mom calls my name again before sending it with Japan tomorrow.

A wave of panic hits immediately. What if he thinks

I'm bragging? It's not even witty. He'll think I'm a loser. I debate deleting it, but that will somehow be worse.

Gah. I throw my phone on my bed so I'm not tempted to check it every two seconds at dinner, then grab it back and shove my suitcase out of the way with my foot. Mom is standing in front of the pizza box open on the kitchen counter with a slice in her hand, so I pull out plates and deliberately hand her one that she waves away. "I don't want to deal with dishes right before we go. Also, I got those horrible garlic sticks you like." She makes a face.

I bring the boxes to the table and set the plates down anyway. "Did you put the passports somewhere safe?"

Mom points to her battered old knapsack, pleased with herself. "All packed, along with the printout of our flight information, Adventure Group itinerary, and meeting spot. Isn't this exciting?"

I nod because Mom expects it, but also because Hazel's right and going to Japan is cool. Despite my feelings about Connor, I'm looking forward to getting out of Toronto. As Mom says, it will be a change, and things might be different when we get home. Dad could be waiting for us at the airport, or Connor will realize I'm the woman for him and show up with flowers. This last year has taught me life can change in a moment.

I check my phone to see if I accidentally turned off the notifications. I didn't. No messages from Connor.

Mom is talking about tomorrow's plan again, so I sink into my own thoughts. I did well enough in my final exams, which was a relief, but the gray dreariness that has me locked in has partly shifted into anxiety. What if the plane goes down over the Pacific Ocean? What if we get there and the information is wrong and we have nowhere to stay? What if I get sick or hit by a car or fall in front of a Shinkansen train or . . . I take a deep breath, the way Mom taught me, and hold it in. None of that will happen.

What if it does?

Suddenly a wave of resentment hits me that Mom can sit there eating pizza without a care in the world and I'm stuck thinking of all the what-ifs.

My phone buzzes, and I nearly drop it as I yank it out of my pocket and hide it under the table to check. It's from Connor, and it's a selfie of him in his room, face barely visible under his hat.

wanna come over

I can see the messy bed in the background despite the dim light. His shoulders are bare, so he's obviously shirtless. I wish it was possible to pan down a photograph.

Mom takes both sides in a debate about whether to pack a raincoat as I brood over an answer. This is my chance to show Connor I can be fun and cool, and I want to go. Don't I? I can't tell if the feeling in my stomach is anticipation or something else. Hold on, I can't go over, not the night before I leave. I haven't finished packing.

Also, the sight of the bed makes me a bit nervous.

"I set two alarms to make sure we get up on time," says Mom proudly. "And I booked the cab in advance."

Sorry. Early flight.

The second I reply to Connor, I feel relief and dismay, but I don't know what's stronger.

Mom takes another slice. "Trust me, everything is going to go off without a hitch. All you need to worry about is packing."

Everything does not go off without a hitch.

First, Mom's alarms don't sound, as she'd set them for p.m. and not a.m. Luckily, I'd set my own as well. "I can always depend on you," Mom says, yawning as she rolls out of bed.

Then our ride doesn't arrive. This isn't Mom's fault, and although she assures me we have plenty of time, I can see myself waving goodbye to the plane from the gate. I was upset about this trip in the beginning, but missing it would be equally devastating.

The security lines are long. I forgot to empty my water bottle, and Mom chugs it down as people wait behind us so I don't have to throw it out. The security agent taps her foot with impatience as Mom tries joking with her, making me squirm with shame when the agent doesn't reply and Mom is left hanging. She doesn't care, but I do.

Then, somehow, I miss our seat zone being called. Mom is deep into the murder-mystery she bought from the airport kiosk—she'd forgotten her book at home—when I hear the final announcement. I jump to my feet, waving frantically toward the gate, where they're about to close up. "Mom. Mom! We're going to miss the flight!"

"Calm down, Ivy." She takes her time gathering her things while I run over. I'd wanted to sit in the seats closest to the boarding area, but Mom said they were too crowded. This wouldn't have happened if she'd listened to me.

"I'm sorry, we're here!" I call to the attendant. I'm nearly in tears from the strain and Mom's nonchalance.

The woman looks bored. "Passport and boarding pass?"

Mom shows up and hands them over.

"Have a good flight," says the woman. She barely glanced at our documents.

Mom strolls down the tunnel to the plane, and we struggle past the rows until we reach ours. The guy in the aisle seat sighs heavily as he hauls himself out so we can climb past.

"What if I need to get to the washroom?" I whisper to Mom.

"Then you say excuse me and go." She sounds remarkably unbothered by having to disturb the poor guy. I decide not to drink water for the next thirteen hours.

"Do you have the passports?" I ask.

"Oh yeah." She pulls them out of her pocket with a flourish and zips them into the front compartment of her bag.

I take the travel pouch from my knapsack and check inside. Noise-canceling earbuds. My eyeshade and gum. An e-reader and then a book if my e-reader runs out of battery. My charger and phone, which I put in airplane mode.

Connor didn't answer after I said no to going over last night. It makes sense. I mean, what's he going to say?

He could have said okay. He could have said let's make plans for when you get back. After all, it's only two weeks. I'm not leaving forever.

I kick myself for not saying yes. I've ruined my chance. I didn't need Japan to wreck things this summer. I'm doing great on my own.

Feeling a chill from the air-con overhead, I reach into my bag to pull out the blanket I added last minute. It rolls into a pouch that looks like a ladybug and doubles as a pillow. Mom's forehead furrows in a familiar but unwelcome way, the way it did when she and Dad were fighting and trying to hide it from me.

"Your dad bought you that."

"I know."

"You were going through a bug phase, and he went all over town looking for a good bug gift." She sounds wistful, and my heart speeds up. I would never say it to Mom, but it's times like this that confirm the whole thing was a big mistake and they'll get back together. They love each other. They only need a break. I tilt my head back and pretend to examine the light above my seat to try to hide the tears that rise. I thought I'd cried them all out over the months, but I guess not.

The flight attendant comes by to remind us to put on our seat belts—mine is already fastened, but I tug it tighter—and a few minutes later, I watch the world disappear and feel some of the tension drift away with the runway. Soon I'll be in Tokyo. The loneliness that has followed me since Dad left rolls back for a bit. It's cruel like that, letting me see glimpses of sun between the clouds, getting my hopes up that things will change. Usually right before it all goes back to blah.

When the Fasten Seat Belt sign turns off, I let down the tray and wipe it with sanitizer, then fish out my e-reader. I'm too keyed up to sleep and figure I'll read until the food comes. I put in my earbuds to block the sounds of the plane.

My e-reader goes flying when the seat in front of me slams back.

"Whoa!" I'm so startled I jump, which causes my earbuds to fall out. What an excellent start to the trip. I scramble to find them in my lap, then pick up my e-reader and see a woman scowling back at me through the gap in the seat. Her blue eyes are surrounded by clumpy mascara, and her hair is dyed red and cut short. "Did you say something to me?" she demands.

Normally I would suck it up, but she asked. "No, but, uh, can you push your seat forward a bit? I don't have any space."

She snorts. "I have a right to be comfortable. I paid good money for this seat."

"I mean, so did I?" Well, Mom did.

"What's going on, Ivy?" Mom's eyes flutter open.

"This woman won't move her seat, and I'm squished," I whisper, not wanting to make a scene.

"Kids these days have no respect," says the woman loudly to her friend.

"Ignore her and put your own seat back," Mom advises me, rolling her eyes. "Don't waste your breath on those kinds of people."

I do as she suggests and get a hit in the kidney. "Hey," says a voice behind me, through the gap near the window. "Watch it."

I try to twist around, embarrassed at being called out. "Sorry, but the woman in front of me put her seat back."

"So?" It's a boy around my age with a hoodie pulled low over his head. His voice is nice.

"So if I don't do the same, I'll have about ten centimeters of space." I try to pull my seat up, but it's stuck. I can feel my face going red.

"Like I have right now?"

A man's voice comes from beside him. "Matteo, stop complaining. We're all crammed in like sardines."

"Fine," mutters the guy.

I wait for some more kicking-the-seat retaliation, but nothing comes. It's almost calm, and the rest of the flight goes by without problems. The guy beside Mom likes to get up each hour to walk up the narrow aisle and do some stretches, leaving us plenty of opportunity to go out to the washroom. The red-haired woman in front starts a complaining contest with her friend about the food. Apparently the friend was served an Asian meal when she specifically ordered "real" food. The red-haired woman loudly says the point of going places is to explore new cuisines, and that she, personally, considers herself a traveler and not a tourist. They are both given white wine and calm down.

As for me, if I accidentally hit the seat in front every time I get up, jerking the woman out of her sleep? It's so hard to move around a plane these days.

Chapter 4

Day 1—Arrive at Narita International Airport

Toukyou e youkoso! Let the convenient Adventure Group bus take you to your centrally located hotel (neighborhood may vary) where you'll meet your friendly tour associate and other Adventurers over a relaxing meal.

When we arrive in Tokyo, I'm exhausted, dehydrated, and almost dizzy from jet lag. I don't see the woman from the seat in front after the rush to get off the plane, although I glimpse the guy from behind with his father in the immigration line. He looks pale and tired, the way I feel. He's not bad-looking and a dimple appears when he smiles.

Then he disappears, and I'm left to navigate Narita Airport with Mom. It's huge, but adorable cartoon characters and the English along with Japanese on the signs help me feel less lost. At least I have two translation apps on my phone, so I'm confident about being able to get the gist of things.

By the time we get our bags, it's three in the afternoon,

so . . . I do some quick calculations . . . about two in the morning back home. Time zones are bizarre. What happened in that time I gained? Is there another Ivy back home living those hours? Having adventures? More probably lying in bed. Mom stands in front of a map to figure out where we're supposed to catch the bus to the hotel, so I wander over to a vending machine filled with unfamiliar drinks. Dad gave me some cash before we left, and I feed a five-hundred-yen coin into the slot. The machine sings a cheery tune before a bottle of strawberry tea comes out the bottom and the change jangles down.

I go back to Mom, bottle chilling my hand, and check our itinerary. "Mom! We're already five minutes late for the bus."

"I know, but I don't know where to get it." Mom looks agitated, her chapped lips deep red from biting them. "I can't read this map."

"We have to go!"

"Ivy, you're not helping."

I shut up and don't point out that she's got the map upside down as I try to stop bouncing from foot to foot. She figures it out, then turns the sheet around, muttering about why anyone would print it like that. We're seven minutes late now, and the cold sweat drips under my arms as she leads us outside, swearing as her luggage wheels catch on the sidewalk. The weather is humid, the air sitting heavy on my backpack to weigh me down.

"We must be in the wrong place," Mom says, scanning the buses. There's a line between her eyes, a clear sign she's frustrated, which stresses me out further, although I keep it hidden.

A man in uniform walks by, and I sigh with relief. "We can ask."

When Mom shows him the map, he smiles and points to a bus with his white-gloved hand. On the front is the same number as on the itinerary.

I try to control my breathing as we get on board. We made it, and that's what matters, but as usual, it's hard not to feel this entire situation could have been less stressful if Mom paid a bit more attention to instructions.

"You okay?" she asks, her mood already improved.

"Of course."

"What drink did you get?"

I forgot about the bottle and open the tea to share.

"Not too sweet." Mom approves.

The seats fill up slowly, and it seems everyone but us is my grandparents' age.

"I wonder if they're dropping people off for a few different tours," Mom whispers as the woman and her friend from the plane come down the aisle. Mom and I look at each other, both hoping they aren't with us. The guy from behind me on the plane gets on with his dad, and they help someone with their baggage before sitting down.

When we leave, it takes a moment to adjust, because

people drive on the opposite side of the road, or what to me is the opposite. Japan looks disturbingly like home, but with a few unfamiliar plants and smaller vehicles. I suppose all highways have the same feel. I want to stay awake and take everything in, but my eyelids are too heavy to keep up. Five seconds. I'll shut my eyes for five seconds, because I don't want to miss seeing the city for the first time.

The next thing I know, Mom is shaking my shoulder as the bus empties out.

"We stopped to let people off, but this one is our hotel," she says, looking past me. She always gives me the window seat, and I feel a bit bad for falling asleep instead of taking advantage of the view. She never seems to mind, though. "Ginza. Shopping heaven. There's a stationery store with eight floors nearby."

"We're going, right?" Mom and I both love a stationery store, and that almost makes up for the disappointment of sleeping through our entry into Tokyo.

"You bet. We don't have to meet the rest of the group for dinner until seven. Do you want to relax or find it now?"

Tokyo and cute paper goods beckon, but I'm dazed by the day of travel and the sheer number of people crowding the sidewalk outside the bus. I need to relax, but Mom's default is to go, go, go, then go some more. Luckily, living with her for years has trained me in negotiating a more reasonable pace. "How about a shower and quick nap, and then we look around for an hour?"

"Sounds good."

Mom checks us in as I doze in a corner of the lobby, too tired to feel anything but a desperate need to lie down. The room itself is perfect, although the view is only of the rooftop next door. Mom unlocks our bags, and I root through the closet. "They've given us slippers," I say.

"Pajamas, too." She shakes them out. "Oh, nice ones. I bet they'll notice if I keep them."

The first thing I check in the bathroom is whether the toilet sings the way I read about online. There are enough buttons on the side to launch a spaceship, and I try one that looks like a waterfall. Encouraged by the rushing sound, I push another.

"Argh!" I scream and jump back from the jet of water that shoots out. Mom appears and raises her eyebrows.

"It's a bidet," she says. "For washing—"

"I know what it's for," I interrupt, not wanting an in-depth description.

It's a pleasure to shower off the grimy germs of the plane, and I fall into bed wearing my hotel-provided PJs with my wet hair bundled up in a towel. Instead of sleeping, I worry. What is this tour group going to be like? What if there's no one for me to talk to? Worse, what if there are people my age and they all become friends except for me? I wonder what Connor is doing. Should I text him? Mom won't let me have social media, citing all sorts of studies about self-esteem and body image and screen addiction, and I didn't care enough to get a secret account, so I couldn't even post a cliché shot of the city from the airplane window.

Or . . . the light in this room is amazing, with the golden afternoon sun. I shake off the towel and slick back my hair before taking twelve selfies until I find a good one. Off it goes to Connor to my instant regret, although I was looking cute. Should I pretend I meant it for someone else and sent it accidentally? Too obvious. I leave it.

Hopeful that will keep Connor's interest, I look out the window. Although I can barely see past the series of yawns that split my face, there's a welcome sense of eagerness I've been missing lately. Japan is out there, ready for me to explore.

As soon as I have a nap.

Mom and I must have been wiped, because we only wake up a half hour before dinner and scramble to get dressed. I slip in an earbud, then carefully pull my hair down so Mom can't see it. She hates when I walk around like this. She doesn't get that the music helps to distract me, which calms me enough to function in public.

Before she opens the door, Mom turns to give me a hug. "I know it might be strange to have this trip without your father," she says. "I'm proud of how well you've been coping with the separation. I never have to worry about you. We're going to have the best time."

I keep the hug going so she can't see my face. I hate when

she acts like their separation is permanent. "We are."

"That's my Ivy. Remember. Yu women rise to the challenge. We don't give in."

Being a Yu woman is so important to Mom that she fought Dad to make sure I got her last name instead of his, officially making me Ivy Brown Yu instead of Ivy Yu Brown. I wish I was a better Yu woman and not letting down the bloodline by being my messy self.

Bonding moment complete, Mom pulls out her sheaf of instructions to confirm our meeting place as I shut off the lights.

"This must be it," she says when we arrive to a big group of chattering people in the dining room. I recognize some of them from the bus. They're all way older than Mom, and mostly couples. There are some single women and no single men. All of them are white. Many are in florals.

"You look lost," yells a boisterous woman dressed in beige capris and a bright green shirt with a bedazzled collar. "Adventure Group?"

If I didn't already know life is cruel and also hates me, this would have confirmed it, because that's our nemesis from the plane. Astoundingly, she seems either to not recognize us or to have forgotten her previous unpleasantness.

Mom looks a bit taken aback. "Yes?"

"Well, come join us!"

I'm too old to hide behind Mom, but I definitely let

her take the lead as we wind through the tables. They're crammed close together despite the big room, and I bang my hip against the chairs as we go. Instead of the usual white, the tablecloths are brown. With the dark gray carpet and light gray walls, it's like being in a cave.

"I'm Paulette," the woman says.

"Are you the . . . tour guide?" asks Mom in confusion, taking the seat Paulette waves us to and pulling me down with a somewhat frantic hand. She's usually confident in any situation, but this seems to have thrown her expectations way off.

"The tour guide! Do you hear that?" She laughs and turns to the three women at her table to see if they're laughing as well. They are, especially the woman who had been sitting next to her on the plane. "Oh, hell no, honey. She's around here somewhere dealing with the food. Cute little thing. Kimiko, she said her name is. Or Kimchi. Something like that. I told her I'd be the welcoming committee while she was gone. Right, girls?"

The women nod vigorously, and I name them Gretchen (airplane friend), Karen, and Cady. Mom makes me watch *Mean Girls* every Christmas. Dad prefers *It's a Wonderful Life*.

Paulette smiles at us with offputtingly big white teeth. "I'm willing to put all that rudeness from the plane behind us." So she does remember. "Forgive and forget, that's my motto, although everyone says I'm too kindhearted for my own good. Tell me about yourself." She leans into Mom's face and doesn't wait for an answer. "Coming to visit your homeland? You must be proud to share your past with your daughter."

"Me?" My mother stares at her. "My what?"

"You're not Japanese?"

"My heritage is Chinese." Mom answers with more grace than I expect.

"How do you like that. So hard to tell, isn't it." Paulette doesn't sound embarrassed as she loses interest, and Mom looks at me as if to ask WTF. I nod at her to confirm she did in fact hear Paulette right. "Oh, looky. Here's a little friend for your daughter."

Since she's basically yelling, the entire group turns to see the boy from the plane and his dad walk in. They wear similar expressions to what Mom and I must have on—kind of stunned—and stop dead when they notice about twenty pairs of eyes on them. The dad recovers first and waves. "Howdy." The guy looks embarrassed. They endure Paulette's loud greeting and sit at the table farthest from her and, by extension, us.

A young Japanese woman in a navy dress with an Adventure Group logo arrives, and we stare at her expectantly.

"Hi, everyone, and welcome. I'm Kimiko, your Adventure Group tour guide." Kimiko gives us a friendly smile, and I admire her hair. It's a sleek cascade to her shoulders with cute bangs and not a single frizzy or cowlick marring her arrow-straight part.

"Konnichiwa, Kimmy!" shouts Paulette. "That means hello!" I don't know what's worse, dealing with a miserable plane Paulette or a Paulette determined to be the life of the party. I'm not thrilled to experience either.

Kimiko's smile doesn't waver. "We're going to be sharing amazing experiences together and making lifelong friends, so let's start by getting to know each other before dinner is served."

Mom nudges me hard when I accidentally groan out loud. "Ivy."

Icebreakers might be evil, but I straighten up and put on a happy face. "I can't wait to find out what animal Paulette would be if she was an animal."

That makes her laugh. "Maybe we'll be lucky and Kimiko will have us play would you rather."

I would rather eat my own hand than do an icebreaker, that's for sure, but I keep quiet. The other kid is slumped in his chair, hoodie up and arms crossed as his father whispers to him. His face says he's not looking forward to playing two truths and a lie either.

It turns out the icebreaker of choice is bingo. Kimiko hands out paper grids, and we're given five minutes to find out who is afraid of heights, who has a pet dog, and other inane things. I write *Lillian* in the square for who is from my city, and Mom glances over.

"Don't use my name," she says as she's about to join the group of milling seniors. "This is your chance to meet people."

I chime along with her next words because they're so predictable. "There's a boy your age over there. You can say hi."

"Don't be rude." She boops my nose, so I know she's not actually mad.

Then Mom leaves, a big smile on her face as she gets ready to make some new forever friends, and I check out the boy. His back is to me, and I decide going up to him will risk making it weird. Saying hi can wait.

I gather names fast, to get this over with. Yvonne, a white-haired woman with a striped shirt and loose pants over ballerina flats, has been on more than five cruises. This is Lisa's first trip to Japan, and her husband, who has an absent-minded-professor shock of reddish hair, suffered a compound fracture two years ago. "Thank you, Adventure Group, for reminding me of that past trauma," he says wryly as I write *Tom* in the center square marked *broken bone*.

The woman I nicknamed Gretchen, who to my shock is actually named Gretchen, doesn't eat raw fish but once had shrimp tempura and thought it was too greasy. I put her down for *likes sushi*. Close enough. Hank, who is wearing a beige vest bulging with pockets on pockets, including a pouch on the back, has the blue eyes I need for the upper right square, and they stare out at me through eyebrows so bushy they look like scrub brushes.

Then I'm facing the guy. His hoodie is down, and his dark hair is a bit long and wavy. His eyes are light brown. He's way cuter than I first thought, with high cheekbones and nice skin I'm jealous of, since the flight caused me to break out. He's wearing an unexpectedly stylish outfit for someone on a group tour with his dad—the jeans fit perfectly, and the shoes are elite: white leather sneakers without a single scuff. Around his wrist is a silver link bracelet.

He looks down at me, because he's one of those tall and lanky guys and I'm short and thick. "Do you have a cat?" he says. Outside of the deafening brown noise of the airplane, I can confirm his voice is deeper than Connor's.

"No." I look at my sheet. "Do you like golf?"

"No, but put my name down anyway. The sooner we finish, the sooner we can eat. I'm Matteo."

"Done, and I'm Ivy. You can say I love gardening."

"Do you?"

I wiggle my fingers at him to show my navy nail varnish, but quickly so he doesn't see the chips. "Sort of, but I have black thumbs."

"Aww, look at the kids," bellows Paulette from across the room. "What a couple of cuties. They remind me of my grandbabies."

I freeze. Cuties? Us? Matteo catches my eye, and he mouths, *Grandbabies*, with an exaggerated *yikes* expression that makes me smile with relief because he's being cool. This might not be so bad after all.

"Bingo!" It's Paulette. Kimiko presents her with an Adventure Group–branded fan Paulette snaps open, pretending to be a geisha, as servers bring out the plates. It's Western food to get us acclimated, and Gretchen digs in happily as Kimiko assures the indignant Paulette there will be many genuine Japanese experiences coming. I watch Matteo, whose dad has struck up an animated conversation with the others at their table. I wonder what their deal is, and why Matteo's mom isn't here, and if he's thinking the same about my dad.

He lifts his head to scan the room. Should I act like I don't notice him looking at me, the way I would with Connor? I'm not sure, but it's refreshing to realize I don't need to worry about impressing him. After all, we were likened to someone's grandbabies.

I give him a wave and smile when he waves back. He seems like a nice guy, and that'll do to get me through the next two weeks.

Chapter 5

Day 2—Tokyo

Enjoy the culinary delights of the renowned Tsukiji fish market before marveling at the austere beauty of the Imperial Palace East Gardens. In the afternoon, appreciate the calm of the historic Meiji-jingu Shrine before attending a traditional Japanese meal followed by a unique taiko drumming event.

"Ivy, get up." Mom leans over my bed. "We need to get going."

I roll over. "Five more minutes." On trips I'm usually the first to wake, but jet lag is messing with my usual dependability as much as my dull feelings do.

"How was your rest?" She keeps poking me until I wriggle away.

"Great," I lie. Maybe it was sleeping in the same room as Mom, or being in a new place with unfamiliar noises, but I kept waking up.

"Good, because Tokyo's waiting. Come on." She drags off my covers.

I stifle my sigh and take the cold silver can she hands me. "What's this?"

"Barley tea. I found it in the fridge."

The bitter, nutty tea gets better with each sip. Rummaging through my bag, I pull out a shirt, and with it comes a lump of blue yarn. Weird. I pick it up before remembering the amigurumi that fell from the drawer. I must have packed it by accident. I run my hand along the hook. I only managed half of what I eventually hoped would be a bluebird.

"Ivy?"

"Almost ready." I shove the unfinished bird back in my bag and get dressed.

Mom points at my black jeans. "You should wear shorts," she says. "It's hot."

"I'll be fine." It drives me nuts when she thinks she knows what I should wear better than me.

"No, you won't, but don't come running to me when you collapse from heatstroke." She puts a bottle of water in her bag, humming a song she's mangled beyond recognition.

I swipe on my favorite red lipstick before we're off to meet the rest of the group in the lobby. We're the last to arrive, a point Paulette comments on immediately. I hate the way it brings everyone's attention to us, and I'm well on my way to continuing the hate I started feeling for Paulette on the plane.

It's only eight in the morning, but the heat hits like a physical slap when Kimiko ushers us out. I have no idea if I'm sweating or if it's the humidity sticking to my skin as I walk through the thick air. Despite the haze, it's so bright the light batters me down, making my sleep-deprived head feel thick and my swollen eyes tear up.

Luckily, the bus is air-conditioned, but unluckily, I get instantly clammy. I sit down with my jeans sticking to my knees, but as Mom goes to sit with me, Paulette grabs her hand and pulls her into the empty seat beside her.

"Keep an old woman company," she says. "Let the young people enjoy themselves."

She points at Matteo, who is coming down the aisle. He pretends not to hear, but Paulette is not a woman who is used to being ignored. She turns to Matteo's dad. "The kids are going to sit together," she orders. "It's good for youngsters to have a friend."

The dad, whose name is Keith, smiles. He's dressed in beige cargo shorts and a black shirt that's faded gray, along with white socks and Vans. Matteo is in a white shirt. Unlike me, the color looks good on him. Last semester I wore white to fake sick so I didn't have to write a math test. Mr. Sullivan didn't question me at all, I looked that bad.

"Great idea," Keith says. "You don't want to hang out with your old man, do you? I keep telling you to get out there. You gotta talk to people." He lowers his voice, but I can hear. "Girls like it when you show some confidence.

Look how popular your brother is."

He all but shoves Matteo into the seat beside me. Matteo, for his part, goes bright red, mutters, "Sorry," then immediately looks at his phone. I do as well, since it's clear he doesn't want to talk. With his dad and Paulette glancing over every two seconds, I don't blame him. It's embarrassing enough to get to know someone without an audience judging the conversation.

I check the camp group chat again. Hazel and I are on it, and so are Addison and Connor, but he rarely takes part aside from posting the occasional meme. Today there's a photo of him with a few others sitting under a tree. I zoom in on Connor like a creeper. He looks amazing as always, with his hair perfectly styled and the cute look that makes me weak. Give me a cheerful, bold guy any day, someone who knows what he wants and can get me out of my shell. Connor is my opposite, which means we have to attract. I glance over at Matteo, bent over his phone. He seems like he would be Connor's opposite as well.

Then I catch my breath because although I'd almost lost hope, Connor's texted me back. **u look hot.**

Perfect. *Perfect.* I nearly hug my phone to my sweaty chest as Matteo looks over. Kimiko pulls on a headset that amplifies her voice.

"Welcome to your first adventure in Tokyo," she says. "We have a busy day, so please make sure you're in time to catch the bus so you don't hold up the group."

"Collectivist culture," says the man behind me to his wife. "It's very important to these people to prioritize the needs of the group over the individual." The wife gives an approving hum. Matteo catches my gaze, and his tiny eye roll makes me snort.

When the bus takes off, Matteo peers around me, and I try to sink back into the seat so he can see out the window.

"It's like being back home," mutters Matteo. "Yay, globalization."

I wish he was wrong, but he's not. We're surrounded by large buildings and signs for familiar stores and big-name brands. The road signs are in Japanese and English.

"It kind of makes the things that are different stand out," I say, looking at an overpass where people cross the road and signs with directions to Hamarikyu and Miyukidori instead of Spadina or Yonge.

"Yeah, but it's depressing to go halfway around the world to buy the same shirt as in the mall twenty minutes from your house."

That's true enough, and as if to underscore what he's said, we pass a Gap. We turn to each other with raised eyebrows, and there's another one of those moments of connection that make me think Matteo will be fun to hang with for this trip. That's a relief.

"Our first stop is the famous Tsukiji fish market, where we'll sample some of their distinctive delicacies for breakfast," Kimiko says, before embarking on a history of the market.

Matteo hears me groan. "What's the matter?" he asks.

"Fish market. I'm vegetarian."

"Look, they're talking!" Paulette's excited whisper causes us to freeze, like we've heard a predator. Matteo gives me a look like a dying cow, and I can't help but laugh, even though I know this will play into whatever scenarios Paulette is dreaming up. However, she only nods in triumph, and we're left alone.

Matteo sighs. "No offense, but it's going to be a long two weeks if she's monitoring every word we say. I should buy her a whiteboard so she can make notes."

His dry tone makes me laugh again. "Maybe we can think of her as our own personal conversation cheerleader."

"My dad would love that. He's big into affirmations. Or she could be our sports commentator." He lowers his voice. "Coming up from behind we have, oh no! Interference from the guy with all the pockets!"

"His name is Hank."

"Really?"

"Yeah, found out during the icebreaker last night." It's easy to talk to Matteo.

Matteo turns from Tokyo Bay to look at me. His eyelashes are long, like he's been using the jelly stuff Hazel wants. "Did he get the bingo square for most gadgets known to humanity?"

"No, most colorless outfit."

Matteo glances back as if he can see Hank through the

seat. "He does love khaki," he says.

"Who doesn't?"

We look over to Paulette, who is dressed head-to-toe in neon-pink zebra stripes, and do our best to not laugh.

The rest of the morning at the market turns into a total pain. Paulette must have gotten most of the tour group on the Ivy-and-Matteo train, because it seems we're constantly being pushed together. There's no escape, and Matteo's clearly uncomfortable being the center of attention. It doesn't help that Keith seems to find the whole thing hilarious.

Mom pulls me aside as we stand around a busy stall where they sell tamagoyaki, an omelet Kimiko says everyone should try. The cooks shake a thin layer of yellow egg in rectangular pans before rolling it up with chopsticks. The air smells like the ocean mixed with cooking oil and fried dough. Across from me are jewel-toned fish on a bed of ice, the vendors in stiff blue aprons chatting with friends and customers. Compared to the heat outside the hotel, the air in the market is slightly fresher with a sea breeze that lifts my hair.

"Are you okay, sweetie?"

"Sure." Then I hesitate, realizing I don't know what I'm supposed to be reassuring her about. "Why?"

"I noticed Paulette trying to shove you and Matteo together." Mom accepts a small paper plate from Kimiko with a bright yellow square of omelet speared by a bamboo skewer. "Thank you."

"No thanks," I say when Kimiko offers me a plate.

"Not hungry?" she asks.

"Ivy doesn't eat meat or fish," says Mom. "She doesn't like cooked egg either."

"I'm so sorry. I didn't see your food preferences form." Kimiko looks concerned, and I smile at her, although I feel like an unsophisticated child who can be fed nothing more exciting than french fries. Inside I'm cringing. I don't want a fuss.

"What form?" Mom frowns. "There was a form?"

Kimiko goes away, and Mom takes a bite. "Oh, it's sweet," she says, looking intrigued. "Sugary egg. That's different." She takes another bite and seems to remember we were talking. "Right, Matteo. Do you want me to have a word with Paulette?"

"No, no, I can handle it." I'm horrified at what Mom might say, and it would cause drama with Paulette for the whole trip. Better to just hope it passes.

"I'll leave it with you, then," she says.

Kimiko returns and hands me a soft, powdered pink ball with a strawberry in the top. "Ichigo daifuku," she explains. "It's mochi with red bean paste. You'll like it."

Although embarrassed she had to go out of her way for me, I bite in, and she laughs at my expression because this thing is delicious. "Wow," I say. "Thank you."

"We can find lovely things for you to eat in Japan that don't have meat," Kimiko assures me. "It's no problem. I often eat this way as well."

I give Mom a bite, and her eyes widen in disbelief. "This is so good."

"Want more?" I offer it again, but she shakes her head.

"That's all you have to eat." She lowers her voice and looks guilty. "I should have said I was veggie, too. The egg tasted strange. Don't tell Kimiko. And I'm sorry about the form, sweetie. I brought some of the protein bars you like just in case, though."

We spend another hour or so at the market, stopping at various vendors. I'm tense from keeping an eye on Mom, whose phone has died and who is constantly falling behind after disappearing into stores when she sees something interesting. I also feel increasingly bad for Kimiko, who goes out of her way to find me food, including a potato croquette that melts in my mouth. Paulette starts to comment on what she calls my "private menu," and I try to avoid her, which I suspect will be a trend for this trip.

When the group collects around a vendor to try a special matcha, I hide in the shade to send a photo of the huge crowd to Dad so he's not jealous at being left out. He hates crowds. Then I flip through my photos to figure out the best one to send to Connor. Which will make me look coolest? I frown, swiping past a basket of silvery fish, then the lanterns at the temple in the corner of the market, and another of a T-shirt of a fish selling fish to fish. The plastic sushi display. A bird on a fence.

I add and delete about six photos to the message before I'm suddenly sick of this, and of myself. I'm in Japan. They're all good. I pick a gritty one of a vendor and caption it **Tsukiji** before sending it to Connor. I shove my phone in my pocket, feeling strangely resentful. At what, or who, I have no idea.

"Hey." Matteo appears as I check out a place selling what look like candy squid. "Do you think that's super-realistic-looking sugar or actual squid made into candy?"

I make a face. "Please not real fish sweets, although I did see a shrimp paste patty that looked like a jellyfish."

He looks intrigued. "I wish we'd tried those instead of the fish that still had the bones and tails."

"Adventure Group!" It's Kimiko, waving toward the main road to lead us out. "Time to go."

It takes a while to drag Mom away from a display of ceramic chopstick holders shaped like sea creatures, and we fight our way back through the crowd to join the others. Although I've been able to steal shade from umbrellas and the awnings over the stalls, it's heaven to get back to the air-conditioned bus.

Matteo sits by me again, and I don't mind. He's quiet, but it's not like with Connor, where I feel the need to try and entertain him. Matteo is simply there, not expecting anything from me. We reach the Imperial Palace gardens and make our way toward an actual moat that surrounds a huge stone wall. Kimiko tells us to be back in an hour.

"Where should we go first?" asks Mom.

"Can I walk around by myself?" The market was a lot, and the garden offers a bit of a break, but not if I have to keep an eye on the time and Mom.

"I don't think that's a good idea."

"Please?" I desperately want a few minutes where I don't have to smile or nod or listen to people. At least at home I'm not with another person all day, every day.

"Coming, Lillian?" It's one of the women from the bus, waving at Mom. Mom glances at me.

"I'll stay with the crowds," I promise.

She gives in. "Okay, but no talking to strangers, and be back at the bus five minutes early." Mom glances at her phone. "When were we supposed to meet again?"

I remind her, and don't point out it's pretty rich that she wanted me to be there early when she's the one who's chronically late. Whatever. I'm free, and it's a relief to be on my own. The gardens are huge and have all sorts of different zones. I eventually find a pond of gorgeous koi near an iris garden that's like a work of art.

I sit on a rock under a branch low enough to brush my head and contemplate the pond. It's dark green, and the huge koi move slowly under the surface as if fighting the weight of the water. What would it be like to be a fish? Fish don't have to worry about grades, or Connor, or their parents. A fish can't disappoint anyone. These ones don't even have to worry about being eaten. I wish I could slip in with them and not have to move or talk or think. I had hoped coming to Japan would mean a new me, but it looks like I'm still the old me, just in a more interesting environment.

I wrap my arms around my knees but immediately let go because it's too hot to sit bunched up. Fish don't sweat, either. I shade my eyes to look around the koi pond. A woman shakes out her blue scarf and wraps it over her shoulders to try and block the sun, while another swipes a handkerchief under her mask.

Matteo appears and sits on a rock without noticing me in the shadows. He's holding what looks like a notepad, but he shoves it in his pocket and stares out over the water. I don't feel like talking, so I wait until he looks in the other direction, then slip away, heading back to the bus on my own.

Lunch is at a conveyor-belt sushi place, which would be fun, except that Paulette forces me into a booth for two with Matteo. Mom looks like she's going to intervene, but since my other choice is next to Paulette herself at the counter, I figure Matteo is the far better option. He must come to the same conclusion, because he sits across from me with an irritated expression that probably mirrors mine. I admit it's a relief to not have to school my face around him, the way I do with Connor, or my parents, or everyone.

Matteo grabs two plates as they go by at eye level. One is tuna nigiri, and the other is inari, rice in a tofu skin, according to the handy illustrated guide posted on the wall beside us. He passes me the inari. "No fish," he says.

"Thanks." I miss some cucumber rolls, and he snatches them for me. They're on a pretty pink plate. "Kimiko said the plates are color-coded for price and they calculate your bill by counting them when you're done."

Before he can reply, Paulette leans back and points her fork at us. "What are you two talking about? School? Are you at the same one?"

Matteo answers, no doubt realizing that ignoring Paulette means she'll double down. "I'm at Roseton Collegiate," he says. "Going into grade eleven."

"Roseton has the best cross-country team in the province," says his dad from farther down the counter. At least we have the whole restaurant to ourselves, so we're not disturbing anyone. "Matty here is on the team, same as his old man was. Runs in the family." He laughs. "Get it? *Runs?*"

Paulette guffaws. "Good one."

"*Was* on the team," Matteo says.

His dad ignores both of them. "He's got talent. Everyone says so, but I always say talent is the bones and effort is the flesh. You have to be open to feedback. True champs listen."

"That's right," approves Paulette.

I wish Keith would shut up, but he keeps going. "That's

why I was a provincial medalist back in my day. His mother was, too, and his brother is on a track-and-field scholarship. Matteo here preferred to waste his time on anime, but luckily it was a phase." He laughs like this is the funniest thing ever.

"Anime?" Paulette sounds confused. Mom is busy talking to the woman beside her and doesn't seem to be listening.

"Manga, it's all the same. Japanese comic books or something," Keith says. "He draws them, if you can believe it. Or did, until he came to his senses."

I drop my eyes to the pile of plates, not wanting to make an awkward moment worse by saying something that might embarrass Matteo.

"Is everyone done?" calls Kimiko. Paulette leads a series of groans and demands for naps after eating too much. Gretchen is the friend she came with, but Cady and Karen (actually Joanne and Susan) are women who have come on their own without knowing anyone and been scooped into her orbit. I finish my drink as they gather hats and bags. There had been a container of green tea powder, cups, and a hot water tap right at the table, which I've never seen before. I send a photo to the group chat.

When a reply comes, it's from Addison.

Connor and I went to a place on Bloor West with the same thing.

I look at this and look at it some more until the text turns blurry. They must have gone with other Granite Lake people. Bloor Street is close to the camp, and it would make sense for everyone to hang out and get dinner. Is this what Addison meant by keeping an eye on him? I'm not sure I like it. Actually, I'm *sure* I don't like it.

I'm still mulling this over as we get back on the bus. Matteo sits next to me without waiting for Paulette's orders. I want to ask about his drawing, but he closes his eyes until we reach our next destination.

I feel bad about what his dad said at lunch, so after seeing the shrine and walking through the lovely dark forest at Meiji-jingu, I let him have the window seat.

He gives it back after another temple, the name of which I can't remember, both of us trying to decipher fortunes we got from shaking a numbered stick out of a box.

After the mochi-making demonstration, I make him take the window again, and he sits down with a small smile.

This silent back-and-forth settles me quite a bit, and slowly, Addison's text fades from my mind.

Chapter 6

Day 3—Tokyo

Your second full day in Tokyo includes visits to Tokyo Tower and the beautiful Ueno Park, where you can stroll under the shady trees, visit the zoo, or explore one of five important cultural institutions, including the world-famous Tokyo National Museum. Later, get dazzled by the neon lights of Akihabara, the famous Electric Town electronics, anime, and gaming district, before we leave to enjoy some of Japan's quainter and quieter offerings.

"Hurry up. Yvonne is downstairs." Mom stands by the door waiting.

I grab my shoes. I'm dressed much better for the weather today, with a breezy shirt and navy shorts. "How do you know?"

"She texted me. She's a fascinating woman, and used to be a journalist." Mom looks blissful. She loves meeting new people. She struck up a conversation with Yvonne yesterday while standing in line to get some mochi on a stick, then sat next to her during the drumming session last night. That nasty twinge I sometimes get reappears. Mom makes a fuss about how she wants us to do things together, but the second she finds someone more interesting, she leaves me behind without a thought. I don't blame her, but still. I don't like it.

I turn off the lights—she left them on again—and we go to the lobby. Yvonne smiles over at me. "I can't believe how alike you two look," she says.

Mom hugs me proudly. "She's my Mini-Me."

I'm not at all, but could never say that to Mom. I stand nearby and watch the tourists milling around checking maps and comparing directions. Matteo is there, dressed in shorts and a black T-shirt. I hadn't noticed how broad he was across the shoulders. I guess because he's not Connor.

Mom sits next to Yvonne on the bus, and I walk past to take a seat by myself near the back, where I can be alone. I stare out the window and try to simply observe what I see to clear my head. Trees with low branches and still leaves. Cars. Wide sidewalks, although it seems like everyone is hiding from the sun today. A children's playground, empty and with those metal bars that burn your hands in the summer and freeze them through your gloves in the winter. The sky is almost white instead of blue, although I can't distinguish any clouds. I forgot my sunglasses and have a headache that's more tight pressure than actual pain. I squint to see if that helps. It doesn't, and I slump back in my seat.

The traffic is lighter than I expected for such a huge city, and soon we pull up in front of a red-and-white version of the Eiffel Tower. Two pink and hilariously shaped bullets dressed in blue and red overalls greet us inside.

"The Tokyo Tower mascots," says Kimiko, leading us by. I do my best to ignore the dirty jokes Paulette is telling her entourage, but Matteo and I take photos and avoid eye contact.

A tower is not the most fun location for someone who's scared of heights—say, someone like me—and once we reach the observation deck, I hover near the inner wall instead of running over with the rest of the group to exclaim about the view. A man washes the windows outside, and the backs of my legs tingle at how high he is, dangling over the city with nothing but a few straps to keep him safe. I sit on a bench near the wall where I can't see him, and watch Mom and Yvonne as they gaze at the never-ending cityscape, trying to figure out the various landmarks. Mom glances back at me, and I manage a cheerful wave. I don't want her to come over with Yvonne to try to convince me to go to the windows. People who aren't bothered by heights don't seem to understand that repeating "it's safe!" doesn't make it feel any better.

The gift store might offer a break. I duck in and immediately regret it because there's a big Tokyo Tower snow globe display right at the front. It's like getting punched in the gut, because we collect snow globes as a family. Or we did. I haven't seen them since we moved.

I shake one so the glitter falls around the miniature tableau of the tower, a temple, and Godzilla, thinking about how things have changed. A year ago, Dad would have been here with us, insisting on a family selfie in every spot. The goal was to make the goofiest face, and Mom always won. Is that why he decided he had enough? Did he want a wife who was more serious, like him? Or a kid who didn't hide behind her hair in every shot because only losers would pose for a family selfie in front of some old bridge?

Even though deep down I liked it. I liked the photos and how excited Dad got.

I put the snow globe down with more force than necessary. No wonder I'm in a bad mood all the time, having to think about Mom and Dad and stuff. I've done my best to not make things worse in the hope they'll come back together, but it's so hard.

Obviously the gift store is a bust, so I leave to the sound of yelling. Or not yelling, but that whispered fighting that is somehow more obvious than regular loud voices. Matteo and his father are in a smallish alcove, and I don't think they realize that instead of providing privacy, the echoes are amplifying their voices.

"Why don't you get off my case?" Matteo says. "You asked if I wanted to come and I said no, but you booked it anyway. Sorry, you had your assistant book it."

"Other kids would be thrilled to get a trip to Japan,"

answers his father. "Your brother was dying to come."

"Great, you should have taken him."

"I don't know why you're being like this. We have a perfect opportunity to bond now that Dom is at school. The only thing I asked in return is that you keep running."

"For the last time, I'm not doing cross-country next year."

"You're doing this to spite me."

"I'm doing it because I don't want to run."

"Sure you do. The coach said you're a natural, but you have to practice. That's what winners do. That's why Dom got that scholarship."

"God, Dad, for once, listen to me. I quit the team."

"Robertsons don't quit, Matteo. We're like attack dogs. We keep going until we win. You need to get smart and act right, do you understand me? Think of how your mother would feel if she could see you now." There's a long pause. "Sorry. I'm sorry, son. I shouldn't have said that. God, I'm so sorry." Keith sounds truly upset at himself.

"Whatever." Matteo comes barreling around the corner, and I step back into the gift shop. Poor Matteo. Given what Keith said, I have a bad feeling his family situation is worse than divorce. His mom might be gone. Really gone. If that's true, what Keith said was horrible.

I linger around the inside wall until Mom comes looking for me with an ice cream cone in her hand. "Ready?" she asks, handing it over. "I know you don't like heights, so I thought you could use a treat. It's a special kind of extra-thick ice cream. Look, it came with a chocolate shaped like the tower!"

She's delighted by this. I think about Matteo and give her a hug. We're the same height now, and Mom says she lives in fear of the day I'm taller than her. In a way, I do as well. It will be unsettling, like a shifting of the balance between us. It's there already when I wear high heels or shoes with thick soles, and I can more clearly see the gray starting to thread through her dark hair.

She leans in, conspiratorially. "I heard there's a banana-themed gift store downstairs. Want to check it out?"

"Sure." It's a family joke that Mom can always find the strangest thing in any given place. Or was a joke.

No, it is a joke.

Back on the bus, and laden with small boxes of banana-flavored candies, I check the daily itinerary for what's next with a sense of tired dread. It's only day two, but the noise and people and the feeling of constantly needing to be on the go are a bit much. Paulette isn't helping, since she decides to lead an off-key sing-along of Gordon Lightfoot songs I recognize from Dad's record collection. Only her friends join in, which means the songs are interspersed with Paulette telling us we're boring, spoilsport party poopers.

I press my temple against the cool glass in the hope it will help my headache, and a few seats ahead, see the back of Matteo's head tilt as he does the same. Kimiko stands at the front of the bus with the microphone and waits politely for the song to peter out. Gretchen is the only one to follow it up with a round of applause.

"You'll have the rest of the afternoon to spend as you wish at Ueno Park. I suggest the art gallery or the museum."

That means three hours on our own, and it's like I've been sprung from jail. I almost dance off the bus and nearly kill myself tripping on my own feet. No one sees but Matteo, who raises his eyebrows as if to ask if I'm okay. I give him a nod.

"Where do you want to go?" I ask Mom.

"Yvonne wants to walk around the park. Should we join her?"

Immediate no. There's nothing wrong with Yvonne, but I don't want to be a leftover trailing behind her and Mom.

"It's a bit warm," I point out. That's an understatement, because it's about a trillion degrees and the heat makes the pavement look wavy. "How about the museum first?"

That ends up being a tactical error, because most of the group has the same idea, including Matteo and his dad, who are very obviously not talking to each other. I try to linger in the exhibit rooms, looking at old woodcuts of women in lovely robes standing on bridges, and people fishing, but everyone seems to take the exact same amount of time. I give up and move with the crowd into the Kabuki room, where Mom and Keith sit down to watch a recording of an old performance.

I'm nearby looking at the embroidery on a robe to avoid checking my phone again when I hear Paulette talking to one of her minions.

"Well, the kids are a lost cause," she says. "They can barely string two words together. Thank God my grandbabies have some social skills. They're like their grandmama."

"It takes all kinds," says Susan.

"The parents, though," says Paulette. "Did you hear Keith with his son? That boy could use a woman's touch. Look at them. Maybe it's time I bring out my fairy godmother wand. I'm quite the matchmaker, you know."

I turn in horror to see Paulette staring at Mom and Keith, who are reading the guidebook Mom pulled out of her knapsack, their heads close together. It's ridiculous to think about.

What if . . .

No. Mom and Dad are going to get back together. A separation is only a break. They're married, and after some time apart, they'll realize things are better when we're a complete family. The last thing I need is Mr. Quitters Never Win messing everything up.

My gaze moves to the corner where Matteo is standing. From the look on his face as he turns to me, he's thinking the exact same thing.

Mom and Keith will get together over our dead bodies.

Chapter 7

After monitoring Mom and Keith with an eagle eye, by evening I decide I'm taking Paulette's comment way too seriously. She's anything but a love god, and her decision to play Cupid means nothing. Why would Mom want to be with Keith, anyway? Dad might make a big deal about rules and have zero chill, but that's better than hanging out with a guy who can talk about sales prospecting for a full hour. I've sat in English classes less dull.

Plus, it's only two weeks. No relationship can happen in two weeks when you're being herded around the country on a bus with your kid and people who spend hours cheerfully comparing knee replacement scars and sciatica treatments.

There's not a thing to worry about.

We're on our own for dinner, and Mom invites Yvonne to join us at an Indian restaurant. I only nod when she asks if it's okay, because it's too late to say no and she'll hate me making a fuss. We go to the fifth floor of a building, which kind of blows my mind, since I'm used to restaurants being at street level. That's a strange thing to get used to, if you think about it, and I wonder how many other things I think are standard just because they're familiar. Mom, as usual, is excited to learn about someone new, and peppers Yvonne with questions, leaving me to eat in silence. I wish I could be on my phone, but the look Mom shoots me when I put it on the table makes me stuff it back in my bag. It would be better if Matteo was here to talk to. Or if I was with Hazel, or even Connor. I mean, especially Connor.

When we meet the others for a night walk of Akihabara, the electronics district, Mom and Yvonne are a few steps ahead and don't notice when I stop as we come around the corner. The lights are like being whacked with a neon sledgehammer, and I want to linger on the side to drink it in from the edges. By the time I catch up, most of the group has split into smaller units and Paulette is talking urgently to Gretchen and the rest of her squad, looking between me, Matteo, and our parents. It's not subtle, so Matteo notices the potential threat as well. He sends me a wide-eyed look as Gretchen is dispatched in my direction and Susan heads toward him. Paulette oversees this coordinated attack like a general.

Gretchen grabs my arm before I can move. "You'll keep me company, won't you?" she asks. "My goodness, what a lot of light. The energy bills for this place would bankrupt me."

"I should find my mother," I say politely as Matteo shakes his head at Susan and steps away.

"Your mother is having a good time with Keith. She

deserves some time to herself, don't you think?"

Gretchen's comment hurts, since it means everyone can see Mom needs a break. I heard Mom crying in the bathroom after they sold the house, and her commute is longer than mine, so I know she's stressed. I'm sure she would have preferred coming to Japan by herself, so she could relax instead of dragging around her miserable teenage daughter.

Mom's face creases as she searches for me, but Gretchen waves and calls, "Ivy's my friend tonight!"

I put on my biggest smile and wave Mom on, holding out my phone to show I can text if there's a problem. Mom hesitates, then nods and turns to Keith. Damn. She might deserve that rest, but I wish it was with someone else. Yvonne would be better. Paulette would be better. The pink animatronic dinosaur outside the store in front of us would be better.

Having failed with Matteo, Susan slinks back to Paulette. They point at Gretchen, who nods back at them. God, did they choreograph this with alternative plans? They must have, because Gretchen tugs me in Matteo's direction. He looks at us warily.

"Matteo, come join us," she says. It's not a question, but also not *not* a question.

"I'm good," he says. "There are some stores I want to check out."

"Come on, those can wait. Or we can go together! Ivy,

help me convince him. You can't refuse a pretty girl, can you, Matteo?"

This is so humiliating. Matteo, who has no answer to this unanswerable question, disappears into a pachinko hall, the balls and noise almost deafening. Then he stands there, as if unsure of where he is.

"What a strange boy," says Gretchen, who, to my relief, lets him go instead of trying to chase the poor guy down or something. "Well, we don't need him. Just us girls!"

I give up and let myself be pulled along. After all, I do want to see Akihabara, and most of the group has disappeared, including Mom. Well, if she's with Keith and he's going on about lead generation and accelerating pipeline growth, the worry will be less them hooking up and more Mom dying of boredom.

The street is busy, forcing Gretchen and me to weave through the shoppers. It's bright as day, and the people form dark shadows against the harsh lights. There's so much to look at that I forget myself for a moment and simply experience the chaos. It's like I'm watching it from outside myself, a welcome change as being in myself hasn't been the most fantastic experience lately. We've been wandering for about forty-five minutes—Gretchen is surprisingly good company and tells funny stories about her job as an office manager—when I spot Matteo huddled in the corner of an alley as green stripes play over his hair. The feel of the place suits him somehow, as if he should be wearing an untucked dress shirt with a loose black tie and his hair a spiky mess, like the anime boys painted on the walls behind him. He has that same look, a bit isolated but incredibly cool.

Gretchen sees him too. "Matteo! Matteo!"

This time, he comes over. "Are you okay?" he asks. He sounds concerned.

"Getting a bit tired," Gretchen says. "I'm a tough old broad, but I'm holding Ivy back. How do you feel about exploring with her while I take a bit of a break?"

"I can go alone," I say, hating to feel like some sort of burden.

Gretchen is shaking her head before I finish. "No, no. Everyone in pairs for safety."

"Okay," Matteo says. I stare at him, and he shrugs. "My dad will kill me if something happens."

"And your mother would kill me," says Gretchen. "That would be two deaths on your conscience, Ivy."

I don't have a choice except to give in, and I do so with the most grace I can manage, which isn't much. We drop Gretchen off with some group members who have found benches near a drink machine, and they welcome her with offers of a seat and a can of coffee.

Matteo and I are quiet until we get around the corner. Then he turns to me. "I want to ask you something. Tell me if I'm overreacting."

"Are you wondering if that whole thing was planned by

Paulette to get us away from our parents so they can have a romantic date wandering through the neon lights?" I ask.

He groans. "Yeah."

"You're not overreacting."

"Paulette is playing on another level," he says with grudging admiration. "Why does she care if they get together?"

"I assume she doesn't. She likes to meddle." Then I'm distracted by a store that has no doors and is filled with coin vending machines. "Wow, cool."

"They're called gachapon machines," says Matteo.

There must be at least a hundred, filled with toys and figurines and taking coins from one hundred to one thousand yen. I do a quick calculation. One to ten dollars.

Matteo stops at a claw machine with round animals that remind me of my amigurumi. I walk past to the next one, with stuffed Pokémon. "I bet I can get one of those," I say.

"No way," he says. "These machines are rigged."

Obviously this is a challenge, and I put in a one-hundred-yen coin. "Want to bet?"

"What do I get if I win?" He leans against another claw machine filled with plush toast wearing sad expressions.

"The knowledge of my failure."

"Is that the top-tier prize?"

"It would be if you could experience it." I examine the pile of toys, trying to figure out the best option. "Too bad you won't."

"Go for the Pikachu," he advises.

"The Eevee is cuter and right near the slot. I can knock it in."

"Are you kidding? There's no way."

Tapping the buttons to the perfect spot to grab the adorable Eevee, I'm getting ready to drop the claw when familiar laughter drifts over. I look up to see Mom and Keith strolling by. My finger jerks, and the claw goes down about ten centimeters in the wrong direction to land on Jigglypuff, then drags across the pink fur without catching. "Shit."

Matteo is looking at the same thing. "I don't like this," he says. "What if Paulette succeeds?"

"She won't."

"How do you know?"

"First, because my mother is already married, so it's a total nonstarter, and second, they met two days ago. Also, did I say she's married?"

The lights of the claw machine dance on Matteo's face. "Your mom's married? Where's your dad?"

"He had work." I have zero desire to enter an in-depth discussion of my parents' marital status. "So you can stop worrying. Whatever Paulette thinks, nothing is going to happen."

He frowns. "She's not wearing a ring, is she? Your mom, not Paulette."

I jam another one hundred yen into the machine,

suddenly angry. Is it at Matteo? Not really, although he's a handy target. "She and my dad are separated, but it's only been a few months. They're married."

There's a beat of silence, and Matteo clears his throat. "Oh," he says, sounding awkward.

I keep facing the machine. "Mom's super friendly. She's always talking to people."

"Right."

Somehow I can't stop explaining. "It doesn't mean anything."

"I get it."

"Good." I begin to work the claw.

"To win, you need to—" Matteo starts.

My hand is in his face faster than I can speak. He gets the hint and stays quiet. This time, I screw it up myself and do my best not to kick the machine when the claw snaps on nothing again. Instead, I give up.

We head out to explore some more. This place is incredible, but the darker thoughts flow in. Mom and Dad. Mom and Keith. It's hot despite the night falling. I'm thirsty. I wish Connor was beside me, and not Matteo. Would Connor have won me something? Too bad Connor's not here and I'm with Matteo and no claw machine prizes and nothing to drink and Mom laughing with some strange man who's not Dad.

"Watch out!" Matteo yanks me to the side as a scooter flies by with a food delivery box on the back, right before it creams me. The shock of adrenaline acts as a reset, and I sigh.

"About our parents," I say.

"Yeah."

"There's no way they're getting together. We're on a bus trip, which is the opposite of romantic. Look at us. We're walking around, right? It doesn't mean anything." I'm surprised by my sudden sensibleness because I usually go for the worst-case scenario as the most likely. Maybe this vacation thing is working after all, and turning me into the happy, optimistic young woman Mom would prefer to have as a daughter, someone more like her.

"Good points." Matteo pauses. "I want to be clear that I'm okay with our parents being friends."

"Me too."

"Like, I'm not against platonicism."

"I don't think that's a word, but I get the idea."

"We would have to be total dicks to not want them to have friends. It would be wrong to stop Dad from talking to people. It's not your mom, specifically. She's nice so I feel I need to say that."

"It's not your dad, either." I don't mention that his dad seems okay, because he's kind of not. "The thing is, I'm sure my parents are going to get back together, but I'd like to avoid any interference, you know? Mom's not in the market for a boyfriend."

"Fine by me. Dad changes when he gets a girlfriend,"

Matteo says. "It's like he wants us to be a happy family right away, and I absolutely do not need a replacement mother."

"We can keep them apart if you're worried," I say. "It's only two weeks. Not even. Twelve days."

We pass a vending machine, and after a brief internal debate on whether I want to risk trying something new, I go for my usual strawberry tea. The sights of the district absorb me as we walk. To the left is a line of vendors selling cords and electronics, and an entire building of video games and anime merch. Matteo stops to paw through some books on display outside a store. They're manga, and I remember that's what he draws.

I'm curious and pick one up, but it's sealed in plastic. Matteo glances over and smirks. "Paulette would have a fit if you brought that back."

"Why?" I look more closely at the cover and realize it's a half-naked girl. "Oh, dang. NSFTB."

"TB?"

"Not safe for the bus. Get it? TB. The bus."

He rolls his eyes and picks up one with a soldier on the front. "I get it. I guess you don't read a lot of manga."

"I read some webtoons."

He looks like I killed someone. "That's a totally different art form with a completely different artistic origin."

"Well, excuse me, Mr. Manga Artist."

Matteo puts the book down. "I don't actually do manga. I was working on a graphic novel, but Dad thinks anything that's not Marvel is all the same. It doesn't matter anyway."

"Why not?"

Instead of answering, he starts walking again. This is a pretty clear *I don't want to talk about it* signal, and I respect that, although I wonder what happened to turn him off drawing. Was it like me and my amigurumi? I follow along until I catch sight of a fantastic visual, the lights flashing over the gachapon machines and a person in shadow in front lighting a cigarette.

I take the photo, and it's perfect. Then I stare at my phone. Connor hasn't replied to my last text, or few texts, to be honest. Maybe I'm being too eager and need to change my approach. I'll drop a few Tokyo photos into the chat, instead of to him directly. I'm no photographer—not like Addison, who had one of her photos run in an actual magazine—but if they're arty enough to get compliments from the others, Connor might be impressed and text me back. In my head, I plan out the chat and how I'll be witty and fun instead of tying myself up in knots over whether I've said something uncool.

We're a bit late by the time Matteo is done, and rush back to the meeting point to see Mom with Yvonne, and Keith on his phone. "Look, they're not even talking," I say triumphantly.

"I guess you're right," Matteo says with relief. He sits beside me on the bus and hands over a plastic ball. "Here."

I turn it around before cracking it open to see a snail

sitting on a mushroom. "What is it?"

He shrugs. "Collectible from the gachapon machine. I got it earlier."

The expression on the snail's face makes me smile. "Cute."

"You can have it," he says.

"What?"

Matteo looks past me to the window. "I feel bad you didn't get a Pokémon."

"It's better than an Eevee," I say. "Thanks."

Matteo nods, and I'm examining the figurine closer when a text comes through from Connor.

looks dope.

I'm nearly bouncing as I tuck the snail away safely in my bag. Finally, something is going the way I want. Then I see Mom and Keith sitting together, smiling, and my heart sinks. Not everything, apparently.

Chapter 8

Day 4—Tokyo to Kanazawa

Whoosh! Get ready to ride over 300 km/hour on the celebrated Shinkansen bullet train to the charms of historic Kanazawa. We begin with a visit to Higashi Chaya, one of the town's historic geisha districts. The day ends with a relaxing (or romantic!) stroll along the Asano River as you listen for distant music from teahouses entertaining guests, much like the time of the ancient samurai.

I wake up in the dark hotel room and realize my pleasure from last night has faded back to the familiar gray. It does that: lift for a tantalizing moment to let me be the old Ivy again and remind me of how I used to be. Sometimes I get scared I'll lose that forever. I'm starting to forget what it was like before this, and if I forget, how can I get back to it?

"Ivy?" Mom sits up. "It's early."

"I'm not feeling great."

"No?" She runs her hand through her hair, which is so straight and shiny that she never gets bedhead. It always falls perfectly to her shoulders. "What's wrong? Are you sick? I bet it's still jet lag. Drink some more water." She swings her legs out of the bed. "You looking forward to the train?"

The thought of herding Mom onto the train is exhausting. "Do you think we can take it easy today?" I ask. "Get a bit of a break."

She laughs. "What are you talking about? It's a train, Ivy, and we need to be on it. Why do you need a break, anyway? It's a vacation. This *is* the break."

"We could get another train and meet everyone later."

"Silly Ivy. Don't be ridiculous." She goes into the bathroom.

I duck under the sheets and curl up with my phone, scrolling without seeing anything. I should get up. Mom's going to be so mad if I make us late. But I can't. The thought of getting out of bed, brushing my teeth, packing—it's all so much. The phone drops from my hand, and I close my eyes, trying not to think.

"Ivy!" Mom comes out of the bathroom. "Why aren't you getting ready?"

I pull down the covers but don't look at her. "I must have fallen back asleep."

"This isn't like you. You're usually the first to get up. Off you go." She waves me toward the washroom before opening her bag. I get in and barely manage to scrape my hair into a ponytail and brush my teeth.

Then those tears I tried to hold back take over with a vengeance. I can't explain why. I don't have a reason to cry. They just need to come out. I've learned how to cry quietly enough so no one hears me, and I'm grateful for my stealth skills now with Mom on the other side of the door. When it gets bad, I flush the toilet to cover any noise I make.

After it lets up, I sit in the corner, near the shower, and bury my face in my knees. There is no thought in my head besides knowing I never, ever want to move.

And there are still ten more days left on this trip.

Mom knocks on the door. "Come on, slowpoke!"

I get to my feet, concentrating on one limb at a time. First my arms, so I can plant my hands on the cold tile. Then my right leg, bent under, and my left to lift me up. I stare into the mirror at my blotchy skin. Shit.

After washing my face in the coldest water I can get from the tap, I think I'm passable. I come out, and Mom glances up from zipping her bag. "Sweetie! Have you been crying?"

I have my usual excuse ready. "It might be allergies, or I'm coming down with something." I rub my eyes as if they're itchy.

"Poor Ivy. That's why you're so tired. Your allergies have been terrible lately." She nods, suddenly sympathetic. She rummages in the bag for some Tylenol and antihistamines and waits while I swallow the pills. I've told her they make me sleepy, so I can be reasonably low-energy for a bit.

Everyone is waiting in the lobby, and Mom sits me down on a bench to rest, then hands me some water. I keep my hat pulled low to hide my eyes. I feel a bit better after my breakdown, which is a relief. Now I'm just empty.

People have already settled into their routines. They have their preferred seats on the bus, and cliques are forming, like at school. There's Paulette and her gang, and then Tom, his wife, Lisa, and a few other people who are interested in culture and ask Kimiko serious questions about the history and meaning of what they see. Another group are dedicated shoppers, and then come the foodies. The gadget nerds—Hank and another man, Gary—compare the many pockets on their vests and pants. To my complete horror, there also seems to be a final group: a party of two.

Mom and Keith.

No way is this going to happen.

I'm mulling over my options as we get on the bus to Tokyo Station, where we're going to catch the bullet train. There's enough room for people to spread out a bit, although most prefer a seatmate, and Mom asks what I'd like. If I had known she'd sit next to Keith, I would have said I wanted to stay with her. But I didn't, and here we are, me alone and her smiling at him.

"Did you see?" Matteo asks through the gap in the seats. I like his voice. I look at the slice of his face with an eye and part of his mouth, and tug my hat further down.

Despite the pills, my headache has lingered.

"If you mean our parents, I sure did." My throat feels rough.

"Kimiko said the seating on the train was assigned, so we shouldn't have any issues there."

We stop talking to listen to Kimiko, who tells us to leave our luggage on the bus, which will drive to meet us in Kanazawa. "It's a long trip by road, and we want you to see as much of the lovely Edo-era town as possible instead of Japan's highway system," she says.

Mom and Keith are pointing out the window to show each other the view. I get a pang, because I don't remember the last time Mom was this sunny with Dad. She used to be, but I can't tell when it faded. Could this separation be a good thing for her? For him, too? In the last couple months, Dad's lost that tired, anxious tightness around his eyes, and he's been way more relaxed.

No. We're a family. We're meant to be together. All they need is space and time to realize they love each other. I turn away from Keith and Mom, and look at the people going to work. The men all seem to be wearing white or light blue collared shirts tucked into dark slacks, and a man in bright red stands out like a flower in a meadow. The women I see look . . . dainty. Pretty. I glance down at my own clothes, wrinkled from my bag, pilled and faded because I haven't had the energy to go shopping lately, and feel like a massive slob.

Well, not like it matters. There's no one to impress here. When my eyes drift to Matteo's shoulder, visible through the seat gap in front, there's none of the tension I felt whenever Connor was near. No, it was excitement, wasn't it? That tight feeling, like I was waiting for something to happen.

Before I can dwell on this, we pull up at Tokyo Station, which is so massive it's like its own city. Inside are signs for what seem to be about twenty different train lines. Mom's eyes dart around as she fights between wanting to look at everything and paying attention to Kimiko, whose smile game remains strong despite having to herd her pack of gawking tourists through the busy maze of the station and its commuters. Mom's glazed expression means it's my job to figure out what's going on as usual, so I do my best to fight through the fog and listen closely as Kimiko gathers us near where our train will leave. She hands out tickets and tells us to be back in exactly twenty minutes.

"There are places to buy food on the platform," she says as I try to block out the confusion of the station to make sense of what she's saying. "The train will not wait for you, so you must be on time."

People murmur agreement and scatter. Matteo glances at me and drags his father off to look at a store.

"Do you want to sit here while I get us bento boxes to eat?" asks Mom. "They have ones that heat up by themselves."

I want to stay, but know if I don't go with her we'll miss the train. "I feel better now."

"That's good." She kisses my head. "Sometimes you just need to get moving."

I set the timer on my phone, and we go looking for the bento box store. The minutes tick by as she lingers over the ones on display, struggling with the sheer number of options and asking my opinion.

"It doesn't matter," I tell her over and over. "Just choose. We need to go."

It's like she doesn't hear me. "Do you want dessert included?"

In desperation, I grab the first vegetarian one. "Here."

"Are you sure?" She barely looks at it. "What about this one? It's a bit nicer."

"Sure. Yes." I'm starting to get spikes of anxiety that we're going to miss the train. "Just pick one so we can *freaking leave,* okay?"

Mom turns around to give me a look. "I know you're under the weather," she says in a low voice. "But that doesn't give you the right to take your bad mood out on me."

"Sorry," I mumble.

She goes back to the bento boxes, slamming the unwanted ones back in the fridge. "Let's go," she says.

My alarm sounds as we're in line to pay, and by the time she's done, we're definitely late and have to sprint back to the platform. We arrive panting, plastic bags thumping our legs, as the train pulls in, white and sleek with a smooth nose that does resemble a bullet. The incredibly unfrazzled Kimiko—I don't know what she's on, but I want some—gets us all on board.

"See, Ivy?" Mom checks over her bento box to make sure it didn't spill. "I told you there was nothing to worry about. You got all upset for nothing."

I'm filled with adrenaline that has no place to go as Mom hands me my ticket. I want to scream at her that the only reason there was nothing to worry about is because of me, but instead I nod. It's hard, because it's like there's so much stuffed inside of me I can't find space to keep it all in.

Shaking slightly, I check the seat number and slide in next to the window as she moves to the other side of the aisle. "Looks like we're together," says Keith as he sits with her.

Hold on. Mom was supposed to be with me, so I could prevent her buddying up to Keith. Instead, it's Matteo, who looks between his ticket and the seat beside me, and we stare at each other until Keith says, "Come on, son, you're blocking everyone."

"This was not the plan," Matteo mutters as he thumps down.

I agree, glad my heart rate has slowed so I can cope with this new issue. "We need to trade spots."

We look over at Mom and Keith, who have been joined by Yvonne in the third seat. "There's no way to do it without making a fuss," Matteo says in defeat.

"Okay," I say, keeping my voice quiet so they don't hear. "It's possible it might be harder than I thought to keep them apart."

"What are you two plotting over there?" calls Keith.

"We're not plotting anything," says Matteo.

"At least they're talking," Keith says to Mom. He's loud, but I don't think it's deliberately so we can hear. It's just his normal volume. "I keep telling him, look, you need to get out there. Talk to people. Confidence matters. People like it when you have something to contribute to the conversation. His brother is more like me that way, you know? Follows right in the old man's footsteps."

"I tell Ivy the same thing," says Mom enthusiastically. "Put the phone down and experience life."

I tune them out because (1) I'm still upset at Mom for nearly making us late over some stupid snacks; (2) the need to take advantage of what life has to offer is a common theme, although she's on her phone as much as me; and (3) Tokyo is passing us by in a bewildering mix of buildings. I watch the scenery and feel my breathing get back to normal, although it's still shallow. It's been harder to take deep breaths lately, like my lungs are too small.

"You okay?" asks Matteo.

I shrug, not wanting to get into it. "Did you find any good souvenirs?"

He shakes his head. "Dad got some stuff for my brother,

Dom, but there was nothing I liked."

The conversation lapses, and we look out the window for a bit. I doze off, until Matteo nudges me with a white plastic bag.

"Your mom passed this over."

Mom leans forward. She's sharing her bento box and snacks with Keith and Yvonne, and when she gives me an exaggerated wiggle of her eyebrows and tilts her head at Matteo, I know what I'm supposed to do.

"Snacks," I say. "Want some?"

"No thanks."

Despite saying no, he can't help but watch as I unwrap the box, which is Styrofoam made to resemble wood. I don't trust Mom not to yell loud enough for the whole train to hear she expects me to share. "Better take it so my mother doesn't make it weird," I say, handing him a triangular umeboshi onigiri wrapped in plastic.

He turns it around in his fingers.

"Sorry." I pass over my sanitizer. "Here."

Matteo cleans his hands, the sharp smell cutting through the savory aroma of the food, then says, "How do you eat this?" He refuses to look at me, like he's embarrassed.

It's on the tip of my tongue to ask if he's never had one before, but to be honest, I only had my first onigiri last year and Hazel had to walk me through it. I demonstrate how to take off the plastic wrapping without making a mess. "Pull down the red tab and then pull out the corners numbered two and three." He copies me, and I show him how to press the seaweed sheet back around the rice. The salty tart plum filling makes his eyes widen, and I laugh for the first time all day. "Good, right?"

He nods and doesn't hesitate when I offer him some of the bento box. We debate the various ingredients and check the translation apps on our phones. "Lotus root?" I guess, looking at a brownish slice with holes. I feel I should recognize it out of some genetic sense of Asian solidarity, but Mom was born in Canada and she's always been more hamburgers than dim sum. For his part, Dad still uses a fork despite being married to a Chinese woman for twenty years.

"Yeah, looks like it," he says, comparing the photos online. "The pickled kind."

We finish eating, and I feel much better. Matteo has a much different vibe to Connor but it's not bad. I like it. Naturally, because nothing can go my way for more than a few minutes at a time, when I grab my phone to take a photo of the view. I see a message from Addison.

Heyyyy girl, it reads. **You know me, I like things totally honest so I wanted you to know Connor and I are kind of a thing now. I know you were interested in him, but he told me it wasn't anything. Japan looks incroyable! So jealous.**

Addison and Connor? It sinks in after the eleventh reading. She knew I liked him. Why is she always using French?

She only took it until grade nine and nearly failed. She's such a poser. I read the message a twelfth time, getting more upset. He told her we weren't anything? I feel sick. They talked about me? What else did he say? Was he showing her my texts? Did they laugh about how pathetic I am?

No, Connor wouldn't do that. Addison is either lying or she misunderstood, because Connor and I have a connection. If I could only talk to him, I bet he'd tell me the same thing. I stare at the ceiling to let my eyes reabsorb the tears that have sprung up. I wish I could get rid of all these stupid feelings instead of having them leak out of me like this. If I had been back home, this never would have happened. If I'd been at Granite Lake like I planned, Addison wouldn't have had the chance to go after Connor. What he did was bad, but somehow, Addison is the bigger betrayal. She's my friend.

Was my friend.

I mean, we talked.

"Did you get bad news or something?" Matteo asks.

I need to talk to someone or explode, but I don't want to go in the dirty details. "Guy stuff."

"The one whose photo you're always looking at? Brown hair." Matteo waves his hand in front of his face.

"Oh, well." I'm not sure why Matteo noticing makes me uncomfortable, since I didn't go out of my way to hide my phone screen from him. "Yeah. That's Connor."

"Is he your boyfriend?"

I hesitate, thinking of Addison. "Not yet." I cross my fingers, hoping I don't jinx it. Anyway, this is more like manifesting.

"You want to talk about it?"

"Kind of, but not really." I wave my phone. "Connor's why I didn't want to come to Japan. We were going to work together, and that was my chance with him." I frown. "Except Addison is there."

"Addison?"

"A friend of mine. She knows about me and Connor, but doesn't care."

Matteo gives a philosophical shrug. "It's only two weeks. Nothing will happen with her if he likes you."

Great, even a stranger can see I'm an unwanted loser. I look out the window, doing my best to believe Matteo is right.

Chapter 9

By the time we arrive at Kanazawa, I'm ready for a rest, but there is none to be had. We don't stop at the hotel, since our luggage hasn't arrived and we'd been warned to only bring our usual day bags on the train. We get on yet another bus and head to the Higashi Chaya district. Too bad that instead of admiring the unique beauties of the four-hundred-year-old castle town I traveled halfway around the world to visit, I'm thinking about Addison's message.

I take out my phone to see the last photo of Addison and Connor sent to the group chat: they're making faces and being cute. I hate it, and only hesitate for a second before sending a photo of a Tokyo street with Matteo barely visible but cut off. He's not recognizable because I've seen enough movies about fake boyfriends to know you always get caught in the lie, but he looks mysterious and attractive—not a stretch, because although I'm not interested in him, he is that.

There. That will show Connor I've got other things going on besides him and maybe make him a bit jealous.

Perfect. Now for Addison. Not answering would be like saying she'd upset me too much to reply; but I have a little pride, and she hasn't won yet. Despite being multiple time zones away, there's a chance I can impress Connor enough to get him back when I come home.

Best to play this like I don't care, although I screenshot the message and send it to Hazel because I want validation that Addison is a bad person. Then I reply to Addison herself.

Connor's great! I write back with way more excitement than I feel. Whatever, everyone covers their real emotions on text. That's why people avoid face-to-face conversations, where it's harder to hide your feelings. Ask him to show you the spot near the tennis courts. Miss you, but Japan's INCREDIBLE.

There. I glance over to see Matteo shifting his eyes from my screen. Was he spying on me? I feel a bit mortified he saw that text exchange. It was private and, more than that, doesn't show me at my best or even my medium. My neck warms as I put my phone away.

"Here we are," declares Kimiko as we pull up near a river. She reminds us to be back at the meeting point in two hours, causing everyone to set alarms and synchronize watches like they're part of some sort of international spy squad. Hank pulls out what looks like a stopwatch from one of his pouches, and the other vest pocket guy, Gary, taps frantically at a device that takes up his whole wrist and could possibly pilot a Mars rover.

I stand near Mom to keep space between her and Keith. "What a place," she sighs in admiration. "Gorgeous. Kimiko said this was the entertainment district."

"Kind of blah, don't you think?" Paulette says loudly. "Needs color on that plain wood. Give it some pizzazz."

Gretchen and Susan nod in agreement and they all ignore Joanne's tiny "I like it."

Paulette calls for everyone to follow the leader, who is apparently her. "Lillian, Keith, you two go on ahead," she sings. "I'll babysit the kids while you explore."

I watch in dismay as Paulette reaches for me, but Matteo casually walks between us as if he hadn't noticed what was happening. "Ready, Dad?" he asks. "You said you wanted to try that twig tea."

Matteo doesn't wait for a reply but hustles his dad off with unexpected finesse. This must be Matteo's attempt to keep our parents apart, because I can't believe Keith is legitimately desperate to try twig tea. Is it really made of twigs? Which ones? How?

Mom, who had been talking to Yvonne during this whole mini-drama, turns with a bright smile. "Ready to look around, Ivy?"

"Run and you can catch up to Keith," urges Paulette.

"We're good," I say loudly. "Let's go, Mom."

Yvonne comes with us, and I'm so relieved it's not Keith that I don't complain. In a way, it's nice to have someone occupy Mom's attention so I can drift around the quiet streets and look at the stores without having to assure her I'm having a good time. Sometimes it's not enough to have fun around Mom. She needs to see you doing it, like a performance.

It's beautiful here. The buildings are low, maximum two stories, and built with very artistically worn and faded dark wood. The doors are partially covered with hanging curtains that split in the middle, and some have what looks like corn hanging from the frames. Above, the clouds are thick enough to form a ceiling over the sky. It's so humid it's like I can drink the air, and in a few seconds I can. A thin drizzle starts to fall, but so light it's more like the cloud has thickened into mist. It coats my clothes to make them heavier, but not wet. A dusty smell rises from the smooth gray pavement stones.

Of all the places we've been in Japan, Dad would love it here best, but I suddenly realize I'm glad he's not with us. The last vacation we went on as a family was two years ago to Lisbon, and I spent most of the time alternating between parental mini-trips. Dad would go to some museum while Mom and I went shopping. Mom would go to the beach while Dad and I went to visit a garden or castle. At least here I can eat a meal without worrying about a fight or, worse, a post-fight silence I'd have to fill. That's what I remember about that last trip more than anything else. Just waking up each morning and feeling dread. I was grateful when we went home and could each retreat to our own spaces in the house.

But Dad will want to know what we're doing. I forgot my usual morning text, so I find a photo from yesterday of a food stall called Princess Strawberry that sold only pink food. Mom had bought me a Very-Berry-Pop, which was a berry-flavored bubble tea with strawberry mousse on top. He won't get it for a few hours, thanks to the time difference, but I know he'll call it a travesty of food and tell me to have fun.

"There are so many cat things," says Lisa, looking up when I poke my head through a door. "I might have Tom carry my credit cards to stop me from buying it all on the spot."

She waves a small cat figurine at me, then places it into a basket with cat cups, cat plates, some fabric printed with cats, and a shirt with a fish. "A fish?" I ask.

"It's for my sister," she says. "She always needs to be different. Did you see this crochet? Adorable."

She shows me an amigurumi calico. It's well done, with tight stitching and real personality in the face. "Don't you love it?" she asks.

"It's cute," I say, although I don't take it when she holds it out. Even looking at it makes me feel bad for my half-formed bluebird, with no wings to fly or beak to sing.

I'm being ridiculous. It never would do those things anyway. I didn't let it down.

I say goodbye and move on to the next store, which sells objects covered in gold leaf.

"There you are. The weather is crazy, don't you think?" Mom wipes her face. "Is it raining? Is it not? I wish I had my hat."

I'd forgotten I saw it as we were leaving the bus and stuffed it in my bag. "Surprise."

"Eagle-Eyed Ivy on the case. Thanks, sweetie." She pulls it on and leans over my shoulder. "Goodness, look at that lovely gold." She checks the price and winces. "Yikes. I'd need to sell a kidney. Are you feeling better?"

It's the third time she's asked, but she's not looking at me, and I'm not surprised and barely care when she waves to someone behind me before I can answer. "Oh, there's Yvonne. Let's catch up."

We do, then run into some people from the tour whose names I can't remember. Mom and Yvonne say the exact same thing as they have the other three times they've seen someone, which is "fancy meeting you here!" They all laugh, recommend some store, and keep going.

Mom is admiring a calligraphy scroll when I finally get a text from Hazel. She's up late. **Hey, so. Addison.**

I stare at the latticed window of a shop selling what look like matcha desserts. My reflection shows my hair, dotted with rain. **Addison.**

Look. I can almost see her philosophical shrug. **A guy who is that easily gotten isn't worth your time.**

She's right but . . . She knew he was mine.

There's a long pause before she replies. I know you're upset and I dislike her for lots of reasons, including the time she said my shirt made me look like a pancake, but you can't blame this all on her.

Yes, I can. I don't get what he sees in her.

Hazel's answer comes quick. Cute, pretty funny, and her parents bought her a Jetta when she finished driver's ed, great photographer.

Not helping. This is all true, but I don't want to hear it.

There's a longer pause, and I can see Hazel typing and deleting. Finally, the message pops up. I am always on your side, but Connor's his own person. You can't put a claim on him like he's the last doughnut. He has agency. This whole conversation is communicated with her usual short forms and emojis. It could count as a dialect.

I want to defend how I feel, but I can't. I know she's right, but when I was with him, I finally felt like things were happening, and I craved that feeling. I should have known it wouldn't work out. Why would he want to be with me when Addison is naturally everything I have to try so hard to be? She always knows how to act and what to say. Maybe he could tell that I was faking it. I know.

Good. She sends a series of emojis that basically translate to *I love you, you're awesome,* then writes, Don't let a guy ruin Japan. That's pathetic.

It kind of is.

It totally is.

"Ivy, for the last time, put that away. I didn't pay thousands of dollars for you to be on your phone." Mom has come up while I was occupied. She makes a face at Yvonne, and I bristle at her bringing someone into this. "Kids."

"Oh, look, a traditional cosmetics store." Yvonne, knowing better than to get involved in an intergenerational disagreement, points to a small wood door. "Let's go in."

The store smells beautiful, kind of subtly sweet and how I imagine rich people's houses to smell. I get distracted smearing different kinds of rice powder on my hand and testing oil blotters that leave your face matte and smelling like lemon but turn at Yvonne's admiring gasp. "Look at you!" she says.

Mom's lips are the perfect red. Like, the ideal scarlet. "It's called Komachi-beni," says the saleswoman as she layers more onto Mom with a thin brush. In her hand is a small pot with iridescent green that turns red when she dips the brush in water. "Used by geisha to enhance their beauty."

"You've got to get it," enthuses Yvonne. "Keith would die."

Keith? I stare at Mom. She waves her hand, but in the well-lit mirror, her cheeks go pink. I'm not worried. Mom rarely wears makeup. She says the average North American woman ingests six pounds of lipstick over her lifetime and she'd rather eat that weight in potato chips.

So when she smiles and tells the saleswoman she'll take two, I know Matteo and I have been too casual about this whole thing. We might have a real problem.

"We have to talk." I pull Matteo farther along the bridge. We can be seen by anyone who looks in this direction, but it's the only way to be sure no one can hear us talking.

Which we need to do, because Mom wore the Komachibeni to dinner, to a chorus of compliments, where she sat beside Keith and laughed at his dumb jokes, and made him laugh with her good ones. Paulette looked on with a smug smile that confirmed my suspicion that I had been absolutely wrong.

"Tell me about it."

"What do you mean?" I lean against the rail between two branches that have been decorated with tags and ribbons and tied to the bridge. Below us weeds choke the banks of the river, forcing the water to move sluggishly. The rain had let up, but I hadn't stopped sweating from the heat trapped under the clouds. My clothes are limp, my hair is so frizzy I can't pull my fingers through, and my shoes feel gross and probably smell.

"Dad was singing in the shower before dinner," says Matteo. He sounds floored, like a grown man singing a song is the most mind-blowing thing that's ever happened in the history of the world.

"So?"

"It's this old song he hasn't sung since . . ." He stops. "For a long time."

"Okay, well, Mom was wearing lipstick at dinner."

"She was?" He frowns. "That's it?"

"Trust me, it's a big deal. We're going to have to do more than keep them apart. It's time to take action. We need to drive them away from each other."

He turns to look at me through the branches. I have no idea why they're here, but they give the bridge a festive look. Despite the dim twilight, I can see little freckles on his nose and across his cheekbones I hadn't noticed before.

Paulette's voice rings down the path. "Joanne! Joanne! C'mon. Quit looking at the river, I'm tired. Let's go!"

Joanne's hunched figure slowly trudges away from the water's edge, and Matteo shudders. "We could start by killing Paulette," he says. "This is all her fault anyway."

"I thought it was too lucky when she stopped trying to set us up," I say dolefully. "I should have known she'd try to wreck this trip some other way. What should we do?"

We stare at the water, racking our brains for ideas that don't involve murder.

"Hold on," says Matteo suddenly. "We still don't know if they're interested in each other. This could be nothing and we're overreacting. We need to be sure."

"You want to, what, follow them around and eavesdrop? Spy on them?"

He makes a face. "Yes, but you make it sound bad."

"It's kind of bad." I think about it. "That's a good point, though. We should have a sense of their baseline relationship so we can map any changes."

"I thought school was done for the summer," he grumbles. "This sounds like a project."

"It is a project. Project—" I cast around for a name with a suitably vague yet kind of official sound. "Omega."

"What does that stand for?"

"The O is a zero," I improvise. "Which is the amount we want them to be together."

"Omega is actually the last letter in the Greek alphabet. It doesn't mean zero."

"Did you *well, actually* me?"

"I didn't say the *well*." He grins.

I wave my hand. "Project Void. Project Null. Project Zero. Whatever. Pick one."

"Omega is fine," he says. "If we need a name. Which we do not."

"Good, glad that's sorted."

"Ivy!" calls Mom from the river path below us. "Ready to go?"

Paulette's voice drifts over. "Let them talk. You and Keith can run ahead, and Joanne will wait for them."

"The hell with that," mutters Matteo. We sprint back

to thwart Paulette, and unlike me, he's not winded at all. Must be that running Keith is so burned about. I gasp for breath beside him, and he slows to match my pace.

By the time we arrive, Mom and Keith have already started walking through the district, lights casting a dim glow on the streets and alleys. Matteo glances over. "Come on," he whispers. "Let's check on them."

I follow him through the shadows to hide behind a big shrub near the bench where they're chatting in low voices. I try to keep my panting quiet so they don't hear me and end up making a weird croaking noise that causes Matteo to slap his palm over his mouth to stop snickering. I poke him, and he raises his hand as if to apologize.

We hear Mom laugh, and Matteo glances down at me, eyebrows raised as if to ask if this is normal. I nod. It's her regular laugh, not, like, a giggle, thank God. Then Keith laughs, and Matteo nods as well. Okay, we've established nothing. They're laughing like normal.

Then we hear Mom. "I agree," she says. "There's something magical about this town."

"You can feel it, can't you?" asks Keith. "The night."

"I can."

Matteo and I stare at each other. "Does your dad usually talk about the magic of the night?" I whisper.

"Never. When we went camping, he brought his laptop so he could watch the game and check emails, then got mad when I told him the light from his screen was spoiling the view of the moon."

That's got to be the most unromantic image ever. I remind myself to pass this bit of intel on to Mom.

"Ivy!" Mom calls. "Ivy!"

Shoot, they can't find us together spying on them. I shove Matteo back and pretend to come around the corner alone.

"There you are," Mom says in relief. "Where's Matteo?"

"I don't know," I say innocently. "I haven't seen him."

Then Matteo comes strolling out from the exact same place I emerged from. Paulette lets out a long, low whistle. "My, my," she says loudly to Gretchen.

To my relief, everyone ignores her, and we head back to the hotel. Matteo leans over before we get on the bus.

"Tomorrow," he whispers. "Tomorrow we figure out a plan for Project Omega."

Ha. I knew he'd come around to the name.

Chapter 10

Day 5—Kanazawa

On your full day in Kanazawa, get ready to be stunned by history and nature. Learn about the time of the samurai at Kanazawa Castle before walking to the Edo-period Kenroku-en Gardens, one of the Three Great Gardens of Japan.

In a castle made of wood and stone, Matteo peers out of a defensive window cut into the side of the floor. "I have an idea," he says.

"About what?" I'm admiring a painting of a tiger. The rest of the group is reading plaques about how the castle was rebuilt after a fire and asking Kimiko complex questions about traditional woodworking techniques that she answers with startling depth and, I assume, accuracy.

Before Matteo can tell me, Hank walks up and pulls out a magnifying glass from one of his pockets, then holds it up to the painting. "Gold," he says. His pants, which are the kind that transform into shorts, have only been partly unzipped, so his knees poke out. He sees me looking and flaps his hands in his pocket. "Ventilation."

Matteo watches him go. "Do you think he ever speaks in full sentences?"

"What's weird is that I always know what he's talking about."

"Me too!"

Kimiko summons us with a wave, and we follow Hank and his airy knees toward the Kenroku-en Gardens.

Once we're alone at a vending machine to buy cold drinks, I ask again. "What's your idea?"

"It's about what we can do to make sure our parents don't end up together."

"I'm listening."

He tells me.

"That's extreme, don't you think?" I ask as another tour group passes. They all have green baseball hats and headsets to listen to their guide, and I'm instantly grateful Kimiko doesn't make us wear matching outfits. It's bad enough to be shuttled around Japan on a bus tour. If I had to wear the same thing as Paulette, I would die.

"It's perfect."

"You think faking sick so your father has to take you back to Toronto is reasonable. Like he won't be upset about that at all. Or take you to a local doctor if it's so serious he has to cut the trip short. Or freak out poor Kimiko and probably trigger some insurance-fraud-type lawsuit. Or notice you're not actually sick."

Matteo takes the empty bottle from my hand and puts it in his bag. We learned on day one there are way fewer garbage cans here than at home and you have to carry your trash around. At night I empty out wrappers and bottles from my bag and feel ashamed to be part of the waste problem. "You've got no idea. All I have to do is tell Dad I've got a torn ACL or something, and we'll be on the next plane out to get it fixed."

"A torn what?"

He sees how confused I am and elaborates. "It's a knee injury. Trust me, it would work."

"No, it wouldn't."

"Yes, it would."

"Why?"

He frowns. "Because then I couldn't be on Dad's precious cross-country team."

"I thought you quit."

"Doesn't matter. He'd freak out."

"Do you not like running?" I ask curiously.

"I did until Dad decided he had to get involved after Dom left for university," he says. "All of a sudden, running became training plans and diet plans and getting yelled at about my potential."

"That doesn't sound fun."

"It was the opposite of fun. If I didn't win, he'd be furious. He made me go running with him, and it was this never-ending commentary on my stride and pace and form. So I quit. I like running, but not enough to deal with Dad's bullshit."

"What happened when you quit?"

"God, basically the world ended. Dad hit the roof." He squints at the pond in front of us. "I don't care. Let's get back to the plan."

I jump on this change of topic with relief. "We could try poisoning."

"Faking sick is bad, but killing someone is okay?" He raises his eyebrows. "Not really what I expected of you, and I thought we decided no murder."

I give him a poke. "First, not like real poison. Food poisoning. Something gross. Second, what did you expect of me?"

Matteo looks over, then smiles. "I think it's fair to say not a poisoner. You're too cool for violence."

No one's thought I was cool before apart from Hazel, and it feels a bit different coming from Matteo. I stare at him for a moment, but he turns away to look at a plaque. Yesterday's rain has burned off, leaving a bright blue sky that saturates the scenery in light and air that's easy to breathe.

We enter the gardens and stop talking. While I'm not thrilled by a defensive gate or hand-hewn beams, I can look around a garden forever. As stunning as the one in Tokyo, this garden has elements designed to reveal the different areas as you walk through, such as curving paths and small hills. Matteo draws in a deep breath, as if he also finds the harmony somehow necessary.

We stop at a huge stone lantern and watch two women in wide straw hats trimming the plants as they sit by woven baskets. Bridges and footpaths pass over ponds and creeks, and everything has been placed with perfect deliberation. It must be beautiful in the fall, with the leaves turning, and under the winter snow, before the spring brings its own covering of pale pink cherry blossoms. If I was making amigurumi, I would do a set based on the garden, of trees and flowers with smiling faces. I kind of want to, I can see them so perfectly.

"I wish we had more places like this at home," Matteo says quietly. "My local park doesn't hit the same."

I know how he feels. The park near our house is nice, but it's like this place has been cultivated to evoke specific memories and emotions. Wait, I mean the park near my old house. The apartment only has a parkette that Mom doesn't like me to use because of the men who hang around the picnic tables and go silent and stare when girls walk by.

Paulette, who is in front of us, turns to Tom, her voice breaking the lovely peace. "I was going to enter my front yard in a contest a few years ago, but the guy running it—very famous man—told me it was unfair to the others."

"How about that," Tom says.

"What they need to do here is get rid of some of the

rock. Too depressing, and look at that boring moss. Some petunias would jazz it right up."

"Huh." He glances around in desperation and sees us. "Ivy, Matteo! How are you kids holding up?"

I like Tom, who is funny, cool for basically a grandpa, and asks interesting questions. His wife, Lisa, joins us to linger on the gravel path as we wait for Paulette to move out of catching-up distance. When it's safe, we head toward the museum. A man passes with so many cameras and lenses around his neck that he walks bent over by the weight, and Tom sighs with envy.

Lisa laughs. "Did you find your soulmate or your nemesis?"

"I don't know if I want to marry him or roll him for his gear," says Tom, watching the guy set up a heavy-duty tripod.

"Don't you think about leaving me for him."

Tom kisses her nose. "And lose my favorite photographic subject? My muse? Never."

It causes a lump in my throat to see them so affectionate. I can't remember Dad kissing Mom like that, but he must have. When I look over, Matteo has the strangest look on his face. He catches my eye and turns to the pond, where a group of girls are posing on a bridge making hearts and peace signs with their hands.

Mom comes to check on me, and Matteo leaves to find his dad. We stroll past a street of souvenir and ice cream shops outside the gardens. People sit at tiny tables sipping their drinks and wiping their faces as white paper lanterns with Japanese characters bob in the slight breeze. Mom slings her arm around my shoulder, something we instantly regret because of the sweat.

"I knew a change would be good for you," she says happily. "Bad moods don't last forever."

"What if they do?" I ask tentatively.

"They don't," she says with confidence. "You're like me, Ivy. A good night's sleep is all we need to bounce back."

I shake my head, but she doesn't notice. That's not true for me, and she won't understand a bad mood can feel like it will last forever.

"I'm glad you're making friends," she goes on. "Matteo seems like a nice boy. He reminds me of Yasmin's stepson. Brady? Bradley? Bardley? Her husband's daughter is in your grade."

Then, like a thunderbolt, it comes to me. Stepfamilies. I know exactly how to keep our parents apart. Mom, unaware of how my brain has gone into overdrive, asks if I would prefer to have dinner at the pizza place or get traditional hot pot. "Kimiko says it's up to us."

I can start implementing my plan tonight. "Where are Matteo and Keith going?" I ask.

Mom narrows her eyes. "I didn't think you liked hanging around the rest of the group when we didn't have to."

"I never said that."

She pauses at a shop selling furoshiki, pretty fabrics people use as gift wrap. "First, Ivy, I can read you like the back of my hand. I know exactly what you're thinking."

I stare at her, unable to even answer this. If she really knew what I was thinking, she'd freak out. It's a muddle in here, and Mom can barely deal with her own messes.

"Second, you did say you don't like it. You told me last night after we got back to the hotel."

Damn, I did, in the hope it would keep Mom away from Keith, although I'd made it sound like a joke so she wouldn't get mad. I think fast. "It would be nice to have some company that isn't Paulette and her crew."

"Point taken. Today she told Yvonne she should smile more if she wanted people to like her." Mom rubs her temples with her fingers. "They were considering the hot pot place. I'll find out."

We head back to the hotel to freshen up before dinner, and I wash my hands with the peach-scented soap sheets I bought earlier while I think over my idea. I'll find Matteo before dinner and go over my amazing plan.

He's going to love it.

Matteo does not love it. "Can you run that by me one more time?" he asks.

"We can keep our parents apart by pretending we're dating," I say.

"Oh, so I did hear you right. No."

"What do you mean, no? No, it's a bad idea, or no, you won't do it?"

"Yes."

I frown. "Is it yes-no or no-yes?"

"Oh my God. It's no-no. No, it's a bad idea. And no, I won't do it."

If this was Connor rejecting me, I would be the saddest flower in the bouquet. I might not get out of bed for a week, although that doesn't take much these days. Also Connor did reject me, I belatedly remember. But with Matteo, it's not like he's snubbing me. Just the idea, although it's objectively great and he's wrong.

"You can't say no like that. It hurts my feelings to get rejected."

Matteo's eyes widen, as if he's worried he really did hurt me, then relax after I nudge him to show I was kidding. "Tell me why you think this is good."

I wriggle my shoulders and look past the river to a shrine with a gray torii and stone lanterns out front. Kimiko had encouraged everyone to go for a walk before dinner, and I'd promised Mom I would keep the restaurant in sight at all times so she'd agree to let me go alone. I basically have, but I needed privacy to talk to Matteo, and we've gone a bit farther than Mom probably expected.

"Because if we're together, they can't be," I say.

"Why not?"

I stare at him. "Think about it."

Matteo gazes over the wooden fence at a bridge in the distance, giving it more deliberation than I personally think is necessary. "Okay, that would be weird and kind of gross," he concedes. "I get it, but it won't work."

"Why?"

His dark eyes flit between my face and the river. "You want me to name the reasons?"

"Yes."

"We would need to like each other." He stares back over the water. "As in *like* like."

Not great for my ego, but I shrug. "Only for pretend, and I was once tree number one in a school play. I'm great at acting."

Matteo closes his eyes. "My dad would ask all sorts of questions."

"Mom will too," I say. "I'll keep saying *Mom* and *I don't know* and *oh my God, Mooooom.*"

"What about that Connor guy?"

I feel my face going red. "What about him? It's not like you and I will be kissing and stuff. We've been stuck together most this trip anyway."

"True, but the answer is still no. I'd hate Paulette to think she'd succeeded with any of us."

I want to kick a wall. "You don't like my idea? Get a better one."

"I will."

"Make it better than faking an ALC tear."

"It's ACL and not a problem."

I'm a little pissy that he dumped on my plan, and we separate and go our own ways to meet everyone for dinner. When I arrive at the restaurant, Matteo is sitting at the far end of the table. I have a fun time talking to Tom and Lisa about other places they've traveled to and don't do a thing to stop Mom from sharing a pizza with Keith. I do, however, give Matteo a smug look when Keith takes a sip of her beer, which is some local specialty, to rub it in.

Let him see the consequences of his actions.

Chapter 11

Day 6—Kanazawa to Kyoto

On this partial travel day, you'll continue your discovery of Japan in the traditional capital of Kyoto. With 17 UNESCO World Heritage Sites, this 1,200-year-old gem has something to offer every taste, from temples to culture to shopping to famous food markets.

We left Kanazawa early this morning, and we've been dozing between stops where Kimiko ushers us out to visit a shrine or temple. The last time, Mom leaned over to me, looking ashamed. "Is it bad that I'm getting bored of beautiful shrines?" she whispered.

I nod to bug her but feel less horrible for having thought the same thing. We've seen so many since we arrived in Japan that they're starting to blur into one meta-shrine. I want more places like Akihabara, with the lights and the action. Mom and I are in the minority of disrespectful and uncultured swine, though, since the others seem content to crunch their way along the gravel paths and take photos of paper lanterns and bamboo cups.

At the last stop, Keith jumped up to direct the group as if Kimiko wasn't there. I never pegged him for a shrine guy, but he's absolutely a lead dog kind of guy. He reminds me of the motivational speaker the school once brought in to encourage us to reach our full potential. Hazel had asked him about the impact of systemic issues that could adversely affect success. He told her the only limits were the ones she put on herself, and how the value of a meritocracy like ours is that people are only judged by their skill and potential.

The frequent stops are one more thing getting on my nerves. At least Mom is absorbed in her conversation with Yvonne, because it stops her constant joking about how I woke up on the wrong side of the bed. If I was at home, I could lock myself in my room until this sense of being on edge passed, but here I'm stuck. I slouch in my seat and close my eyes as snippets of Mom's conversation drift over me.

"I don't know," says Yvonne. "I found therapy very useful to help me work through my divorce."

"I suppose a lot of people do, but I've never been a fan," says Mom.

"It's definitely a trial-and-error process."

"People are too in their own heads and feelings in general," Mom says. "Half the time all they need is to get off the screen and get outside. I'm glad Ivy never needed any of that sort of thing. She's so even-keeled."

I don't hear Yvonne's answer because of the rush in my ears. I didn't know Mom was so down on therapy—though it's true she always says a good walk helps everything. I was right to keep quiet about this weight I'm constantly feeling. I can figure it out on my own. It has to fade eventually, right? I guess it doesn't matter, because even if it doesn't, Mom won't want to hear about it.

I wish I could talk to Matteo about this, but when I got on the bus, he passed by the empty seats near me to sit somewhere at the back. That caused my face to go up in flames. I mean, I don't care, but I kind of want to tell him I meant the fake part of fake dating. What if he took it to mean I'm interested in him, which I absolutely am not? Although I admit the hoodie he's wearing to ward off the chill of the bus's air-con is the cutest one I've ever seen. It's pale green, with a deep hood that looks incredibly cozy and has the perfect amount of hoodiness. My own sweater is thin, and I'm under a vent.

Kimiko stands up at the front of the bus. "We'll take a quick break to admire the view and stretch our legs," she announces as we pull into a parking lot overlooking an indigo lake.

"Coming, Ivy?" Mom yawns and stands.

"In a sec." I don't bother to look up. I'm kind of upset about what she said to Yvonne.

She frowns. "Don't let yourself get in a mood," she says.

"We have a busy day. No sulking."

Can't I be quiet without the commentary? No one asked her to deal with it, but I know better than to say so. I rub my eyes to pretend I was asleep. "Just need a second to wake up."

"Oh, still groggy?" She runs a hand through my hair, and it takes everything in me to not jerk away. I just nod. My shoulders drop as she goes off, chatting to Yvonne about how relaxing a road trip is when you don't have to drive, and leaving me with my thoughts.

The grayness comes and goes. Yesterday it seemed like more of a silk scarf than the heavy curtain of today. I'm so sick of it being tangled around me at all. I want to be the Ivy of before. Sure, I got sad, but it was about specific things: if I had a fight with Hazel or when my parents weren't talking to each other, or messing up an assignment or saying something stupid. It always passed to let me be myself until the next time something went wrong.

Now, though, it's like there's no myself to go back to. It's always with me. Sometimes less, sometimes more, but always there. I hate feeling like this, like there are only valleys and any peak is barely a plateau.

As if I'm not feeling bad enough, I make it worse by looking at a new photo on the Granite Lake chat of Addison and Connor leaning against each other by a tree. At least they're not kissing, but that's not much comfort. Daria commented, **look at them they make me believe in luv.**

A shadow dips over and I look up. It's Matteo, and apart from me, he's the last person on the bus.

"Are you coming?" he asks. He sounds normal, so I decide not to mention there was no need to act weird. Just add it to the list of things I keep to myself.

I shrug and motion out the window, not having the energy to move. "I can see from here."

He looks at my phone. "Is that Connor?"

"Yeah, with Addison."

"You still like this guy?"

I'm a bit offended, because there's something judgy in his tone, like it's my fault Addison moved in. "Look, things would be different if I was there. It's how he is. Everyone likes him. He's that kind of person."

Matteo drops in the seat across from me and holds out his hand. I pass him my phone.

"Is that what you like about him?" he asks as he zooms in on Connor. "Everyone else likes him?"

"Of course not."

"Then what?"

"I don't know. What was great about the last person you liked?"

Matteo grins. "She did stand-up comedy."

I wasn't expecting that. "She did?"

"Yeah, I noticed her at a school talent show, and she was hilarious. Is Connor funny?"

"Is he funny?" I echo.

Matteo raises his eyebrows. "Not sounding like a yes. Is he cool?"

"Yes." I can answer that at least. "He is."

"Why?"

I open my mouth and close it again. "I don't know. What made the stand-up girl cool?"

"Well, she did stand-up. She was also a super good person. She organized food drives and stuff."

I frown because Connor would never do that. "I don't know. I had a bad year, and he seemed like . . ." I struggle to find the word.

"A sign?"

"Yeah, exactly. Like when he finally started paying attention to me after two years of not, it meant things were changing."

Matteo shrugs. "Sounds like you wanted the change, not the guy." He hands back the phone. "Want to come see the lake?"

"In a minute."

Matteo leaves and I stare out the window. We're not the only group here, and other tourists are adjusting their brimmed hats and slathering on sunscreen. Paulette blithely stands in someone's shot, while Mom and Yvonne take a selfie near the water. Behind them, two kids try to fly a blue kite. There's only a breath of wind, but they keep going until they laugh so hard they fall on the ground. Finally the kite—it looks like a bird—slowly dips and drops before it rises into the air. They stare in awe as it dances above them.

My thoughts leap along with the kite. Talking with Matteo was kind of like pulling the final plug on my Connor crush. Although I don't think I feel better, my skin is less tight. I look back at the photo. I shouldn't waste my time being bummed about a guy who picked another girl. The more I think about it, the more I wonder if Matteo was right, and it's not Connor I wanted. It's the chance for change.

Everyone comes back onto the bus, and as Matteo passes by, he drops a bottle on the seat beside me.

"There was a vending machine beside the stamp stand." He waves his booklet. Lots of the tourist places have a spot where you can ink-stamp a booklet or paper to show you were there. Matteo is collecting them, and they're pretty, about the size of a hand and featuring an image unique to the location. I wished I'd started as well, but now I can't because I'll look like a copycat.

Then he passes me a sheet ripped from his notepad. "I got you one."

For some reason, this makes my throat get tight, and I remember the time Connor took my Coke out of the camp fridge last summer, the one I'd been saving. He hadn't apologized when I mentioned it was mine, or replaced it. He didn't text to see if I got home safe after either of those parties, and stopped talking to me after I didn't go to his place. I think about that messy bed in the photo and the vodka he offered. I pick up the bottle Matteo brought me. It's strawberry tea, and I close my eyes to enjoy the first cold sip.

There's an hour left before we arrive in Kyoto.

"I've been thinking about what you said yesterday," Matteo says. He sat next to me after the final shrine stop, and chatting with him has distracted me enough that Paulette's insistence on a bus-wide game of charades was only slightly aggravating instead of rage inducing.

I glance around to make sure we can't be overheard. Mom and Yvonne are playing some card game, Keith is at the back talking to Gary, and Hank is asleep. I still keep my voice low.

"What part?"

"Fake dating is a terrible idea, but I support the goal to keep them apart for the rest of the trip." Matteo leans in further to whisper. "Not with anything so drastic that other people notice, or they end up, like, hating each other. That's mean."

"The thing is, keeping them apart hasn't worked," I point out.

"I know, so we need a list of ideas to work from."

"We had ideas."

"Reasonable ideas." Matteo has his phone out, and he starts a note. "What's your number?"

There's nothing to read into this, given that Matteo gives off the same energy as if we'd been assigned to the same group project in history. A few seconds later, a message pops up to tell me Matteo wants to share a note with me. I open the list and stare at the only thing on the screen, a number one. He looks at me expectantly. Confused, I add in numbers two and three.

He sighs. "Ivy. You need to add your suggestions."

"You didn't."

"I'm an ideas guy."

"The number one is not an idea. It's the placeholder for an idea."

"I thought of doing the list."

"Now it's my job to do the work? I think not."

He makes a face. "I don't know where to start."

"Me neither." We pass a brick building that reminds me of a library. "Maybe we need to do some research."

"That makes sense." He starts typing, and I look over to see his search terms.

"How to break up a couple?" I ask. "They're not a couple."

"Well, what would you use?"

Paulette's cackling laugh gives me inspiration. "Dating turnoffs?"

"Oh, that's a good one." He nods with approval. "Let's see what we find."

We turn to our phones. "This one says bad hygiene," I say.

Matteo fake gags. "I have to agree. Let's put that on our list."

"Are we going to steal their toothpaste?" *Hygiene* appears letter by letter on the note. "As the people who have to share rooms with them, this could backfire on us."

"We can rank the pros and cons of all the ideas later. Look, maybe we're doing this the wrong way. What would you hate?"

"Me?" I think. "If the other person talked about themselves all the time and didn't care about getting to know me, or they didn't get off their phone."

"I agree. What's the point of even going on a date if you're going to do that?" he says. "Although sometimes it's not really the person's fault. Once . . ." Matteo stops.

I pounce. "This sounds like a story."

"It's not." He sees the look I give him. "Okay, I had this friend."

"A friend, uh-huh."

"For real," he protests. "He had a huge thing for this girl at school, and they ended up getting paired for a volunteer day. He freaked out and thought he was going to make a fool out of himself and she'd laugh at him. He didn't know what to say, so he spent the whole time on his phone and completely ignored her."

"What happened?"

"She thought he hated her."

"Did they get together later?"

"They never talked to each other again." He shakes his head. "She also told her best friend, who told everyone. It was pretty bad."

"Yikes."

"Yeah." He sighs. "I know."

I look back at the list. "How about you? What would you add?"

Matteo taps his knee as he looks past me and out the window. "I'd hate to feel like I couldn't be myself? Like, I kept having to be someone I'm not to keep them interested?"

"That would suck." I stare at the back of the patterned blue velour seat, frowning, then look at my phone to move this conversation on. "According to this website, talking about the ex is a turnoff. Would you care if someone talked about their ex?"

Matteo looks up, like he's giving it serious thought. "I suppose it would depend on how they did it, and how much."

"Yeah, if it was a comparison, that would be bad. Like their ex is still taking up a lot of brain space."

"Totally," he agrees. "Maybe we're looking too generally. We're not the ones who need to be bothered. What does your mom hate specifically?"

Although depending on the day it's more a question of what doesn't Mom hate rather than what she does, it's fairly easy to come up with some all-time favorites and then move on to Keith's hates. By the time we're done brainstorming, there are twenty-three items on our list. "Whoa."

"We got on a roll."

I scroll through them. "Some of these are a little unrealistic," I say.

"Are you looking at fourteen?"

"I am. Causing an international incident that gets us kicked out of the country might be too much."

"I can see that." He creates a sublist called JUST NO and moves over *international incident* along with *fake dating* and *torn knee*. "What about the rest?"

"What does this one mean?" I point to *favors that are not favors*. He added it without me noticing.

"We convince them to do something the other person hates, but as if it's a favor."

I frown. "I need an example."

"Let's say your mom hates coffee."

"She loves coffee."

"This is an example. A hypothetical."

"She hates lemon-lime pop. Use that."

"Oh my God. Okay. We tell my dad that your mom really loves Sprite, so he keeps getting her Sprite."

I think about this. "Then Mom will be mad to get all the pop she doesn't want to drink and Keith will be mad she's not happy with his gifts. Nice."

"I know, I'm awesome. Sprite is pretty great, though. I'm not sure why your mom hates it. Oh, I know, tell me something embarrassing about her."

"Why, you got some fun blackmail plans?"

He rolls his eyes. "We can add sharing embarrassing secrets to the list."

"Right. Let me think." Bad stories about Mom. There's the usual—she's messy, and late, and never listens—but that's nothing Keith would have missed after knowing her for a few days. There was the time she got sick, and . . . I don't want to embarrass Mom like that. It's mean.

Matteo looks over. "What do you have?"

"Sometimes she has so much crammed in her purse she can't find anything."

"Is that it?"

"She hates putting away clothes, so she piles them on a chair."

"Ivy."

"Once we went to see a midnight showing of *The Rocky Horror Picture Show*, and she fell asleep and sang along in her sleep. She can't sing."

"None of those are that bad."

"Well, what do you have on Keith?"

Matteo paused. "When he makes pancakes, they're always raw in the middle, and he only makes the gross protein ones."

It's my turn to be unimpressed. "Okay, next."

"He has motivational posters all over the garage."

"That's bad, but Mom once cross-stitched a wall hanging that says *Life is tough but so are you*, so it might work in his favor."

"Ugh." I can hear his frustration. "He's annoying, and I want them apart, but this one feels wrong. Like I'm betraying him, or breaking some sort of family trust."

"Yeah, me too." I move *embarrassing secrets* to JUST NO. After some more discussion, and a couple quick checks to make sure Hank is asleep, we have our winners.

1. Bad hygiene.

"We'll feed them garlic and hide their toothbrushes," suggests Matteo.

2. Talking about exes/current partners. Mention Dad to Keith and Kathy (Keith's ex-girlfriend) to Mom.
3. Favor not favors.
4. Point out to Mom that Keith is always working (something she hated in Dad) and to Keith that Mom is always late (he loves punctuality).
5. Heavy perfume (Keith hatred) and socks with sandals (Mom hatred).

"We're evil geniuses," Matteo says, admiring our work.

"We are."

Then Kimiko says, "Welcome to Kyoto," and we put the list aside for later.

Chapter 12

Mom goes to the window of our hotel and calls me over. "Ivy, look!" Our room overlooks the Kamo River, and it's gorgeous. We gasp as a huge gray-and-white crane flies over the water, like a painting come to life.

"What do you want to do this afternoon?" I look longingly at the bed, but there's no chance of a break because Mom already has her map spread on the table. According to the dog-eared Adventure Group itinerary Mom printed out, we have the afternoon to ourselves before meeting for dinner.

She hands the map over. "This."

"Nishiki Market?" I read the description and have to admit it sounds amazing: a covered alley that's a combination of food stalls and cookware shops that's existed for more than four hundred years. "Can we take a quick break first?"

"Come on, Ivy, we're in Kyoto. I don't want to waste a single second."

"One hour?" I give her a pleading look, and she swipes at me.

"None of that," she says. "I perfected that look."

"I do it better."

"Only because your eyes are bigger," Mom says. "I do it with feeling."

We spend a few minutes making pathetic faces in the mirror that end up looking increasingly clownish before she checks the time.

"We'd better hurry. I told Keith we'd meet him and go over together. It's only a ten-minute walk. I don't want to make them wait."

Figures. I fight off the frustration that again she's not listening to me.

"What about Yvonne?" I ask. She's not my favorite, but at least having her along will break the date vibe between Mom and Keith.

"She's going to the Samurai Museum," says Mom absently as she empties her suitcase on the bed. "I need to get a nice blouse."

This puts me on alert. "Why?" That's not good. Is it for Keith?

She points to a line of white on a black shirt and I peer closer. "What's that?"

"Salt from sweating," Mom says as she tosses the shirt into the bathroom. She's wearing a linen dress she desperately tried to steam in the shower. It's wrinkled but looks a little less like she slept in it. "Remind me to buy us energy drinks for the electrolytes."

"Eww." I immediately look at my own black clothes and am relieved to find them unsalted.

It turns out we're not the only people going to Nishiki Market, and we end up following Gary, who insists his career in logistics has made him an expert map reader. Mom frowns at her phone and gestures to Keith.

"No shade to Logistics Master Gary, but he's taking the longer route," she whispers. "If we go left, we can get there faster."

"If it gets us out of the sun, I'm for it," says Keith. "Great thinking, Lill."

Lill. Dad never called her Lill. He always called her Lillian. Then again, Dad never congratulated Mom for having a good idea. That wasn't their thing, but the way Mom smiles at Keith, it seems like maybe it was Mom's thing that Dad never fed into.

Keith starts off at a brisk pace, leaving us behind even though Mom is the one with the map and the knowledge of where to go.

"Go right," she calls. He waves his hand as if to say he knew, which of course he didn't. I pipe up.

"Wow, it's like he thinks he's in charge," I say. This wasn't on our list, but I'll take advantage of the opportunity.

I tried to say it as innocently as possible, which apparently is not very, because Mom raises her eyebrows. "Don't be rude, Ivy."

She goes after him and I seethe. She was never this

forgiving when Dad walked ahead of us. Then it was like the start of World War III. Here, she's laughing as she points Keith in the right direction and he acts like it was his plan all along.

Grr.

After Mom playfully taps Keith on the shoulder, I focus my attention on a Starbucks with menu items I've never seen, like lemon cake Frappuccino.

"It has real cake in it." Matteo is by my side, looking at the same sign.

"Do you think I can get one without listening to a lecture from Paulette about how I should be taking advantage of local culture?"

"Right before she complains about not being able to find a Diet Coke." He laughs. "It's like they don't get that differences in a global brand *are* the local culture these days."

"Kids!" Mom waves at us to hurry up.

We follow her instructions, Keith making sure to keep a step or two ahead of the rest of us. Since Mom prefers to navigate by landmarks or her heart—which can lead to some interesting adventures but is mostly aggravating when she gets lost and then angry as people become frustrated—I'm surprised to find us entering a crowded corridor lined with stalls a few minutes later.

"We did it." Keith high-fives her. What's this *we*? He didn't do anything. Matteo's face looks grim, but I can't tell if it's embarrassment at his dad or because our parents are joking with each other.

Mom surveys the busy scene. "If we get separated, let's meet at the far end of the market in an hour," she says. "It's only a single straight hall, so none of us can get lost." She hands me some yen for food, and we dive in. The yellow, green, and red coverings over the windows that form the roof give a cheerful look to the place, along with the flags of fish and waves hung over the corridor. Identical white signs line the upper part of the hall, which I assume are store names.

It's a good thing Mom decided on a meeting place because I stop to look at some cute bowls shaped like bears and when I'm done, the others have been absorbed into the crowd. This is fine by me. Although I'm surrounded, I have a pleasant sense of not being seen. The solitude is welcome after days of having to talk to people and sharing a room with Mom.

I send a photo to Dad and one to Hazel, but none to the group chat. I definitely don't send anything to Connor. My arms tense when I remember how many times I texted him, desperate for a tiny crumb of attention. I shake my head and take my time poking through the stalls. There's fresh seafood on ice and sweets and trays of deep-fried food. Almost everything is displayed with careful intention.

Absorbed in what's going on, I accidentally walk into a tall guy in front of me. "Oh, sorry," I say, doing my best to retreat so I'm not on the backs of his shoes.

He turns around, and to my surprise, it's Matteo.

The feeling that comes is nothing like what I got with Connor. When Connor looked at me, I felt almost sick, with butterflies in my stomach, and shaky hands. With Matteo, I relax. Being with him makes things better. Comfortable.

I like it.

Matteo reaches out and guides me through the crowd pressing in to the woman offering glasses of sake for one hundred yen. "I thought you were with our parents," he says.

"I thought you were." I raise my voice over the din of the market and vendors talking in Japanese.

"I let them go ahead because I wanted to be alone for a bit."

"We're supposed to be keeping them apart."

"Then why didn't you catch up to them?" Matteo leans against a wall, then hastily stands straight when the vendor yells something and waves his hands. "Sumimasen," he calls. "Sorry."

"Same thing," I admit. "I wanted to be alone for a bit. I got stuck talking to Susan about how to repot a pothos at the last shrine we stopped at."

Matteo sighs. "Gary cornered me about football. I don't watch football. Luckily he didn't care about what I had to say."

"Only wanted to hear himself talk?" I ask.

"Yeah, but his wife looked so relieved at getting a break I considered it my good deed for the day. Should we get something to eat before we keep going?"

We? "I thought you wanted to be alone?" I ask in surprise.

He shrugs. "It's probably better if we keep together so we don't get lost. Want one of those potato croquettes you like? I'm getting a shrimp one."

I do, and we order before standing at a table made of an upright barrel to watch people walking around with full filming rigs for their social media. One guy tries to set up a floor ring light before he's told to put it away. Matteo shakes his head. "Everyone is filming the same thing," he says.

"They'll all appear on a list of the top five secret places in Kyoto."

"They will!"

The gadget they provided sends up a shrill beep and Matteo goes to fetch the food, which is hot enough to burn our fingers. We drop the croquettes back to the plate. Matteo stares at the wall art with a complicated look on his face. It's a page from a manga, blown up to cover the whole space. This reminds me of something I've been wondering since Akihabara. "Do you do words or pictures first for a graphic novel?" I ask.

"Words, usually, but I have an idea of what the pages will look like." He doesn't sound excited, the way Hazel does when talking about her poetry. Or the way I used to, with my amigurumi. "Why do you ask?"

"Curious. What are you working on now?"

"Nothing." Definitely said with no emotion, but he doesn't stop staring at the wall of art.

"Why not?" The question is out before I remember Keith's comment about giving up at the conveyor-belt sushi place. Shoot. Did I overstep?

He shrugs. "I stopped. Quit. Dad kept telling me I can't make a living off graphic novels so it was a waste of time. He thinks art's a big joke." He looks away from the manga wall. "Anyway. This market is interesting. Dad loves these kinds of places, with a ton of action. How about your mom?"

I take the hint. "Same, but my father hates them."

"Yeah?"

I nod. "He would have hated most of this trip, to be honest. He likes staying in one place. When we were in Lisbon, his happiest day was sitting in a café reading a book. Mom's was when we ended up at a random street festival."

He laughs. "What a difference."

I hesitate. "I think Mom's been happier without him. And he's been happier, too."

Matteo looks at me closely. "But you want them back together?"

"Of course I do!" I poke the table with my finger. "They only need a break."

"Really?"

I don't need to answer because someone looking for a table comes to hover over us. We finish eating and go back into the crowded corridor. Matteo stops at the most perfect peaches I've seen in my life.

"Are you getting one?" I ask. They look like sunrises nestled in green tissue cut into leaves.

He checks the price, and we see they're about fifteen dollars. Each. "I'll stick with two-dollar squid skewers, thanks."

Exploring with Matteo has an added something I like, a kind of fuzzy and unnameable feeling that makes wandering through the market extra fun. I keep my eyes on his back, trying to figure out why, as he bends over to look at a pair of engraved chopsticks. He suddenly turns around, and I jump, a bit embarrassed to be caught staring. He doesn't seem to notice and points at a tea set printed with strawberries. "That is perfect for you. You always pick strawberry if you have a choice."

I grin at him. "You pick peach."

"The best flavor."

We bicker about peach versus strawberry as we look through knives that cost over a thousand dollars, then poke around the stalls until we reach the end of the market. We come out into a covered shopping arcade. Matteo tilts his head to the side. "Do you hear that?"

It's the most haunting music, like a flute but not, and it's been piped into the shopping arcade. There's a temple a few steps away, and the music and the dull light coming in from the roof make the scene feel like a memory from the past. Matteo seems to feel something as well, because he looks around, his eyes darting between the people passing and the stores selling everything from beautiful paper fans with paintings of birds and bamboo to a vending machine making cotton candy flowers. His hand hovers over his bag where a notepad peeks out before moving it to his side. I stand quietly as I take it in, not wanting to speak and break the spell we're under.

Then, too soon, it's broken for us. "There you are!" It's Mom, and she comes over and hugs me. For once, it's not too hot, so I don't shrug her off. "What did you think of the market?" Keith is beside her. Very close beside her.

I look at Matteo and he looks at me. Then we each start telling them about something we want to see, separately, on opposite sides of the shopping arcade.

My heart drops as Matteo leaves with his dad, but I put it aside. It's for the best.

Chapter 13

Day 7—Kyoto

Welcome to your peace! Begin your day strolling through the famous torii in the meditative beauty of the Fushimi Inari Shrine before making your way to visit the wild macaques, chattering in the rustling bamboo groves of Arashiyama.

I stand at the foot of a winding trail that has the benefit of being shaded by trees from the punishing sun. Kimiko has taken us to Arashiyama, where most of the group is about to climb up a narrow path to see the wild monkeys while animal haters check out the town, another temple, or linger among the bamboo.

"Remember," she warns. "Don't look the monkeys in the eye."

While almost every man in the group starts to joke about showing the monkeys who's the alpha, Paulette turns to her followers.

"We're going shopping," she informs them.

Joanne's sad expression kind of breaks my heart as she looks longingly at the path. She's even wearing a shirt printed with monkeys in hats.

"Mom," I whisper. "Joanne looks like she wants to stay."

Mom follows my gaze to see Joanne following behind Paulette and the other two, then makes a disapproving cluck. "She does." She raises her voice. "Joanne, where are you going? Come join us."

"No, she's coming with us," Paulette yells over her shoulder as Joanne hangs her head. "Monkeys are dirty things. We don't want to get rabies."

"Rabies has been mostly eradicated in Japan," says Gary.

"See? Nothing to worry about," Yvonne says. "Joanne, you said monkeys were your favorite animal."

This is enough to have everyone calling for her to join the hike to see the monkeys. Joanne glances uncertainly at her friends before looking down at her shirt.

"Joanne." Paulette's face is like a thundercloud. "I said we're going shopping."

"I think I might like to see the monkeys," Joanne says. "If that's okay." She walks over to Mom, despite Paulette literally grabbing at her arm.

"Kimiko says you can feed them," Mom says. "Isn't that something? What do you think they eat?"

Joanne casts her friends, or so-called friends, a few anxious glances, until Yvonne hands her a map of the path. She and Mom lead Joanne away, chatting about whether it's a myth that monkeys love bananas, as Paulette stares after them, her mouth working and her face beet red. Behind her, Gretchen nudges Susan, and they exchange suffering looks.

It's been a long, hot day so far. We started the morning early to get to the Fushimi Inari Shrine before the crowds, and Keith ran ahead so he could be first on the path. Mom waited for me with surprising patience as I held back to find the perfect moment to get the perfect shot of the gorgeous red gates all in a row with no people.

"That's *National Geographic* worthy," Mom said when I showed it to her.

"Not hard when the scenery looks like this."

She booped my nose. "None of that. You've got your mother's artistic eye, and I say it's a beautiful image you should be proud of."

Of course she thinks all my good stuff comes from her. It's all I try to show her. No one would like the true Ivy, even if she did take the occasional great photo.

Mom went ahead to read a poster about wild boars as I sent the photo to Hazel and, after a moment, to Matteo.

He replied almost instantly with a shot of one of the many stone fox statues wearing a red bib to ward off bad energy.

I sent him one of a moss-covered lantern and in return got a black-and-white cat sitting with its tail wrapped around its paws.

The next stop was Kinkaku-ji, where the Golden Pavilion rose from its surrounding pond and was so gorgeous people stopped talking to look. Matteo found a hidden spot and sent me a photo, which was basically a dare to find it. I examined the angles and the trees and, three minutes later, arrived at a secret path behind a rock garden. Matteo was waiting for me, and his next picture had been of my own triumphant expression.

Now on the hillside, Matteo points to a sign with some monkey trivia questions as I come near. "Should you try to shake a monkey's hand?" he asks. "Yes, no, or only if they offer."

We debate monkey facts as we walk up the hill. I pull out my phone to challenge him on monkeys versus apes, and a photo appears from the Granite Lake group chat, showing Addison and Connor cuddled up on the saggy, gross old couch campers jump on during the rainy days.

I get the expected sting. However, this time it's not because Addison is with Connor. Not really.

"What's up?" Matteo asks. "Did you find I was right and apes don't have tails and most monkeys do?"

I show him the photo and he frowns. "Sorry, Ivy. That's tough."

"No, no." Then I pause. "I mean, yeah, but it's not what you're thinking. Check out Addison."

He avoids a rock as he looks again. "She looks happy."

"I don't think I would have been if I was her."

"Why not, if you like him?"

I pause. "I don't think I could have been myself," I say finally. "Not comfortably."

Because if that had been me, I'd have been worrying about whether I was sitting too close or too far, and if I was being too cutesy and if I'd said something silly or weird and if he was going to kiss me and if I could kiss him and if my breath smelled. I'd have been careful to be the Ivy he'd like, and the constant monitoring would have made me tired and anxious.

"Then it sounds like he's not the guy for you." Matteo shrugs. "That person should make you happy, right?"

He should. I walk slower as I think it through. I hadn't understood how much this crush on Connor had brought me down until I was free of it. It feels good. Really, incredibly good.

We come out of the wooded path into a clearing with a hut and children's playground. Matteo grabs my arm, and, following his gaze to the top of the mountain, I gasp.

Monkeys. Little brown monkeys with pink faces are hanging out in trees or running around after each other. There are no gates or cages. They're simply there, and it's the most extraordinary thing I've seen in my life.

Without a word, we go up the steps and are surrounded by more monkeys. We've caught them at feeding time, and they fight for food and scamper at our feet. I would reach down to pet one, had not every sign on the way stressed that these are wild animals and Arashiyama is not a Disney set.

Matteo sits on a giant banana-shaped bench, and I go into the hut to buy some monkey food that I give to a mother monkey with a baby clinging to her fur. To the left, Tom sets up his camera, the lens trained on the mother and baby I fed.

"Do you like photography?" he asks when he sees me watching.

I hold up my phone. "I take photos, but I don't know if it's photography."

He looks at the screen on his camera, flipping through the images. I didn't see any of the places we visited in the same way, which makes me wonder if we even experienced the same things. Where I've been focusing on everything that's different or new to me, Tom found the elements that were universal. He pauses on one photo. It's a kid, staring joyfully at an ice cream cone as the people and neon lights swirl behind him. The next one is a silhouette of a couple holding hands as they stand on a small bridge over a narrow canal.

"I don't know if this is photography either," he says. "I only picked up a camera a few years ago."

"What made you decide to do it?"

Tom looks out the window to where the monkeys either clamor or wait for more food. "My father died."

I wince, feeling as if I said something wrong. "I'm sorry."

"Thanks, but you know, it wasn't his death that bothered me most." He settles his arms on the rail. "I mean, it sucked, don't get me wrong, but that's not what I think of when I remember him. Dad was a great artist, but he had five kids. He always said he'd have all the time he needed for his art when he retired."

Tom has the expression people get when they're remembering something bittersweet, a sort of inward look and smile that's more of a tilt of their lips. Mom gets it occasionally when she tells me stories of when she and Dad were first married. "That sounds nice," I say.

"It was for a while. When he retired, the whole family pitched in and got him new supplies. Oils and canvases and acrylics and an easel. My sisters and I helped my mom clear out the junk room to turn it into a studio. After a lifetime of sacrifice, Dad was finally able to do what he'd dreamed of."

"That's amazing."

Tom shrugs. "He'd noticed some stiffness in his joints for a few years before that and never told us. Got diagnosed with arthritis two months after he retired. Had another few months when his hands were good enough to hold a brush. Soon that was too painful, even if he taped it to his fingers. So he had months instead of the rest of his life for the thing he wanted to do most in the world. The thing he'd been waiting decades to do."

Although I'd been expecting an unhappy ending,

because that's how life is, it's a jolt. "Wow."

"Lived another fifteen years with all that art in his head, unable to put it to canvas." Tom shook his head. "When he died, I was clearing out his workroom and thinking of my own life. Man, I was so down."

I'm listening so hard my ears are about to bleed. "Yeah?"

"Yeah. I found his art kit in the back of the garage, the one I'd bought him, and I didn't feel a damn thing."

"Nothing?"

"Nada. All the things I liked to do felt dead to me somehow. I liked to swim, but the idea of having to find a swimsuit, go to the pool, get wet, dry off? It was too much." He shook his head.

"I used to do a craft called amigurumi," I say. "But then I got bored."

Tom glances over. "Bored or was it too much, like my swimming?"

"Swimming," I admit.

"I told myself I was bored too, like stopping was a decision I'd made deliberately. People get bored all the time, you know? But this was different, because it wasn't my choice. It was how it was. I knew something had to change."

"What happened?"

"I talked to someone." Tom pats my shoulder, but not in an uncomfortable way. It's like he gets what I'm feeling. "I should give you some sort of pep talk here, but I don't think reaching out for help is a lesson you can get too young. I wish I'd understood that at your age, but I was an obnoxious know-it-all back then." He grins at me. "Lisa would say that hasn't changed."

"Mom says I should learn from other people's mistakes."

Tom groans. "My mother said the same thing, but I never could until I'd made them myself, and usually a few times. I don't think any of us can. Otherwise we'd be perfect as a species. Anyway, you didn't come to Japan to hear a lecture from an old man. You should—oh my God! No!"

Although Kimiko had assured us the monkeys rarely approached people except for treats, one has snuck up to Tom's camera bag and tucks a hand inside. Tom goes to grab the bag but realizes it's a wild monkey with extremely big and probably very sharp teeth. He freezes and the monkey freezes and they stare at each other over the bag.

Then Tom says, "Don't even think about it."

The monkey keeps its hand in without breaking eye contact, as if daring Tom.

"I said. Don't. Even. Think. About. It." It's the most dad of dad voices and the monkey makes a face like it's been caught coming in past curfew. It moves its hand away slowly and then runs away. Tom blows his breath out.

"I know Kimiko said no eye contact," he says guiltily. "But that lens is expensive."

I leave Tom to sanitize his bag and go back to watch monkeys play in the water while I think about what he said. I feel a bit bad for him, but part of me is glad to have found someone who felt the same way.

I glance over to where Matteo is looking at the city below us, a monkey perched near him like a friendly dog. His back is to me, so he doesn't see me approach.

Which means he doesn't put the notebook in his lap away. I watch him draw for a minute, and he's so absorbed he doesn't notice me at first.

"Ivy!" He slams the book shut and goes red.

"Oh my God, Matteo, that is so good." I stare at him. "I had no idea you could draw like that."

He looks straight ahead, and I start to feel a bit guilty. "I'm sorry, do you want me to go away so you can work? I don't want to make it weird."

"Did you really like it?"

It had been a sketch of the view, with giant monkeys crawling curiously around the landscape. "I thought it was incredible."

His shoulders relax a bit. "Thanks."

"I'd love to see more, if you have them," I say. "You're really good."

"Adventure Group!" Kimiko is waving from the hut. "Time to go."

Matteo puts away his notepad, and we head back down the mountain—I keep Mom at the front, and Matteo has Keith bringing up the rear—and meet up with everyone else to trade stories about our various adventures. Tom gives a highly exaggerated retelling of his monkey escapade that makes it sound like they were about to engage in hand-to-hand combat. Paulette refuses to look at Joanne, who hovers on the edge of their clique before straightening her shoulders and coming back to stand with Lisa. Paulette talks louder while giving her sneaky looks. What an immature woman. I have no idea why the other two stick with her.

Kimiko gives us the option to ride a train that offers what she calls a "picturesque look at residential Kyoto" or to take the tour bus directly back to the hotel, and Mom and I choose the train along with a few others. I hear Keith and Matteo arguing outside the ramen restaurant where we had lunch.

"There's a treadmill at the hotel," Keith is saying.

"Dad, knock it off."

"Don't take that tone with me, son." Keith sounds fed up. "I said we're going back. You know what you need to do. I'm trying to help you build resilience, and you don't do that by being a quitter. People hate quitters. You think a girl is going to want to be with a guy who can't handle the pressure? Who's one of those people who get walked all over? Your brother trained every day, even when he sprained his ankle."

For a minute, I watch anxiously to see if it's going to escalate, but Matteo only mutters something under his breath and gets on the bus. Mom hasn't noticed, and I don't say anything as I join her.

She glances up from her conversation with Joanne and

Yvonne. "Keith and Matteo not coming?" She only seems politely curious, which is a relief.

"I guess not," I say.

"Let's get on board, then."

There are only two cars on the purple train, and the conductor is a woman in her twenties with her hair in a tidy black ponytail that hangs down her back, a uniform with a white blouse and navy skirt, and a black pillbox hat that I love.

I reach in my bag to find my water bottle is empty. Mom hands me hers.

"But you're almost out," I say.

She smiles and runs her hand over my head. "You have it, sweetie."

I drink the water and shift in my seat to take in the scenery. Kimiko wasn't lying. We trundle through neighborhoods right out of a Studio Ghibli movie, with stations and houses bordering the track. The scene is so peaceful it doesn't feel real, and I take photos to show Matteo. He could make amazing drawings here. Even I feel inspired to create new worlds. That house, for instance. I can see the amigurumi creatures I could make to populate it, and they could have adventures with the monkeys on the mountain. It could be a whole series.

The train passes through a tiny station surrounded by houses, where the sun comes through wooden slats to lay stripes on the platform. There's a sense of agelessness, with the faded wood and paint, and long blades of grass growing around the tracks, as if the train station had grown up with the world around it. I bet it would look the same fifty years in the past or twenty years in the future.

Kimiko notices me admiring the view. "Have you heard of wabi-sabi?"

"I have," says Paulette confidently. "It's a condiment. Burns your nose."

Kimiko smiles. "You might be thinking of wasabi."

Paulette laughs. "I think I know what I'm talking about."

Mom shifts to block Paulette from view. "What's wabi-sabi?"

"It's a traditional aesthetic philosophy that celebrates the beauty of imperfection," Kimiko says. "It shows us things that are incomplete, or have aged, or are impermanent are worthy of appreciation." She points at a passing garden. "Look."

"It's pretty." It has something that draws the eye, and I can't help craning my neck to keep looking as the train passes.

"Yes, and the bamboo fence is missing a slat. The stone lantern is mossy and has a chip out of the side." She sees my face. "I didn't notice that all in a moment. A friend lives there. But what's not perfect is what makes it authentic and real." She grins at me. "Perfection is dull. It has no character, nothing that tells of its history or experiences."

"I don't know about that," says Mom. "It can be nice to

have a clean, fresh bit of perfection. Some things aren't worth the effort of fixing, and not everything old and worn is attractive." She catches Kimiko's look and groans. "I'm being crassly North American, aren't I?"

"It's an appreciation that sometimes needs to be cultivated," says Kimiko diplomatically. Mom looks uncertain.

Paulette leans around Mom. "I'm pretty sure it's a condiment," she says, and Kimiko shifts the conversation to how wasabi is made. Apparently from a rootlike stem, which I didn't know.

We're back at the hotel soon enough, and although I keep my eye out for Matteo, he's not there. He must be in the basement gym or in his room fighting with Keith. I want to tell him what Kimiko told me about wabi-sabi and see what he thinks. Would he agree it's fine to not be perfect? To celebrate the things life or time has cracked open and left flawed? Or would he agree with Mom?

What do I think?

I don't know.

Chapter 14

Day 8—Kyoto

Feel free to explore Kyoto at your own pace, or join our optional bike tour* of the city! There's much to see, and lucky Adventurers might catch a glimpse of an elegant geisha on her way to work. At night, rejoin the group to take part in a traditional tea ceremony and dinner in atmospheric Pontocho.

*Bike tour not included in Adventure Group base fee.

It's an optional day, so some people are sleeping in and others have already left on various side trips. Mom and I are going on a meander day, Mom's name for wandering around and checking out whatever we want. There might be one or two destination spots, and usually we start with them before we get sidetracked. The goal is simply to explore and, honestly, shop.

I usually love meander days, but it's hard for me to get moving. I know I need to. I'm in Japan. I want to sightsee. I want to be *normal*. I want the Ivy I am for Mom and everyone else to be the same one right down to my bones, instead of only surface level. Why am I like this?

Mom stops and looks at me. "What's wrong with you?" She's been chatty and must have noticed my lack of enthusiasm.

"Nothing."

"Ivy, I keep telling you I'm not a mind reader. You're like your father, thinking it's my responsibility to investigate your little moods and make everything better."

"I'm not in a mood, okay?" I hate how she calls it that, and if I was tempted to tell her anything, her comment killed it. "I'm tired."

"You're always tired." Her face is set because she's losing patience with me, and we haven't even left the hotel.

"Maybe too much sun yesterday." It's easier to blame everything on the sun, or allergies, or lack of sleep. Mom understands physical weakness, at least.

"If you're not well, we could stay in the hotel so you can rest," she says reluctantly. "At least for a bit."

I can see her mentally recalculating her day. No thanks. Sitting in a hotel room watching Mom suffer from FOMO will not make me feel better. "Give me a few minutes," I say.

I drag my bag into the bathroom and am getting out my clothes when I hear a metallic clang on the tile floor. It's my crochet hook, which has fallen out of the yarn I'd pierced it through to keep it all together. The bluebird had tangled in my clothes, and with the hook gone, a few of the stitches have come out. It's an easy fix, but instead I pull the yarn slowly, and watch the loops shrink and disappear. Shrink and disappear. Shrink. Disappear.

Then there's only blue yarn and no bird left. I stuff the whole thing away and stare in the mirror, trying to get myself in the mood for people. Maybe Mom is right and I need to power through it.

"Ivy!" Mom knocks on the door, and my smile falls off until I push it back up with my fingers. "Let's *go*."

After I turn off all the lights, because she's left them on *again*, we're off.

We take the subway—thank goodness the signs are in English as well as Japanese—and head to what looks like a typical city corridor of concrete and office buildings. It's such a shift from the old wood charm of where Kimiko has been taking us that for a second we freeze in the middle of the sidewalk to get our bearings.

"That's the thing about being a tourist," says Mom. "It can be so easy to forget a place isn't only temples and monkeys, but where people need to get gas and go to work."

She's clearly decided to act as if nothing is wrong, in that really obvious way that tells me she's pretending. I don't have the energy to fight. I put on my happy face, and after a while, she accepts it for real and cheers up.

That makes it less tense, and I can work on calming down and trying to break free of this blah-ness that threatens to overwhelm me. It fades as Mom gets us lost again, but I distract myself by taking over navigating. The success of finding our destination helps a bit as well.

The incense store smells like a bouquet in a cedar sauna. We're the only customers, and about eight saleswomen look up to greet us. Mom waves hello and enters an internet-mediated chat as she shows a saleswoman photos of a particular powdered body incense she wants. I wander around to smell the incense on display. I turn my translation app on a package. It's called Enlightenment, and I breathe it in, not sure what that would smell like. Apparently, kind of spicy.

My phone buzzes, and I steel myself for a message from Addison or the group chat, not looking forward to another reminder of how Connor made me feel. Instead, it's a text from Matteo. He and his dad left before us, and the photo is of a cute street with a pagoda in the distance. He sends another of a cream sandwich filled with peach and strawberry slices.

I take a photo of the shop and, like him, I don't caption it. Let the pictures do the talking.

Mom finishes and we hit a café overlooking a shrine and life-sized terrarium. Mom and I split a peach drink, and she lets me eat all the whipped cream, which is thick and delicious.

"God, why are we stuck with dull drink flavors at home when we could have this?" Mom says. "Are you feeling better now?"

Yesterday Tom said sometimes you need to talk to

people. I stare at the beads of condensation around the drink and decide to try.

"Not really."

She nods seriously. "What do you mean? Tell me more."

My heart pounds that I might finally have to open up about this and give details I'm not sure how to describe. I don't want to, yet I do.

"I'm not sure. I feel . . ." I keep staring at the cup, the printed words merging into a dark blur.

"You said you were tired," Mom interrupts. "Is that it? That makes sense. This trip is more intense than I expected."

"It's been going on longer than that."

"Well, it's been a lot for you this year. It's normal to feel run-down. Sweetie, I know what it's like when things are changing and it's hard to cope. I felt the same way growing up."

I know that's not true, which makes it harder to say what I need. It's like trying to describe water without using the word *wet*. "I don't think so."

She sighs. "Is it the divorce?"

"The separation," I correct her.

Mom's mouth goes tight. "You know what I mean."

I only shrug.

"Fine. Ivy, your dad and I are separated. Are you still upset about it?"

I shrug again. She's acting like it happened decades ago.

"I know it's hard, but we all need to move on. Your dad

and I have been talking, and we agree."

They've been talking? I brighten. This is what I want to hear. "Really?"

Mom has told me a hundred times they have to be separated a year before they can make it final, but surely the fact they're not actually divorced has to mean something.

"Really. It'll pass, Ivy-mine." This is a play on *ivy vine* and is an old nickname from when I was a kid. She hasn't used it in a long time, and for some reason, it makes my throat tighten.

"Sure."

"That's my good girl," she says. "What else is bothering you? You know you can talk to me about anything."

I nod, but that's not true. It's not that she doesn't care, but I need her to slow down and *listen* to what I can't say instead of what I can. But there's no way I'm going to try again, not now, because having her ignore what I need makes it worse. Almost embarrassing, like when you answer in class but the teacher was calling on the person behind you.

"I'm glad we talked. Ready for more shopping? Let's have some fun!"

I do as she says and stand up. Tom was wrong. Sometimes you can't talk to people.

The one place I desperately want to check out—the special stationery store that sells the handmade origami paper

Hazel wants for writing poems—is closed until later in the afternoon, so Mom and I wander around the shopping arcades out of the sun.

"Get off your phone, Ivy," she says as we pass by an old bookstore. "Be in the moment."

"It's from Matteo. They're at a big temple."

"Oh, that's nice. It's good you're hanging out with him," she says. "Poor Keith is at his wit's end. He hoped this trip would help him reconnect with Matteo after what happened."

"What?" I turn to face her. "What happened?"

"Matteo's mother died suddenly about two years ago," she said. "An aneurysm. A tragedy for the family."

"Oh." I don't know what to say.

"Keith promised he'd take advantage of life after that," she says. "He told me all about it, and that's why they're here. It seems Matteo's been unhappy, and Keith thought a change of pace might help them get closer, especially with the elder son out of the house. Japan is a place his wife always wanted to visit."

I try to analyze her voice like some sort of human lie detector, but she seems unbothered talking about Keith's wife. Perhaps we were wrong. Could they really be only friends?

"Did she? What was she like?"

Mom looks surprised. "I don't know. I didn't ask."

"Why not?"

She wrinkles her nose. "I didn't feel comfortable quizzing a man about his dead wife."

That's fair. I leave it alone.

Mom looks at purses made of old kimono as Matteo sends me another photo. We've managed an entire day of telling each other what we were doing without words. I know he had sushi for lunch and didn't like the roe, which ended up in a pile of red bubbles on the worn wooden platter, and ice cream floats in a café that looked like a mix of a vampire's den and wacky thrift store. I send him a shot of a candy store and a street with signs forbidding photography that I saw too late.

He's also sent me a couple sketches, which I can tell were drawn on his phone. They're cute enough to be stickers, and I ask if I can save them. He says yes and sends me another of a cat staring at a statue.

It's getting late when I check the time. "Mom, if we're going back to that stationery store, we need to leave."

"One minute." She's spent an hour shopping for an embroidered satin bomber jacket—the lady said they're called sukajan—while groaning at the price and debating with the owner whether the dragon jacket or peony one is better. I've tried to hurry her along, but that backfired. Mom hates being told what to do, and I'm sure she deliberately started going slower after I spoke up.

Five minutes later, I'm getting stressed. "We need to meet everyone for dinner soon, and the store is going to close."

"Right, I'm almost done."

"Can't I go back by myself?"

"Do you even remember where it is?"

I wave my phone at her. "I can map it."

"Give me a second, Ivy. I can't think when you rush me like this."

Finally, she decides on a different, third jacket with a tiger and goes to pay, but it's not over. She hangs around, chatting and laughing with the owner for a few more minutes as I hover on the edge of the stairs, dying to get going. Mom joins me, looking happily into the bag. "Isn't it gorgeous?"

I'm already halfway down the steps, the location ready on my phone. "My store closes soon," I say. "Can you hurry?"

Again, she takes her time. "Don't worry, it's open another half hour."

The crowds in the shopping arcades have at least doubled over the day, and people linger in front of signs advertising capybara cafés and owl bars. Mom strolls along, swinging her bag and exclaiming over stores she wants to go into, but I walk a few paces ahead and pretend not to hear. Actually, I don't have to pretend. A rushing sensation in my ears makes it hard for me to distinguish sounds. I begin to recognize the stores and hurry faster. Twenty minutes left. I'm not going to be able to take my time and browse for the perfect gift, but it'll have to do.

When we get to the store, a man in a canvas apron is

pulling down a metal door from the inside.

"Excuse me." I bend down to call to him. "I'm sorry, can I get one thing? I know it's late."

He shakes his head. "Closed."

"Please, just . . ." The gate rattles down the rest of the way, and I stare at it in disbelief.

"Oh, too bad." Mom comes up behind me. "Just missed it. What kind of a place is only open from noon to five and then closes early? That's random."

I'm so angry I can't look at her. "I told you it was getting late. I told you!"

"Good Lord, calm down. Look, there's another paper store right there." She walks across the corridor and looks at me impatiently. "Are you coming?"

"Mom, I wanted this particular store. I told Hazel."

"I'm sure she'll understand."

"You promised we'd come back when it was open." I know I should let it drop the way I usually do, but I'm too upset to pretend it's not a big deal. I'm sick of always having to hide how I feel. *Sick* of it.

She moves her giant shopping bag from one hand to the other. "What do you want me to do? I'm not a magician. I can't make them open."

"You could have taken less time over that stupid jacket so I could do something I wanted as well!"

"Ivy, I didn't know it was going to close early, and there's nothing to do about it now. We can see if it's open tomorrow, okay? You can accept that, or you can ruin the rest of the day, but I don't want to hear another word. This discussion is over."

I clamp my mouth shut, wanting to scream, but what's the point? She's right. The one place I wanted to see is closed. We're leaving early tomorrow, so coming back is an empty promise to shut me up. It makes me madder that she's right and there's nothing to be done. Something *could* have been done earlier if she wasn't so selfish.

"Do you want to go into the other store or not?" she asks.

"No."

"Don't be like that."

"I'm not being like anything."

"Well, I want to go in."

We spend the next half hour looking in more stores, but I barely pay attention. I'm sure I probably could find something similar to what was in the stationery place, but I don't have the heart. I'm done with the day, and all I want to do is get out of here and be quiet.

Chapter 15

When we get back to the hotel, I check the time. It's about four in the morning at home where Dad is, but he's the only one who will understand.

Mom is being Mom, I write, knowing I won't get a reply for a few hours but needing to vent. **I wanted to go to a store but she messed around until it was too late. Why is she so selfish.**

I read over my message and delete the last few words. I want Dad to be on my side, but if he thinks I'm going too far, he'll tell me I'm exaggerating and that she loves me. Then I delete the part about the store, too. Dad won't get why it's a big deal.

However, he'll completely understand what I mean by Mom being Mom. Sometimes it seemed their entire relationship was based on being opposites. If Mom was enthusiastic about something, Dad thought it was boring. If Dad freaked out, Mom would say it was no big deal. It's kind of incredible they got married in the first place.

"Ready for dinner?" Mom is acting like nothing is wrong, and I shove my phone in my tote bag and follow her to the lobby without answering. Her expression says she's about to tell me to put a smile on my face, but we arrive at the main floor before she gets a chance. She leaves me for Yvonne, probably to describe what happened and make herself sound like the reasonable one. In the middle of the lobby, there's a small indoor garden featuring an old pot with a big crack. I stare at it, trying to see the wabi-sabi Kimiko was talking about, but I can't. It's just an old pot that should be tossed. Mom's right. Wouldn't a new one be better, one without all the wear?

Kimiko takes us for a tea ceremony in Pontocho, a narrow winding alley lined with restaurants and bars. In some spots there's only enough space for two people to walk together. It's a romantic scene, and the path is lit with lanterns patterned with the symbol of Pontocho, birds that look like tropical fish and that Kimiko says are called plovers.

"You may be lucky enough to see a geisha, which we call geiko in Kyoto," she says. "If so, please be respectful and make sure not to interfere—"

"Oh my God, look! There's one right there, out in the open!" Paulette's cry causes everyone in the alley to turn around and see what the issue is. She's pointing at a geisha and has stepped in front of the poor woman to take photos like she's at a zoo. Kimiko does her best to get Paulette to act like a decent human being while the geisha passes by unperturbed, as though dealing with the Paulettes of the world is part of the job, which it might be. Her kimono is gorgeous, with reeds and dragonflies around the hem, and the blue obi forms a huge knot at the back. Her black hair is styled up and decorated with ornaments, and her skin is painted chalk white.

"Did you see that?" Paulette screeches. "Like out of a movie. I saw *Memoirs of a Geisha* twice."

Kimiko waves us into a two-story building, and we take off our shoes in a plain foyer with a niche holding a single scroll. Lisa says something about a pretty flower display, and I put on a smile that would make Mom proud. I don't want other people on the tour asking me what's going on, so it's easier this way.

The floor we step onto is wood, but the room has tatami mats with low tables and cushions in a U shape surrounding a hearth in the middle. It looks like a fire hazard in this city of wood.

"Does 911 work in Kyoto?" I ask Matteo. Being with him and away from Mom has already made me feel a bit better, although a brief zing of anger went through me when we passed a paper store a few minutes back. Mom's wrong. They're not all the same. It was the one thing I wanted to do, but as usual, Mom got her own way.

"They use 119," he says.

"How do you know?"

He rolls his eyes. "Dad told me, like, ten times before we came here."

"Strange that there's no global number."

"There is, kind of. 112 works on most cell phones to connect you to the local emergency line."

I stare at him. "Did Keith make you memorize that, too?"

"Nope. Learned it in history for some reason." He looks at me closely. "Hey, everything okay?"

I shrug. It's not bad when Matteo asks. "Feeling quiet."

He nods. "I get it."

The woven mats are slightly slippery to walk on, and when I sit down between Mom and Yvonne, I touch them to find they're cool. They smell good, too. Fresh. Matteo is across from me, and his eyes dip down to his phone. Two seconds later, mine buzzes in my hand. It's a photo of a row of lanterns lit up and glowing softly. I send him the one I took of a display of hyperrealistic food.

Then we snap to attention because a woman in a beautiful pale blue kimono has come in, so elegant and confident I can't keep my eyes off her. Kimiko told us she is a maiko, an apprentice geisha. She bows, and unsure of what to do, I look around to see some people bowing back while Paulette, who has stood up, is simply filming on her phone. The woman kneels—again, so graceful—and dips a bamboo cup on a long handle into an iron pot.

Soon we're each given a small bowl of tea to try. Unlike the delicate teacups we have at home, these are thick and almost rough-looking. "Where's the sugar?" calls Paulette. "Tea needs sugar."

Kimiko explains that sugar interferes with the flavors of the tea, and Paulette stares at her. "This isn't the way my local café makes their matcha green tea, and I can assure you they're very authentic," she says.

Susan, face red, lifts her cup and takes a loud sip while Gretchen stares at Kimiko expectantly and waits for Paulette to be appeased.

Kimiko murmurs to the maiko, who leaves the room. Not a minute later, she comes back with some servers, who hand everyone a small mochi on a gray ceramic plate. "Sometimes we will eat a sweet with the tea," says Kimiko. "You might find this more palatable."

She also presents Paulette with a heaping bowl of white sugar without a word, and beside me, Joanne starts coughing to cover her giggles. Paulette shoots her a glare as she stirs a huge spoonful into her cup, then lets it sit there without drinking until Kimiko tells us to follow her for a traditional kaiseki dinner. We go into the next room, which has been set up Western-style with tables and chairs, as if they've anticipated the horror of a group of Canadians unused to kneeling for an entire meal.

Kimiko hands us numbers that correspond to a seat. "To change it up," she says. "You can get to know others on the tour a bit better."

"Is that okay, Ivy?" Mom asks in a low voice. "You can sit with me if you want."

I don't want to, so I shake my head.

We sit down and Matteo slides in beside me. Tom and Lisa are with us, as well as another couple Mom calls the Silent Twins because they dress in matching outfits and barely say a word. Mom is with Keith, who's showing her something on his phone.

Matteo sees the same thing I do, and we exchange a glance. "Time to regroup for phase two," he whispers.

"What's phase two?"

He shrugs. "We'll figure that out when we regroup."

The dinner is long, and although Tom and Lisa are nice, it's a table with adults and I'm distracted by Matteo sitting beside me and Mom and Keith having the time of their lives on the other side of the room. I like the food, because the meal is basically a bunch of small dishes served on individual trays. Matteo glances over, and then to my surprise, manages to keep the conversation away from me. I don't have to say a word the whole meal as he chats with the others about school and pop culture and what we've seen so far on the trip. Sometimes he says, "Right, Ivy?" and all I have to do is nod.

It helps a lot, and by the end of the meal, I feel better. Everyone stands to leave, and Matteo pulls me aside.

"Thanks," I say.

"No problem." He shrugs. "Dom and I used to do that when one of us had a shitty day to get Dad off our backs at dinner."

He points toward the rest of the group, who are

chattering about how good the meal was. Mom and Keith are in the middle, and it looks like his hand is on her arm. No. I want to leap over and yank them apart.

Kimiko claps her hands, so we all pay attention. "I'll be heading back to the hotel, and those who want an early night are welcome to come with me," she says. "Or you may wish to admire the beauty of Pontocho by yourselves. Please be on time for the bus to Nara tomorrow."

Mom comes up. "A few people are going to explore," she says. "What do you think?"

It's on the tip of my tongue to give a snappy answer, like *what does it matter*, but she'll get mad, and anything is better than sitting in the room ignoring each other. "Okay."

Keith and Matteo, Yvonne, Tom, and Lisa join, but soon we're spread out. Mom has told me to meet her at the end. The alley where all the restaurants and bars are located is winding and crowded, and Matteo and I drift to the back of the group.

"Your photos looked like you were having a good day," he says.

I rub my eyes, hoping my mascara doesn't smear. "The city was fun, but you know those days when you don't feel right?"

He nods. "You had one?"

"Yeah, but I feel I get them a lot."

"Did you talk to your mom about it?"

"I tried."

This makes him laugh. "Did she do the thing where she answers what she wanted you to say instead of the thing you actually did say?"

I manage to smile. "She did."

"Dad does that all the time," says Matteo. "That sucks. Is it feeling more sad? Or more mad? You don't seem like either."

"Thanks! I try." I give him a big fake smile, and he winces. "Sorry."

"It's okay. Both come and go in waves, I guess?" Talking to Matteo about this is way easier than with anyone else. Maybe it's because we're walking through a busy alley, or because he doesn't really know me. That being said, Mom is right in front of us. "I don't think I want to talk about it."

"I'm here if you want." He touches my arm. "Okay?"

I nod and we weave through the crowds until Matteo points to a tiny alley filled with what look like goldfish bowls. "Let's check that out."

For a moment, I'm torn. I want to look, but Mom and Keith are ahead of us. We should rush over and separate them. That's my goal, right? To keep them apart so Keith can't interfere with my parents getting back together.

"Ivy?"

I let Mom and Keith go, and follow Matteo to poke our heads in to the alley. We gasp because it really is filled with goldfish bowls, complete with goldfish. There must be over a dozen containers, lit up different colors, and all sorts of shapes and sizes. I have no idea why it's here, but I love it. We peer through glass bowls and down into huge pottery ones, with goldfish darting around. When I join Matteo near one with fishing raccoon dogs, he moves aside and stands a bit behind me so I can see better. With most people, I'd feel uncomfortable to have them so close, but I don't mind with Matteo.

More people come in and we leave, after putting some yen in the donation box. The alley has gotten more crowded, but I see a path. "Down there."

We escape and find ourselves on the edge of a picturesque canal crossed with bridges, and more buildings on the other side. It's peaceful, with the cool air rising from the canal. I breathe deep.

"Let's move to Kyoto," I suggest. "We can walk along this path to school in the morning."

"If you could live here, would you?" He steps down on one of the stones edging the canal. "Or in a lonely cabin in the woods? Or at the top of a skyscraper?"

I join him on the stones and balance with my arms out. The canal is so narrow I could almost jump over it, and the lights play on the shallow dark water below us.

"I don't know," I say. "There are places I'd like to live, but maybe not forever."

"Yeah, a cabin in the woods would be nice for a while, but eventually I'd want a shawarma."

"A skyscraper would be cool, but it would be a pain to

have to come down fifty stories to grab a bag of chips." I lose my balance for a second, and Matteo reaches out to steady me. "I guess I'd like to be back in my old house most of all."

"When did you move?"

"A few months ago." I climb up the closest bridge. Matteo joins me to stand in the middle. From here we can hear people laughing from the surrounding restaurants. "My parents sold the house after the separation, and they live in apartments on the opposite sides of town now."

"Do you like it?"

I shrug. "It's only for a couple years until I go to university."

He leans over the rail to look down at the water, and I do the same. "I thought you said your parents were getting back together. But they sold the house?"

I don't want to think about it. "It needed a lot of renovations, and they wanted a change," I say shortly. "We should get back. Mom will be worried about me."

"Right." We walk back over the bridge, then Matteo looks at me. "Sorry," he says. "I should have kept my mouth shut."

I shrug, not wanting to think about it, and in another minute, we're in the alley and it's too busy to talk.

Dad's reply is waiting when I check my phone before bed.

What happened?

She promised we'd do something I wanted but made us late so we couldn't.

He must be on his phone because his answer comes right away.

That sounds like your mother.

She never listens to me.

You know she loves you. Are you having a good time apart from that?

I should have known he wouldn't want to get involved. He hates what he calls drama. I can't tell him about Keith, obviously, so I write, Japan is cool.

Glad to hear it. Be a good girl and listen to your mom. See you soon.

I plug in my phone to recharge and lie back in bed, staring into the darkness and feeling alone despite Mom across the room. It takes a long time before I fall asleep.

Chapter 16

Day 9—Nara

Get ready to greet the sacred deer of Nara! Remember to buy a cookie to feed them, and be careful to show respect to these famous symbols of the city.

"I knew the Nara deer would cheer you up," says Mom happily, opening the curtains to let in the morning sun. "Apparently you can feed them special cookies."

I'm not sure if it's the deer or talking with Matteo last night, but I do feel better. The heavy gray veil has lifted for a bit to let me feel, if not like my usual self, not quite so worn down. I swing my legs out of the bed. Every hotel has given us pajamas, and these are my favorite. I run my hand down the thick waffle fabric as I consider this. I'm better, but not. It's like the melt on a frozen pond. There's water there, but the ice remains underneath. When this lightness goes and the water drains, the ice will remain. The question is, will it be thinner? More brittle? I hope so.

As usual, we're the last to join the group, and Mom gives a chirpy good morning. Keith glances between the clock and Mom with a small frown before walking over. "Better late than never, huh, Lill?"

Success! I share a triumphant look with Matteo.

Mom smiles at him. "It gives you more time to check your stocks or whatever is so necessary on your phone all the time."

Ugh, they're joking about it. Not even passive-aggressively joking, but laughing.

Matteo shakes his head and comes over as we get on the bus. "Today we talk about other relationships."

"Got it."

We spend the ride to Nara bringing up Dad (me, loudly, around Keith) and Kathy (Matteo, loudly, around Mom). I didn't realize how hard it was to mention one's own father in a casual way, until I find myself looking at Keith's gallon water bottle and saying, "My dad likes drinking water, too!"

Keith gives me a puzzled look. "That's great?"

I don't have to check the buzz on my phone to know it's Matteo roasting me, but he's not doing much better. "Dad's girlfriend, Kathy, had a dog," he says to Mom.

"People like dogs," says Mom.

"Umm. Yeah." He catches me shaking my head and grimaces. "Dogs are cool."

Lisa starts talking about hobbies, and here's my chance.

"Dad doesn't have a lot of hobbies," I say. "He thinks they're a waste of time."

"I have to disagree," says Lisa pleasantly. "I was having the loveliest conversation with your mother about learning how to weave."

Mom has so many hobbies she has to rotate through them. The mess drove Dad nuts, as well as how she would put things aside when she got bored and pick them up when they interested her again. How long can you live like that with someone? How long until all the little things add up and become too much? I suppose for my parents, about twenty years.

Then Mom laughs at something Lisa says. Dad hasn't made her laugh like she's been laughing here, not in a long time.

"I took up kayaking last year," Keith declares. "You have to keep moving so the mind stays fresh."

"Oh?" Mom turns around. "Where do you go kayaking in the city?"

"Right along the Humber River," says Keith, and they begin talking about kayaking spots. How does Mom know about kayaking? When has she ever kayaked? Who even is this woman?

My phone buzzes, Matteo sending a disappointed cat shaking its head.

We failed again.

An hour later, we're in a park surrounded by deer. My mouth drops when one crosses the street and all the cars stop to wait. Like the monkeys, the deer at Nara can go wherever they want, so it's not like a zoo. Kimiko tells us the rules: remember they're wild animals to be treated with respect, only feed them the crackers sold at the park, and don't walk around teasing them with food. "The deer are sacred," she reminds us.

I follow the group to see more deer strolling around like they own the place, which I suppose they do. There are so many. People are feeding them and bowing, and I laugh out loud when a deer bows back. Matteo points to a table with elegantly wrapped deer cookies, which look more like crackers. "Dad gave me some money to feed them. Should we?"

"I can't believe you need to ask."

The deer are way bigger than I expect and fierce once we get the cookies. They immediately surround us, and while trying to save our fingers from their bites, Matteo bows.

"Oh my God, he's bowing back!" I call as Matteo jumps out of the way of the lowering antlers and then holds out a cookie.

"You try," he says, holding his phone up.

My first deer ignores me, but I give him a cookie anyway. When I bow to the second deer, she bobs her head up and down, then nibbles the cookie out of my hand.

"I love them," I say, feeling good under the warm but not burning sun. It's a perfect summer day, with a slight breeze and fluffy clouds. "Let's go under that tree and watch for a bit."

"So, talking about your dad and Kathy was kind of a bust," says Matteo after we sit down and check to see if any Adventurers are nearby. Then he frowns. "Hey."

I follow his gaze. Paulette has pulled what looks like a Twinkie out of her bag, but she's teasing the deer with it, holding it up in the air out of reach.

Matteo's instantly on his feet. "She can't do that," he says. He gets two steps in her direction before the deer decides it's had enough. Paulette turns around, the Twinkie in her mouth, and the deer places its front hooves on her back and shoves her onto the ground, into the dirt and other, grosser, deer things. She screams, and Gretchen stands above Paulette, shouting and basically being useless. No one from the tour group goes to help her until Kimiko approaches in slow motion. Paulette is on her knees, with hoof marks on her back and cream on her face, waving her fist and threatening to sue the park, Adventure Group, and Kimiko herself.

Hank shakes his head. "Embarrassing."

Kimiko eventually leads her away, no doubt to buy a new shirt. Paulette glares at everyone as she passes, sputtering about how dangerous the deer are. Gretchen goes with her, but despite being summoned to the queen's side with a "Susan, I said we're going!" Susan stays with Yvonne. Another one freed from Paulette's clutches.

"Is this what we have to look forward to when we grow up?" I ask as we go back to watching the deer.

"Some people never grow out of school. My mom did a year with the PTA once, and she said never again. People were almost getting in fistfights over whether to have juice boxes at movie night."

There's my opening. "Your mom?" I won't mention that Mom gave me some background.

Matteo turns to the deer that has come up to look at him with huge pleading eyes. "I'm sorry," he says to her. "I gave them all away."

I think he's not going to answer and decide not to push, but then Matteo leans back. "She died two years ago."

"I'm sorry." Instantly I feel bad about all the times I've been upset at Mom or taken her for granted.

"Thanks." That's all he says for a few minutes as we watch the deer. Then he sighs. "It's part of why we're here. She always wanted to go to Japan, and Dad decided we were going to make her dream happen. Or he did after Kathy broke up with him and Dom left for school."

"That's sweet."

He shrugs. "He wanted it to be some sort of bonding experience, but the thing is, he only likes to bond with me by running. He and Mom met at a cross-country meet. We used to go for family runs all the time."

"Did you like it?"

"Yeah. We did one at night in a forest. It was the best." He sounds wistful. "Afterward, Dom and I slept in a tent right by the river."

I'm not sure if I should say what I'm thinking, but Matteo nudges me. "Just say it."

"How did you know I wanted to say anything?"

He laughs. "You get a tiny frown and look down to the left. It's cute."

My face goes hot. "Okay. It's none of my business, but I don't think you're happy you quit running."

Matteo rubs the back of his neck. "I would have stayed on the team if it wasn't for Dad."

"Did you tell him?"

He snorts. "After my last race, he got in a fight with my coach. He was bringing up all this training advice from when he was a kid and how he used to be a champion, like Coach was an idiot, and acting like she was to blame for how I did, and how much better Dom's coach was."

"Oh no."

"Yeah, exactly. I thought I was going to melt, it was so embarrassing. Then on the car ride home, he wouldn't talk to me, like I was this huge disappointment. That's when I decided I was done."

I think. "Can't you run without being on the team?"

"Not with him around. He makes it stressful. It's all about times and form and pace and the rest of it, and how I compare to him. At least with Mom it was fun, you know? I could run and feel the air, and it felt good, like time didn't exist."

Then he's quiet, tapping his fingers on his knee and thinking.

A girl passes by with an amigurumi bear charm on her knapsack. That's the first animal I crocheted when I started three years ago, and I'd called her Ms. Growl. A terrible name, and Ms. Growl and her friends were now stuffed back in a drawer with the rest of their raw materials, the yarn and stuffing and thread.

A bowing deer would be so cute as an amigurumi. Or . . . I look at the sky. I've done clouds, but what if I created amigurumi feelings? How would I do happiness? I don't have a clue. There's a muted blue-gray I bought for an elephant before I realized how dull it was. If I'd been making feelings for the past months, that would have been the only color I used. No wonder my bright bluebird was a failure.

Matteo takes out his notepad and has about half a deer sketched when Keith walks over and frowns.

"Come on, Matty, what are you doing? You're done with that kind of thing."

Matteo takes his pen and scribbles it all away in rough, heavy lines before hiding the pad.

"You okay?" I ask.

"Yeah."

Mom arrives with more deer crackers and gives me a hug. The tuberose she put on this morning drifts up from her clothes. "Did you see the deer?" she demands with enthusiasm, like we aren't surrounded by them. She points to a doe nibbling some grass. "She's my favorite."

"Why?"

She smiles. "Just because. Look." She shows us her photo roll, which legit has about fifty photos of that deer. Then she glances up. "Oh, she's smiling!"

She goes off after the deer, and Matteo laughs, the incident with Keith put aside. "Your mom always gets so excited about stuff. It's fun."

It is, but Mom also likes the people around her to match her energy. I've been trying, but it's hard.

Kimiko returns, and she waves for us to gather together. Matteo and I stand and go to drag Mom away from her new deer friend.

Matteo and I promise to up our game at the kintsugi workshop in the afternoon.

"Laser focus," he whispers as we enter the workroom. "Utter and absolute focus."

I give him a mock salute, and he holds out his hand. "Go, team," he says.

Giving it a slap, I scope out the space. It's set up with workstations, so each person has a spot with what looks like glue, metallic dust, brushes, and a broken plate or bowl. "I have an idea," I say. "How good is your dad with crafts?"

"If there's a level below terrible, he's probably under that."

"Let's make sure they work together," I say. "They'll frustrate each other."

"How so?"

I don't want to say it's because Keith is the kind of man who doesn't listen and thinks he knows better than anyone else, so I keep it vague. "I think it'll be a bad match."

"I don't know," he says. "Wouldn't it be better to separate them by getting them to work with someone who needs help? Dad can never say no to playing Good Samaritan."

"Trust me." Mom is capital-C crafty. She can knit, sew, paint, decoupage, and quilt. She's the one who taught me how to crochet, and I don't think she'll react well to Keith acting as if he's the expert.

Which he might not. He might surprise me. But I doubt it.

Matteo considers this. "Dad does hate it when he's not the best," he says. "Let's try."

Yvonne enters the room complaining that she could barely handle making macaroni art in Girl Guides, but I grab Mom before she can swoop down with an offer to help and bring her to the table where Matteo is already sitting with his father. Matteo gives me a secret thumbs-up.

The instructor enters and bows, and it's a young man who speaks fluent English. "Welcome to our kintsugi workshop," he says with a huge smile. He's dressed in a white shirt and black pants, with a canvas apron. "I'm Yuki. Are you familiar with this art?"

"It repairs broken pottery with gold to make it beautiful, right?" calls Lisa.

"Exactly right." Yuki shows a green bowl traced with metallic lines. "Instead of taking a broken pot and disposing of it, we repair it in a way that showcases the break. It makes a flaw into part of an object's history and something to be illuminated and not hidden. Many have taken this as a metaphor for resilience. What we experience makes us unique and beautiful."

"Stacey's therapist told her that," a woman whispers behind us. "It's kind of like that Kelly Clarkson song. What doesn't kill you makes you stronger." I don't want to look around to see who's talking.

"It's a manifesting of the concept of wabi-sabi," he adds, and from across the room, Kimiko nods at me. I pay a bit more attention.

Yuki gives us quick instructions. We can choose gold or silver powder, then mix it into the resin and apply it to the break. "Press it together carefully, and hold."

I look at my small broken bowl. "I'm going gold," I say.

"Lillian, this is how you do it. Watch me." Keith applies the resin without mixing. "You add the gold on last."

"No, you don't." Mom begins to mix hers together the way Yuki said.

"You're not optimizing for materials use," Keith says. "Look, you're going to waste the gold. My way, you only use what you need. Efficient and effective."

"I know what I'm doing," Mom says casually, not bothering to look up. "You're wrong."

Keith's jaw twitches and I rejoice. I knew he couldn't handle Mom being better. Matteo and I exchange a triumphant look, although he also looks a bit mortified.

Yuki comes by. "Excellent," he says to Mom. "Have you done this before?"

"This is my first time."

"You have a steady hand and good eye." Yuki turns to Keith. "Did you forget my instructions?" he asks politely. "You missed a step. It won't turn out as well."

There's a pause as Yuki leaves to help Paulette. Keith stares after Yuki, then shrugs. "More than one way to do something."

No one answers until Mom says, "You know, I read the most interesting book that had kintsugi as a motif. It was called *Drop of Tea*. Have you read it?"

Keith laughs as if this is hilarious. "Tell me when they make it into a movie. Who's got time for reading?"

His phone buzzes and he grabs it. "Shit, I need to deal with this." He gets up, his plate half glued, and leaves.

This is going better than I expected. Matteo gives me

a look out of the corner of his eye, and I remember I can't gloat too much. It kind of sucks that the reason this is working is because his dad is a bit of a jerk.

We glue in silence for a few minutes, listening to Yuki as he walks around to answer questions and agree that, yes, traditionally lacquer is used, but since it needs to be cured for days, it's easier for us to use resin.

Yvonne groans. "God, what a mess I'm making."

Mom is on her feet in a second, leaving us to help her friend.

"I like this idea," Matteo says, messing with his broken plate. "That mistakes can be improved if you take the time and effort."

I look at the bowl in my hands, thinking about all the dings and use that made it different, and more unique. Matteo reaches for the resin and accidentally knocks into my phone. The screen lights up with a notification, and I automatically open the message. It's a campfire at Granite Lake with Connor in the foreground. I can barely see Addison, but she's there. I shove the phone in my pocket, angry for allowing myself to be treated like that.

Matteo has been watching. "Connor?"

This time I surprise myself by answering honestly. "I'm mad I wasted time on him," I say, pressing the pieces of my bowl together so hard my fingers go white. "He wasn't nice to me. Why did I let that happen?"

Yuki, who is passing by, points to my hands. "Gently,"

he says. "You don't want to shift the pieces. No need to try so hard."

He moves on, and I release my grip slightly.

"I think the important thing is you decided it was time to stop," says Matteo.

I gaze at the small line of gold keeping the pieces together. There is a thicker line where I messed up and went over it again. That part will be extra strong. "I did, didn't I."

Perhaps Connor was like that, a crack I needed to seal with gold. A part that will be extra strong in the future. Another bit of wear on my journey.

"Thanks," I say.

Matteo smiles at me as he slowly lets his piece go. "I got you, Ivy. This is what friends are for."

We stand for a moment by the plate and bowl, looking at the imperfections we've transformed into something worthy of admiration.

Chapter 17

Day 10—Osaka

Visitors and locals alike rave about Osaka's easygoing vibe. We'll make a quick stop for you to sample the many charms of this friendly city, including the world-famous aquarium and appealing districts to whet every appetite. Be sure to try takoyaki from a street vendor!

The next morning is a mess. We've been in the hotel room for a few days, so Mom has scattered her belongings everywhere. Because she's Mom, she fell asleep last night after reassuring me she had it under control.

News flash, she did not. I rub my head. The headache is back, and I'd been forced to get up in the middle of the night to turn off the fan after Mom had gone into the bathroom. I hate that noise. How hard is it to flip a single switch?

"Oh my God, how much did we buy?" she says. "Ivy. Come sit on my suitcase."

"I'm getting ready."

But she points at it, so I have to drop what I'm doing to

help, as usual. My own bag is already at the door, packed and locked.

"You're not even trying," she complains.

"Maybe if you folded things instead of jamming them in, you'd have more space." It comes out snappier than I expect, but she doesn't comment on my tone.

"I thought I left enough room for the things we would get while shopping. This is ridiculous. Okay, I have it."

I get off the suitcase and wash my hands. Her makeup stuff is still all over the counter. Time to test Keith's sense of smell and whether poor hygiene is a dealbreaker. I grab her toothbrush and deodorant before I call her. "You forgot the bathroom."

She comes in, frowning. "Why didn't you remind me?"

"Is this my fault?"

"Watch that tone, Ivy."

"What tone? The tone of something not being my fault?"

"What is going on with you this morning?" Mom sounds exasperated. "Yesterday things were fine. Stop being so moody."

"I'm not being moody."

She closes her eyes, counting to ten before she grabs her purse and starts swiping stuff off the counter into it.

I poke around the room and check under the bed—Mom left a sock—and the drawers, where I grab the book she's been reading. These I don't bother to mention, as she's busy swearing in the bathroom, but put in my own canvas tote bag. It was Dad's job to do the final check of the room, and it's annoying I need to be the grown-up because he's not here.

We arrive downstairs, and I'm honestly shocked we're not the last ones. Mom's triumphant. "Look at that," she says smugly. "On time."

I don't answer but pull out the book and the sock as revenge. Dad used to do the same thing, just hand over things she forgot without comment. Seeing her eyes narrow makes me feel a bit better, then worse. I'm being a jerk. But I want to be. I feel twisted and bad. My hair is a mess, and my face is puffy from lack of sleep, so my inside and outside match in a way that must be obvious to anyone who passes. This time I can't hide it.

"To Osaka today!" Kimiko says. "We'll go direct with no stops and be there in about an hour."

Keith comes up as we stand near the bus. "Here, Lill, for you." He hands her a huge bottle of Sprite.

She takes it without enthusiasm but with confusion. "Thank you?"

He beams at her. "No problem. No problem at all."

We file onto the bus, but once I'm settled, I feel suddenly trapped. I want out. I *need* to get out, away from the chatter and laughter around me for a few minutes of solitude. Tom and Lisa and a few others are still standing with the luggage, so I have time. No one will miss me if I disappear for a bit.

I leave my stuff and climb off to escape around the corner of the hotel and stand in the shade to take some deep breaths, hands on my knees and bent over like I've run a race. The pressure lifts for a moment, and I simply breathe. *In*. A bicycle passes. *Out*. A child laughs nearby. *In*. A horn sounds, and it's different from home. *Out*. A siren goes in the distance.

Mom didn't even notice me leaving the bus. She was talking to Yvonne, so why would she care where I am? She's happy making all these friends. Part of me wishes I could walk to Osaka all by myself.

The sun beats down, making the headache worse. These aren't good thoughts. I know Mom loves me, but if my parents can break apart their marriage so easily, what else can change? No wonder my own mother doesn't want to be around me when I'm like this. I don't even want to be around me.

It takes a second before I realize I'm hearing my name. Then a second time, but a different voice. A third. "Ivy? Ivy! I-veee!"

Then a last time, but closer. "Ivy!"

My head jerks up to see Matteo jogging in my direction. "There you are. Everyone's looking for you. We'd already started going before your mom saw you weren't on the bus."

"I was only gone for a minute."

"I don't know what to tell you," he says. "But your mom is pretty upset."

Just what I need. We run back to the bus under the brutal sun. Mom is pacing and staring out at one of the side streets. "Ivy, where the hell did you go? Matteo, thanks for finding her." She doesn't even wait for me to reply before raising her voice. "Kimiko! Tom! Lisa! Yvonne! She's here."

Matteo gives me a quick look before getting back on the bus as I stand in front of Mom.

"What were you thinking, disappearing like that without saying anything? And without your phone? We could have left without you! We almost did! You made everyone go look for you."

"I needed some fresh air," I mutter. Matteo lied. She's not pretty upset, but furious.

"You need to think about other people, is what you need."

The others come up, sparing me the rest of the lecture. Kimiko checks the time. "Good," she says. "We can go now."

"I'm sorry," I say.

"As long as you're safe," Tom says.

"We're not behind schedule," Kimiko assures me. "No harm done."

It hadn't occurred to me that we'd have to skip something. A wave of humiliation flows through me, which is made worse when everyone stares as I get on the bus. Then Keith calls, "The prodigal returns."

I have no idea what this means, but everyone laughs,

and I scrunch my shoulders down to make myself as small as possible as I sink in my seat.

Kimiko does a head count. Twice. "Now that we can finally leave, we are off to Osaka!" she says.

"Again," Paulette calls.

I take out my phone to stop thinking. My first task is to delete the *where are you?* texts. I don't need a reminder of what happened, all because I needed a minute of privacy. Then a message from Matteo pops up, a cartoon cat dressed as a strawberry. I think I recognize the style.

Did you do that?

If you like it, I did.

I do!

Then yes.

I save the strawberry cat as my phone background and watch the cityscape shift from the quainter older parts to more modern hotels and office buildings before it becomes regular highway.

Connor alert. A message comes from Hazel. It's a blurry photo of him near her food truck.

I don't care anymore. It's true. I really don't.

The response comes a few minutes later, and it's about

three rows of surprise emojis. **Congratulations on de-Connorfying your life. Remember the best thing for a broken heart is a crush.**

I send her a photo of some of the tour men with wide-brimmed hats tied under their chins, pointing unironically at a plaque, Hank's vest front and center.

LOLOLOL, she writes.

Another message arrives. It's from Matteo, and it's a photo of the scene through the bus window.

I still don't feel like smiling, but send him back one of my own view, grateful to have something to think about other than my own untidy self.

Osaka is interesting, but I'm getting tired. Not that being tired is new for me, but this time I feel validated that it's not only me. Mom keeps yawning as we make our way to the aquarium. However, the second we walk in, my exhaustion fades. I could spend hours here. Days. It's set out by depth starting with the surface level, and I have to be tugged away from the otters by Matteo.

"Everyone's gone ahead," he says. "You've got an ocean to see."

"But otters!"

One does a flip, and Matteo hesitates before he points down the dark hall. "Remember, there are penguins coming up." He laughs when he sees my indecision. "Two more minutes with the otters, then on to the other animals."

"Deal."

Everyone in the group has split up, and after we check that Mom and Keith are apart—he's charged ahead, she's sitting with Joanne staring enraptured at some fish—we keep wandering. A bunch of kids go tearing by. Last year at camp we went on a field trip to the aquarium, and Connor nearly lost his mind when the kids refused to leave the jellyfish. I'm about to tell Matteo when I pause. Suddenly, the story seems kind of unnecessary. Boring.

"What's up?"

I smile at him. "Nothing. Jellyfish."

We don't talk until he pauses at a kelp forest. "Did your mom eat the chips?"

I told Matteo about stealing Mom's toothbrush and we went to a 7-Eleven and found the strongest flavors of snacks possible: natto, a garlic curry snack, and onion rings. All of them looked tasty but like they would definitely linger on your breath. Then we gave them to Mom and Keith.

"She did." I make a face. "It's going to be worse for us than them."

"We only have to keep it going for a few more days," says Matteo. "The trip is almost done."

My stomach dips a bit at this, because what happens after? "What if they decide to see each other at home?" I ask. That would really interfere with my parents getting back together.

The second I think it, it comes to me I'm not so much

worried about that. I'm worried I won't see Matteo again.

"We'll figure that out later," he says. "It's looking good now."

Is this a hint that we don't need to hang out as much? Then he says, "We should keep trying, though. The two of us."

"Good idea," I agree, relieved.

The rest of the day is busy, since we're leaving Osaka the next morning, and we get whisked through a neighborhood called Shinsekai, which is an assault on my eyes. I love it. Kimiko says it was built in the early 1900s and inspired by Coney Island and Paris. There's a huge octopus over a door, and lights and food everywhere.

Kimiko points at a gold statue of a grinning figure I've seen all over the city. "Although created by a Kansas City woman in 1908, Billiken has become the unofficial mascot of Osaka," she says. "He's considered the god of things as they should be—good vibes, you might say—and is now a symbol of good fortune."

Matteo is fascinated by the statue and takes a bunch of photos. "The god of things as they should be," he says. "What a cool idea."

"Yeah!" I look over at the figure. "Imagine if he gets overwhelmed with the options of modern life, and he goes on strike? Then no one has any idea of how things should be and they go off in all different directions trying to figure it out."

"And each thing they try makes it worse."

We keep building the story until we have Billiken chilling on the beach with his jellyfish friends, before getting lured back with mochi and strawberry tea.

I examine the statue again. The god of how things should be. It's so hard to put that into words, how things should be. Or how they are in the first place. I was thinking about doing amigurumi feelings at the deer park, but what if they were feelings that have no names, like reading a book you're sure you've read before but never have?

I think about this on and off for the rest of the day as we go through Osaka Castle and the Namba Yasaka Shrine with the gigantic lion's head building, and while eating okonomiyaki, shredded cabbage pancakes I get without the octopus. They're hot, right off the pan, and shockingly tasty for cabbage.

When we come out from dinner, boats covered in lights are going up and down the river. It looks exciting, but instead of exploring, the group gets back onto the bus, Mom complaining about how she can't wait for bed. Matteo, who has the window seat, leans back so I can look longingly at the bright lights. "I wish we could wander around at night," he says. "Dad's always asleep by ten."

"Me too. Did you see the boats?"

"I did and I wanted a better photo of the Glico running man." He makes a face. "I guess that's a reason to come back one day."

"What would your dad say if you asked to go back tonight? If we promised to stay together?"

He turns around with his eyebrows raised halfway up his forehead. "What do you think he'd say?"

I sigh. "Same as my mom. No way."

"Exactly. For a guy who's all about taking initiative, he hates it when I do." He brightens. "Maybe someone will go back, and we can talk your mom and my dad into letting us go with them. They might agree if it's Tom or Lisa or someone."

The hotel isn't far—why we needed the bus I don't know—and when we get off, we examine the group for someone who looks lively and full of energy. All of them are yawning. We share a disappointed glance. Now that the idea is in my head, it's all I want to do. I want to run out the door and see the city at night. I want to . . .

Well, I won't. If Mom was mad at me for leaving the bus, she'll go ballistic if I sneak out. I follow Mom up to our room, hands shoved in my pockets. Matteo is right. Some other day.

Then I go and steal Mom's new toothbrush.

Chapter 18

Day 11—Hakone

After the whirlwind of the last few days, it's time to take a deep breath of refreshing mountain air in the onsen town of Hakone. Relax in the baths, or if you want more adventure, visit the Owakudani volcanic crater and Lake Ashi via the Hakone Ropeway, which provides stunning views of the region.

It's a five-hour drive to Hakone, so we leave Osaka early. I spend most of the time dozing and staring at the three centimeters of Matteo's shoulder visible from the seat in front of me. I have one hand in my bag, playing with the yarn that used to be my bluebird, and I'm thinking about my nameless feelings amigurumi. What would be the first one I could make? I can't think of any.

I don't notice I've drifted off until we arrive in Hakone, which is gorgeous. There are mountains all around, and rocky streams that look like they could be described as burbling. Tonight we're staying in a traditional ryokan, and as we file into the sprawling wood inn, Kimiko asks us to take off our shoes and put on some black rubber slippers from the neat rows near the door.

"It was a long drive, and I'm sure you wish to relax," she says. "You can nap, stroll, or enjoy the baths until dinner."

I follow Mom up to our room, and we stop at the threshold to admire it. It's small, with no furniture except for a low table near the window and tatami mats on the floor. Snowy bedding is piled neatly in the closet. Mom puts the bags beside a special bench that looks like it was meant to keep stuff off the floor and takes off her gigantic hat.

I text Matteo.

Why did we do the hygiene plan right before we hit a town known for baths?

Dad bought two more deodorants because his kept disappearing. I have them stuffed in my bag.

I don't even think they noticed because we gave them the same snacks. It canceled out.

I admit defeat. Time to move down the list.

"Ready for the onsen?" Mom asks before pulling her clothes out of her bag to drop them on the floor, cluttering up the pleasantly minimalist room. "Kimiko says we can use the one next door for a quick soak. We're going to the big one tomorrow."

It sounds perfect, so we grab our swimsuits and head over. I loved having baths at home but hate the gross bathtub in the apartment. While the onsen probably won't have rainbow flower bath bombs, the thought of lying in hot water is too tempting to pass. We take a shady stone path to a beautiful wood building. I pause at a bonsai that looks like it might be ancient—the trunk is gnarled and bent in a way that draws the eye, and the leaves are perfect miniatures. Kimiko is there already and must have told the staff we would be arriving, because we're immediately handed slippers and blue-and-white cotton robes and sent down a corridor.

My first indication things are not quite the same as back home is when we go through the red curtain to the changeroom and see a lot of skin. Like, a lot. No clothes at all. Even Mom looks a bit surprised. "Okay," she says slowly.

Kimiko walks in and sees the swimsuit in my hand. "Oh, no," she says. "There are no clothes in an onsen."

"What?" She's fully dressed, but I look her straight in the eyes for practice.

"You don't wear clothes."

"None?"

"None, but the baths are segregated. Men and women."

"They used to be all together?" Oh my God. I couldn't handle that.

"It was never common," she assures me.

"Look at all us girls!" It's Paulette, who comes in and strips down in seconds. She stuffs her clothes in one of the baskets on the shelf before doing some wide-legged stretches. I squeeze my eyes shut.

Kimiko holds out a towel. "You can use this for modesty if you want."

It's the size of a piece of paper. Mom looks at it, then at me. "Are there options for a more secluded environment?"

I'm grateful Mom is taking control of this situation, because I absolutely do not want to strip down in public.

"There are private onsens at the hotel, in the basement," Kimiko says. She gives us a pleasant smile and leaves.

"What do you think?" asks Mom. "Would you prefer that?"

Would I ever. I nod my head so fast my neck might come unhinged.

"No problem." Mom grabs her bag. "I'll tell Yvonne I can't join her."

It's nice of Mom to keep me company; however, Kimiko's

phrasing was ambiguous, so I don't know how private the basement onsen is. What if it's a small tub for two people? I would rather be naked in front of a dozen strangers than only Mom. "You can stay here and meet Yvonne, and I'll go to the one at the hotel," I say.

"Are you sure?"

"Yes." Am I ever.

She stares at me as if to check whether I'm telling the truth, then nods. "Okay. Don't forget to take water to drink and come out if you get too hot or feel woozy." She takes a breath as if to give me more instructions, and I roll my eyes.

"I know how to take a bath," I remind her.

"Right."

I glance at the steam drifting through the door. "What about tomorrow, though? If the baths are all public with no clothes, can I stay at the hotel?" No way am I going to hang out with wet, naked retirees all day, and Mom's been talking about the onsen for days. I'd feel terrible if she missed it.

She purses her lips as she thinks. "Kimiko is taking some people on the cable car to Lake Ashi."

A day trip sounds way better than the alternative. "I can go by myself?"

"If you stay with her."

She sounds as if this isn't a big deal, which is an agreeable change from her usual worry that I'm going to get kidnapped. Is it because she wants to go to the baths or because she wants time alone with Keith? There must be some mixed spaces in the onsen. "Maybe," I say.

After a discussion about who should keep the keys, since they're real metal and not plastic keycards, I head back to the hotel and check online for onsen etiquette. Despite what I said to Mom, although I know how to take a bath, I'm not entirely sure how to *bathe,* and the do-it-naked thing points to some significant gaps in my knowledge. Once I'm satisfied, I head to the basement.

Then I stop at the foot of the stairs, because Matteo is staring at the onsen reservation board. There are two baths, and you reserve a spot by writing in your name. All the evening slots are taken but it's the afternoon, and both are currently free.

"I went down to look," he says when he sees me. "Imagine a big room with two sunken tubs. One is wood, and the other is stone."

"They're in the same room?" I squeak. How do I feel about that?

Maybe good?

A bit nervous? A bit excited?

He laughs. "Sort of, but not. There's a huge rock in the middle that goes from the floor to about three-quarters of the way up."

I don't know if I'm relieved or not. "So, semiprivate."

"That's a good way to say it." He glances down. "Are you going in?"

Since it's not an open free-for-all, I nod. "You?"

"Sure. Do you want the stone or wood bath?"

We decide to rock, paper, scissors, and I get the stone one. We each pull the rope over the doorway to indicate the bath is occupied and make our way down the separate staircases.

I've never been in a dungeon, and I expect a dungeon wouldn't have hot soothing water at the bottom, but as I descend, I get real dungeon vibes. It's humid from the steam, and the walls are stone, like those of an old castle, but smooth. Everything is a bit slippery, and it's dark enough to feel like it should be lit with torches. Much different from the light wood of next door.

When I reach the wood slats that make up the floor, there's a big sink with a pile of small towels that the illustrated sign indicates are for sitting on. I open the sliding door to the bath to check it out and gasp.

The room looks like it was built into rock. A frosted window lets in enough light to give it the feeling of a rainy Sunday afternoon, but a restful one, not the usual depressing kind filled with bitter thoughts of Monday. The rectangular bath is bigger than a hot tub, and steam lifts off the water, which is cloudy with minerals. The rock Matteo mentioned is in the middle and although you can't climb over or see into the other bath, there's enough space for voices to drift across. A small stool, a faded pink bucket, and a handheld shower are to the side.

Nothing in the room looks new, but it calms me. If this is wabi-sabi, I get it. It's like stepping into a space set out of time, but where being alone offers a welcome minute to reflect, rather than sad isolation.

I back out to take off my clothes before I reenter, feeling self-conscious although there's no one to see me, and give myself a good scrubbing. The helpful guide made it clear that only a disgusting monster would go into the bath without getting clean in the shower first.

On the other side of the rock, Matteo splashes around, and I try not to think about the fact we're so close. Hazel once wrote a poem about how we were all only a thin layer of fabric away from being nude to the world, and the English teacher took her aside to ask if everything was okay at home. I lay my towel down and sit on it to put my feet in the water.

Then I yelp and yank them out.

"It's hot," says Matteo from his side.

"Very helpful." Hearing his voice sound the way it always does makes me feel okay about the situation. He's not acting strange, and neither should I.

Once I get in—slowly, slowly—I prop my arms back and relax. The sound is more muted than I expected. All I can hear is my own breathing and occasional splashes. When I sit up, there's a line across my shoulders, with the skin bright red under and pale above.

It's heaven.

Matteo says nothing to break the silence and neither do I. My thoughts wander as I stare at the window. It's the same color as the terrible gray veil I've been unable to shake. At least it feels better now. Was Mom right? Was a change all I needed? I wave my arms in the water and feel the heat swirl on my skin. Not really. I don't feel quite right, but unlike before, I can feel myself gaining some sense of what I need to change. Or try to change.

Getting Connor out of my system is a good start. Then there's Mom and Dad. I'm trying to do something about that, but is it working?

"I'm worried my parents won't get back together," I say abruptly. There's no warning or anything. It bursts out to echo in the steamy stone room.

Matteo is quiet for a moment. "Are you sure you want them to?" he finally asks.

"What do you mean? Of course I do. Why would you ask that?"

"My friend's parents got a divorce last year," he says. "I remember going to their house when I was younger, and there was always the sense of a fight about to happen. It felt tense, all the time."

"What did your friend think about it?" I examine my fingers closely. I took off what was left of the navy polish the other day with a single acetone pack I bought at the 7-Eleven, and my nails are almost translucent from the water.

"At first he was angry they were wrecking his life. Oscar and his sister had to move, and his dad got a new job, so they had this crazy commute, and it was a mess." There's a pause. "He got quiet before the split. He barely talked and didn't want to do anything at all, you know?"

Yeah, I knew.

"After they told him, it got really bad. He didn't go to school for, like, a month."

"Did he think it was his fault?" I stare at my finger so close it's blurry.

"Do you think it's yours?"

I shrug in the water, the red line on my chest rising above the surface and dropping back down. "It's hard to not think a kid adds extra pressure." As the fights got more frequent, I did my best to not be a bother or add trouble, but could I have done more? Been better?

"I don't think it's your fault, and I didn't think it was his," Matteo says. "They're adults."

"Maybe. What happened with your friend?"

"After a while, he got better. He said at least it was done. He didn't have to worry about what would happen anymore, and he could go ahead and deal with what was in front of him."

"Low bar." Is that it? Do I just have to accept there are some things I can't change?

"Yeah, obviously it wasn't great, but it was something. He started running with me again."

I skim my hand along the hot water and watch how it sticks when I lift my palm. An example of adhesion: my science teacher, Ms. Brar, would be proud of me. "This was before you quit the team, right?"

"It was. I guess he'll have to find someone else to go with. Good thing Dad doesn't know about that, since it would be another example of how I'm a failure compared to Dom." The water on his side splashes like he slapped it. "At least when Dad's talking to your mom, he lets up on me a bit. The same happened with Kathy, which was the only good thing about having her around."

"What was it like to have him date?" I don't think I could stand it.

"I was mostly grateful she was his age and not twenty or something gross. One of Dom's friends has a stepmother who's only five years older than her."

That makes me laugh. "No way your dad would date a twenty-year-old."

"It was bad enough that she wanted to act like my mom," he said, sounding grim. "I would have died if she was closer to my age than his. And you know what?"

"What?"

"I was glad when they broke up. Dad and Kathy." His low voice barely makes it over the rock to drift down through the steam. "I know Dad liked her, but I was fucking mad. How could he go on living his life when Mom was gone? I couldn't stand the thought of Kathy moving in, and taking

Mom's photos down, and using her closet. Every time she tried to tell me what to do, or insisted on family meals, it drove me nuts. Dad added a stocking for her to the mantel at Christmas! Even Dom freaked out about that, and he usually thinks Dad is perfect."

"I get it." It's not even close, but I know how I'd feel if we stayed in the house and a new person's clothes were in the drawers, and their shoes in the front hall.

"When she told me not to worry about her replacing Mom, I laughed in her face. Like she had a chance. Dad was so mad. Kathy was probably nice enough, but I didn't want anything to do with her."

There's a long silence, then he says, "You must think I'm a real asshole."

This makes me laugh, although it's more of a gross snort. "I'm working with you to actively keep our parents apart," I say. "Trust me, I'm in no position to judge." I pause. "Even if I was, I wouldn't. I'd feel the same way you do."

A tiny ding goes off, the electronic noise out of place.

"I set my alarm because they said to only stay in for twenty minutes," he says. "Do you want to stay longer?"

"I'm good." I stand up slowly so I don't pass out, completely attuned to the sounds coming from Matteo's side. He's out of the water now. There's the shower. Is he listening to me as well? The bath is quiet apart from a faint dripping, and I worry about the noises I'm making before I hear the door on Matteo's side open and shut. A few seconds under the cold shower helps me feel better, and soon I'm getting dressed and assessing my face in the dim mirror. I'm red but in a cute, flushed way.

Or so I think, but another mirror at the top of the steps shows the light in the onsen dungeon had been overly flattering. I am a lobster, but when Matteo looks over, he's a matching red. The humidity of the bath transformed his hair into puffy curls he's frantically trying to pat down. All of a sudden my heart skips a beat, so much so that I clap my hand to my chest in surprise. He looks up and for a second, he holds my gaze, his face serious.

He smiles at me. A tiny lazy grin with the dimple that makes my cheeks heat up, and I don't know where to look. I never felt like this with Connor, as if he was seeing me, and not the Ivy I made sure to have on display whenever I was with him. It's so different, and so much better.

Then Mom arrives, brandishing a bag of seaweed-and-salt-flavored potato chips. She loves going to convenience stores to find new snacks, so Japan has been heaven for her. "Look what I got on the way back from the onsen!" she says happily. "Hi, Matteo. Want to try some?"

He takes one, then excuses himself. Mom follows me up the steep, narrow wood steps as she tells me about her bath and asks about mine. I describe it but leave out that I could talk to Matteo. I like keeping that to myself, one good secret all for me.

Chapter 19

Day 12—Hakone

The healing powers of the onsen await. Rejuvenate your mind, body, and soul at a Japanese mineral bath, where you will also enjoy a beautiful meal hand-crafted by expert chefs. For those seeking a more invigorating day, an optional tour will take you across the Hakone Ropeway to the pleasures of Lake Ashi and its pirate boat cruises.*

*Pirate boat admission and meals for optional tour not included in tour package.

The next day is cloudy and cool enough for a light jacket. Mom stares out the window, ecstatic. "Smell the trees," she demands, and doesn't stop until I lean out to breathe deep.

"Finally, a break from the sun," she says. "Perfect. Will you be okay on your own?"

"Absolutely." I can't wait. The only time I get a moment to myself is when Mom is in the shower.

Strange how it didn't bother me when Matteo was in the onsen yesterday, though. I won't see him today. Last night at dinner, we decided only one of us would have to suffer getting into the baths with the rest of the group to keep an eye on our parents, and flipped a coin.

"Heads, heads, heads," I chanted under my breath. "Please be heads." It's not that I was against the aging human body or anything, but I didn't know how I could look at anyone on the bus in the eye after knowing . . . I remember Paulette trying to touch her toes. Don't think about it.

It was heads, which meant Matteo was the loser. He took it better than I expected. "Kimiko says there are a bunch of smaller spaces in the onsen where you can go to be alone," he says optimistically. "Or I can keep my head underwater."

Mom hugs me before reminding me about the key, and to drink water, and get something to eat, and . . . The list goes on as I roll my eyes and shove her out the door. "Don't forget, no talking to weirdos," she calls as she goes.

"Got it, Mom."

A few minutes later, a knock comes at the door, and I go to open it before I remember Mom's no-weirdos rule. "Who is it?" I call.

"It's me."

Not a weirdo, or if he is, it's the kind I like. I open the door to Matteo, who is looking . . . wow. He's leaning against the wall, and the top of his sketchpad peeks out of his cross-body bag. Unlike the post-onsen puff, his hair has been tamed enough to make me want to mess it up. I don't know how he keeps his clothes looking so good. I feel like I've been rolled around in dirt after almost two weeks living out of a suitcase, but his white shirt doesn't have a speck. It also shows off the width of his shoulders in a distracting way. I feel like I'm seeing him differently since yesterday, which is unexpected but not unwelcome. It's like the onsen water boiled away my previous, far more platonic, perception of Matteo to leave these new feelings for me to wrestle with.

What's more distracting is when he slowly lifts his head to focus his gaze on me. There's something about how he smiles, like he's happy to see me, that makes my hand slip on the doorframe. "Want company today?" he asks.

"Aren't you supposed to be at the onsen?"

"Dad has a chance to close a sale, so he didn't go. He doesn't want me around so he can work."

Suddenly the day seems a lot brighter, despite the dark, cool sky. Matteo waits while I grab the key, and we go down to meet Kimiko. Tom is already there, checking over what looks like a bag of camera lenses. "Hey, kids," he says when he sees us. "Ready to float over a volcanic crater?"

Matteo blinks at him. "I thought Kimiko was joking."

"Nope, and sometimes they have to suspend the ropeway because of increased volcanic activity." He sounds thrilled.

The cable car that takes us to the start of the ropeway is basically a train dragged up a slope so steep the top is invisible. I can't figure out why the seats are staggered in tiers until we start—it's the only way to keep people from tumbling down and out the back.

Matteo says in a low voice, "Good job with the chocolate by the way."

"Thanks." I told Mom it was Keith's secret vice, and she'd gone into the 7-Eleven and found a gigantic box of chocolate-covered mushroom-shaped cookies. Keith had taken it with a slightly sour face and made a joke about having to run off the calories. Matteo's *favor not favor* idea was turning out well.

When we get off at Sounzan Station—large and modern, with a coffee shop and gift store—Matteo points to a terrace overlooking deep green mountainsides. A huge symbol is visible in the trees. We'd seen it from the hotel as well, and Kimiko said it's the character for *big,* burned into the woods during a festival to return ancestral spirits who had been temporarily welcomed back to the land of the living. "Let's look," he says.

We wave goodbye to Tom as the rest of the group heads toward the ropeway to go over the crater and to Lake Ashi. The weather is cooler up here, and my lungs expand for the first time in ages. I almost gulp in the air, replacing the dust and smog and all sorts of stale nastiness deep inside me.

Outside is a long counter with seats and steaming water underneath. Incredibly, it's a footbath, and people are drinking coffee and chatting with their shoes and socks tucked beside them. Matteo and I look at each other and, a minute later, have our feet in the water. Matteo takes out his sketchbook and hesitates. I don't mention it, giving him some space.

"Do you really like my drawing?" he asks, staring at his hands.

"I love it."

He nods but doesn't open the sketchbook. A break in the clouds lets through a single ray of light that lands on the terrace in front of us. Two girls go over to stand in the middle and take a selfie.

"Are the sketches for your graphic novel?" I ask.

"No, but it doesn't matter. I stopped working on it a while ago." He pulls the pad open and shut.

I know a hint that someone wants to talk when I hear one, because I've given enough of them myself. "Why? Same as why you stopped drawing?"

"It's stupid."

"Hey," I say, shaking my head. "I don't believe that."

"I sent the first pages in to a contest," he says. "I didn't win."

"Oh." I can see why that would sting.

"Yeah, and when I told Dad, he got mad I was upset, if you can believe it. Normally he'd say I have to bounce back from setbacks, but this time he said it was good I got rejected and it proved I was wasting my time. He was happy when I told him I was giving up." He rolls his eyes.

"It's the only thing I was allowed to quit without a guilt trip."

"If you like it, it's not a waste," I say.

"He's right, though. If I was talented, I would have won."

I squint at the mountains, drawn sharply against the clouds. "Maybe, but when you started your book, was the goal to win the contest?"

He laughs. "I didn't know it existed. I only wanted to tell the story I had in my head."

"Do you miss it?"

It takes a while, but he nods.

"I don't think art is about winning contests. Maybe you should keep telling the story you want to," I say. "I'm not saying your dad is right about all that resilience and quitting stuff, but if you want to write the book, you shouldn't let a contest stop you. Or your dad."

Matteo stares hard at his sketchbook, then opens it with a sudden movement. I watch him draw the scene—the people small but dynamic stick figures against the dense weight of the mountain and surrounded by what look like dogs—then wiggle my toes in the hot water. If this was anyone else, I'd be embarrassed about sitting in a footbath with my pants hiked up to my knees, but Matteo makes it feel stress-free, like of course this is something we'd do. I like the person I am around him. I'm still Ivy, but less worried about how to act and how he perceives me. I'd say I like him, except this isn't what I'm used to. Where's the angst?

The sense of desperation? The intensity that is almost sickening? Isn't that what you're supposed to feel when you like someone as more than a friend?

The clouds look a bit darker, and we decide to keep going toward Owakudani. After drying off and putting our shoes on, we head to the ropeway. I stare in disbelief at the pods dangling from a cable above.

So does Matteo. "This is going to take us over a volcanic valley?" He sounds doubtful. "Without dropping us in?"

Apparently it will. We get in line and somehow snag a gondola, which seats six or eight, to ourselves. There's a slight jolt and then we're up, swaying slightly in the wind and looking down at the ground as it drops away in a gentle slope.

"This is less scary than I thought," says Matteo.

"You're not afraid of heights, are you?" I tease.

To my surprise, he makes a face. "I am, a bit."

"I am too."

"We'll take turns opening our eyes during the scary parts," he says.

It's beautiful up here in the sky, with overlapping shades of green for the grass and the trees and the more distant forest. I grab my phone, causing my wallet to fall out of my bag and spill open when it hits the metal floor. "Oh, shoot." I bend down, grateful we're the only ones here so I don't have to reach around people's feet.

Matteo helps me gather the scattered yen and my emergency lip gloss, then spots the snail he got me from the gachapon place. His fingers curl around it. "You kept it."

"Of course." I grab it back. "I love her. Her name is Snailerella."

There's the strangest expression on his face, but I can't tell what because he bends back down to pick up something else. "What is this?" he asks, squinting. "Wait, is it a cat?"

"Yes. It's a micro-amigurumi." The black cat was my first micro attempt, so I keep it as a good luck charm in my bag. "I crochet them. Or used to."

He stares at me. "This is the size of my fingertip. How did you make it?"

"With a tiny crochet hook and a magnifying glass."

"Holy shit, Ivy, that's incredible. How long have you been doing this?"

"I started a few years ago." I shrug, but his praise makes me feel warm. "When I got good enough, I sold them at school craft fairs and things like that. I haven't done any lately."

"Why not?"

I stare out the window, the black cat in my hand. "I didn't feel like it."

"Oh." It's only one word, and barely that, but it sounds like he understands. I relax, knowing he's not going to say something like *how hard is it to move some yarn around a hook?* "Yeah. I get it. This is amazing, though. You're really talented."

I look at the cat. "I had an idea for some amigurumi the

other day," I say. I want to tell someone.

"More animals?" He pauses. "Are they always animals?"

"I started with animals, but you can make anything. Plants, cactus, chairs. If you can think of it, you can crochet it into amigurumi. I did a lot of food, like tacos and croissants and ice cream. Lemons were popular, especially if you put googly eyes on them. Avocados, too."

"Googly eyes make everything better," he agrees. "Is that your idea?"

I'm about to speak when a flash of yellow catches my eye. I gawk out the window.

"Ivy?" He sees where I'm looking. "No. Oh my God. What the hell?"

We're bobbing over what looks like Lucifer's domain. No joke. A huge pit scarred with bright neon yellow has opened beneath us and it looks like steam is rising from far below. I see why Kimiko called Owakudani the Valley of Hell but didn't think it would be this spot-on. "How did we go from forest to this? It looks poisonous."

"We're passing over a literal active volcanic area?" Matteo says.

"This is terrifying. I can't stop looking."

He gives me a little grin. "I can help."

"How?"

Matteo leans over and puts his hands over my eyes. "Like this."

The feeling of his hand makes my skin tingle. This is

different from Connor as well. When he touched me, I always tried to anticipate where his hand would go next and would tense up in preparation. I want to lean into Matteo and bring him closer. I can feel him pressing against me from my thigh to my shoulder, as well as those hands over my eyes.

"Is this better?" he asks.

I nod because I'm having some trouble speaking.

"Now, tell me about your idea."

It's hard to put my thoughts together with him like that but I try. "Um."

"Tell me, Ivy. Otherwise we'll have to think about the pit of horror." His mouth is almost at my ear, and I hope he doesn't hear my heart thundering. I pull it together, or as much as possible.

"Right. Okay. In Osaka there was the god of the way things should be."

"Billiken," he remembers. "You want to make Billikens?"

"Not the god, but it gave me the idea. I want to do all those feelings or experiences we don't have words for."

He drops his hands, ignoring the deathscape below. "Feelings we don't have words for?"

I blink at him because the light seems brighter than before. He's sitting close, so when I look into his eyes, everything else blurs. "You know the first day after the winter when you don't have to wear your coat? How light it feels?"

His eyes widen. "When you say the wrong answer in

class but no one hears you so you're safe?"

"The bus getting a red light right at the stop in time for you to catch it." I nod. "Exactly. All of that."

He frowns. "How would you do them?"

"I originally pictured them as versions of emojis, but now I want them to look sort of like aliens."

"Interesting." He pulls out his sketchpad. "Kind of like this?"

In seconds, he's created almost exactly the image in my head. It's for Catching-the-Bus, a wiggly blob desperately reaching out its tentacles. I stare at it for a moment, wondering if telepathy really exists. "Yes!"

The gondola goes over a fence and into the station, and we stop talking to look around. When we hop out, Kimiko and the rest are in line to continue to the next stop. "We'll be at the lake, and there's no way you can get lost," she calls.

Tom waves at us. "Try the black eggs."

There's a slight smell of sulfur—right, that's what the yellow was—and we walk out to a paved area with lookouts over the pit and a path going up. When we hold tight to the fence, we're able to handle the height and lean over. The crater is so big it boggles my mind.

"Do you want to climb the path to the top?" Matteo asks, pulling back. He tugs at my shirt to bring me with him, and his hand lingers on my hip. It's like all my attention is suddenly zoomed on the tiny area where he's touching me.

"Let's do it."

Too bad the weather is not on our side. We've hardly started when the wind suddenly picks up enough to send hats flying and cause people to slap their hands to their sides to keep their skirts down.

"It's going to rain," says Matteo, hat in his hand so it doesn't blow over the side into the pit. The wind messes up his hair. It's cute but I don't have time to dwell on it before he's proven right. The storm hits and we join the crowds running back to the information center, the wind gusting the rain in sheets across the paved surface. The tops of the mountains have disappeared under heavy clouds close enough to touch, and we're laughing and yelling at each other as we get drenched.

By the time we stumble under the shelter, Matteo's white shirt is soaked and clinging to his shoulders, and I'm very grateful I wore black. I rub my arms, then cross them over my chest, and Matteo reaches into his bag. "Here." He hands over a navy hoodie, the one he wore the first day for dinner. It looks warm, and it's dry.

"What about you?"

He shrugs, and runs his hand through his wet hair, which is starting to curl. "I'm not cold. You wear it."

I'm dying to wear it, and not only because I'm chilly. "Thanks."

When I put it on, he fixes the hood around my neck, which makes my stomach flip-flop. "Keep it as long as you like."

I pull the sleeves up a bit because they're too long. It smells good, but not like cologne or soap. Just good. I do my best not to bury my nose in it.

Matteo texts Kimiko as the rain continues to hammer down. Around us are people taking photos and muttering about wet hair and shoes. Or I assume, because it's mostly in Japanese, but people are pointing at their heads and feet, so it's a fair guess.

"They made it to the lake before the storm hit," he reports. "Kimiko says the ropeway doesn't run in bad weather so we should stay here until it passes or take a bus or cab back."

We decide to wait it out and spend a good forty-five minutes wandering around the gift store. Matteo changes his mind on the black eggs about eight times—they're supposed to taste like regular boiled eggs, but what if they don't—and I try on a hat that looks like lava and buy some truffle chips we eat while looking at the rain.

It feels good.

Chapter 20

After the downpour, it simply rains for a while before turning into a heavy drizzle. Matteo and I slowly dry out. I'm toasty warm, but I keep the hoodie on because I want to. Through the rain-streaked windows, people run by covering their heads with bags or strut along in gigantic plastic ponchos (sold out by the time we realized this was an option) as they line up at the bus stop. There's no other way to get away with the ropeway closed.

"What do you think?" Matteo says. "Should we give it a shot?"

Normally, I'd say no. How would we know what bus to get? What if we get lost? Mom might be mad at me for going off without telling her. But Mom is relaxing in an onsen without her phone, and also, it's a bus. What can go wrong? If we get off at the wrong stop, all we do is go back.

"Let's do it," I say.

We follow the crowd out, and a nice woman helps us pay the fare. My shoes are squishy and uncomfortable, and I hate how the steam from people's breath and clothes covers the windows in condensation so I can't see out. I like to know where I'm going, although it's kind of useless since I have no idea where we are, or what destination landmarks I'd be looking for. It's not like home, where I know to grab my bag after we pass the Dollarama.

The bus is packed, so Matteo and I squeeze together in the aisle and clutch whatever handle or seat we can to steady ourselves as the bus goes around what feels like the first in an endless series of hairpin turns. A man wipes off part of the window with his sleeve, enough for me to see the side of the road is nothing but a steep rock face and trees. Switchbacks make the trip a fun but nauseous ride. We hit another corner, which causes me to lurch into Matteo.

Immediately, he releases the seat he's holding on to for balance to catch me, arms curling around my back as my hand comes up to grip his shoulder. "Are you okay?" he asks, looking down into my face.

Time stops. Matteo's light brown eyes are fixed on me and filled with concern. "I'm good," I manage to say.

Matteo doesn't answer, and he doesn't move. I don't want him to. I could stay like this for ages.

Another bounce breaks us apart. Matteo grabs the seat back again, and so do I. We don't say anything for a few minutes as the bus goes down the hill and by some buildings, until the driver stops and calls something. Matteo squints out the clear patch on the window and frowns as everyone files out.

Kimiko had described Lake Ashi as a resort location, and I was expecting touristy things, with lots of lights and excitement, kind of like Niagara Falls. We stand in a silent parking lot, with fog so dense we can barely see ahead to the shadowy buildings lurking on the edges. There's no station leading to a ropeway, no lake, and I'm almost certain we're not where we should be.

Matteo shakes his phone in disgust. "My battery's dead. Do you have Kimiko's number?"

"Mom does, but she's at the onsen and won't look at her phone for a while." I asked Mom for the number twice, but she forgot to give it to me. "How about Keith?"

"He'll get mad if I bug him while he's working and tell me to show some leadership." He looks around. "There's a map over there."

It's at the edge of the parking lot, and we go to check it. We're not in the right spot, but illustrated characters inform us there's an aquarium with seals to the left. The lake is in front of us, invisible thanks to the fog, and there's a hotel to the right.

The bus is gone, so we decide we might as well explore until the next one comes. "It's like something out of a horror movie," I say as we approach what looks like a gift shop/arcade/snack bar. On a warm sunny day, it would have an old-school vacation feel, but in the fog it looks deserted and creepy.

"Let's stick together." Matteo takes my hand. "We can't

get separated in case the clown killer comes, or the fog lake monster."

"Yeah," I agree. I hope my voice stays steady. One of the new feelings amigurumi I'm going to make will be this instant, when something you hoped would happen but didn't know you were hoping for actually occurs. Like Matteo, with drops of water dotting his hair like crystals, smiling at me as he holds my hand.

Connor never made me feel like this. Why did I put up with someone who didn't want to talk to me, or learn more about me? Who had no curiosity about me, or ever wanted to share their own thoughts? I almost stop as I realize something shocking. I did the same to him. I liked his hair and eyes, but did I like Connor himself?

It's only now, in this moment, in the fog, that I begin to understand crushes aren't deep in the way I always thought they were. Feelings are different when friendship is involved.

There must be an amigurumi for that, and it could be falling in love.

Matteo points at some dark shapes under a canopy. "I have to see what those are."

With each minute I spend with Matteo, my feelings about Connor fade until they finally disappear in a whimper of nothing. Matteo looks at me, and I can't help but smile like a total weirdo. In fact, I can't stop smiling as we walk over to find a bunch of animatronic bears you put coins in to ride. I assume on sunny weekends there would be a huge line of kids, but today it's only us. We can't figure out how to drive them, since there are no steering wheels, so we take a couple photos like we're in a rodeo. I'm about to suggest we take one together when a pack of wild children comes screaming out of the fog, followed by stressed parents. I'm disappointed, although the seats on the bears are far enough apart that it's not like we would be sharing a saddle.

Matteo takes my hand again, and it feels natural. He tugs me close as we look in the window of a closed boutique selling bright resort gear and huge-eyed dolls. I pull him over to check out a hidden doorway leading to the hotel. Wisps of fog linger around the columns of a long outdoor corridor with no one in it. Apart from the families at Ride-a-Bear, we haven't seen another person. Everyone from the bus seems to have disappeared into the fog.

"This is haunted," I whisper, and he moves his head close to hear me better. My lips brush his hair, and it tickles.

We go down the corridor and find a door at the end. He pushes it open to reveal a crimson-and-peach carpet with the exact same pattern as the hallway in *The Shining*—Hazel insisted we watch it last Halloween, and we had nightmares for weeks—before we decide it's not worth it.

"There's a feeling for you," Matteo says as he firmly shuts the door. "The sense there's something menacing around the corner."

"Have you ever seen a ghost?" We head down a concrete path that should take us to the lake. The fog lies heavy on the ground, drifting and shifting like a living thing.

He doesn't speak for a while. "I had a dream about my mom," he says finally. "After she died. She was going down a hallway and turned around and smiled at me and waved. She always curled her fingers, and we used to tease her about it. I knew it was her saying goodbye."

I squeeze his hand, not knowing what to say, and he squeezes back. "When I woke up, I felt better," he says. "Calmer? I don't know if that's the word."

"Accepting?" I ask.

He pokes his tongue into his cheek as he considers this. "Yeah. Accepting. That's how I felt."

We arrive at the edge of the path, which turns to grass and, a few steps later, into lake. There's no fence or beach, and if you aren't paying attention on a day like today, you could walk right into the water. The fog has muted all sound except for the waves lapping against the shore. There's no one around but us. It's the perfect place for the kiss I feel has been building all day. Or that I hope has been.

"It feels like we're the only people in the world," he says quietly.

Kiss him now. Do it. I can take his hand again and step up to him. I can see it perfectly. My face raised, his lips on mine.

I can't bring myself to do it, although we're holding hands.

What if he rejects me the way he did the fake-dating thing? It would hurt a lot more now, and I don't think I could handle seeing him for the next few days if that happened.

There's too much risk. I pretend to fix my shoe, and after I stand up, I walk along the edge, holding my arms out as if I'm balancing.

A splash comes from somewhere close in the fog, and I jump back.

"Monsters?" asks Matteo.

"What else could it be?"

Matteo turns back to the path. "Want to get something to eat?" he asks. "There's a restaurant near the aquarium."

He sounds calm, and I sigh with relief that I didn't make a move. God, how humiliating would it have been to lean in and have him say, "Ivy, you read this completely wrong." Then he'd give me a pitying look so I could feel rejection from my second love interest in a row.

There's another amigurumi. The relief of not acting on an impulse.

We find the restaurant and, after a quick bite, locate the right bus and head back to the hotel.

He doesn't hold my hand again, and I'm left alone with a whole bunch of new feelings.

"Did I tell you about the pebbles?" Mom sighs as she sniffs at her laundry before picking out her least grubby shirt for dinner.

"Many times." Apparently one of the baths had a reflexology bottom covered with small rocks to roll your feet on.

"Heaven. Did I tell you it was heaven?"

"Again, many times."

She boops me on the nose. "Don't be rude because your feet are tense and stiff and mine are loose bags of bone in freshly exfoliated skin."

"Eww, Mom, gross."

She goes out to get some tea and returns with a bottle of pop.

"What's that?" I ask, knowing full well what it is.

"Keith keeps giving me these," she says.

"You hate Sprite."

"I know. He got it in his head that I love it." She laughs. "You know how I've been giving him chocolate as thanks? Turns out we were both wrong. He can't stand chocolate either! We've been giving each other gifts we don't like. Isn't that funny?"

It wasn't supposed to be funny. Mom was furious when Dad gave her stuff she didn't want. Why is Keith so different? "He should have asked what you like before buying you things."

"Oh, we talked about it and had a good chuckle."

I glare at her. "How come when Keith doesn't know what you like, it's funny, but when Dad did it, you yelled at him?"

She raises her eyebrows. "Because Keith is a guy I've

known for two weeks and your dad was married to me for twenty years?"

I shut up and make a mental note to tell Matteo of our failure.

"Ready to eat?" asks Mom. "We can go, just you and me. You'd like something quiet after being around people all the time, wouldn't you?"

I nod. That would be perfect, since I want to think over my day, and the relief of only being with Mom is almost overpowering. Finally, she seems to understand I'm having trouble dealing with everything and can use a break. We walk to the restaurant, up a hill and along a dusty road. Mom sighs.

"I wish I could have done more things like this with your grandmother. Too bad she hated traveling."

"Remember when you asked her to come to the cottage with us?" I ask.

Mom snorts. "She said she didn't move fifteen thousand kilometers to use an outhouse and do her own dishes on vacation."

"You don't like those things either," I remind her. "When we went, you complained all week."

"Yeah, well, my mother didn't move fifteen thousand kilometers for her daughter to use an outhouse and do her own dishes on vacation, either."

We get to the café and are waiting for a table when the door opens.

"Hey, you two!" It's Yvonne, and although she's a perfectly nice woman, my shoulders rise up. "I'm meeting Joanne. Should we sit together?"

"Of course!" Mom beams at her. I wish I had the guts to say no to Yvonne's face, but instead I turn away and take out my phone. People, when Mom promised me a break. My whole night has been ruined, and I instantly feel myself getting red and black all deep down inside. Better than feeling gray? I don't know.

We get seated, and as we wait for Joanne, Yvonne goes to wash her hands. I turn to Mom.

"I thought we were having dinner alone," I say. "Now we're stuck with Yvonne and Joanne?"

Mom shrugs. "Things change, you know that. What did you want me to say? No?"

"Yes! You said we could eat alone."

"Don't be ridiculous, Ivy. It's not a big deal, and I'm not going to be rude."

"Oh, but it's okay for them to be rude and horn in on us?"

"Sorry," says Yvonne, coming back. I guess our voices carried more than I thought. "Do you want us to get another table?"

I sit back. "Whatever. Like it matters what I want."

"Ivy!" Mom sounds honestly shocked. "Mind your manners." She turns to Yvonne and rolls her eyes. "Excuse Ivy's rudeness. She had a tiring day," she says. "It would be a favor if you saved me from the teenage attitude."

Yvonne smiles. "I get the same way, and it's not a problem for Joanne and me to move."

"No, no, sit down. Ivy's fine." Mom shoots me a look as Joanne comes up and some seaweed-wrapped crackers arrive as an appetizer.

The pizza is cold and limp, and the three women talk around me and take Mom's lead to act like I'm not there. My good mood from the day has been smashed, thanks to Mom. I knew I was irritating her. I hate that I was proven right.

Chapter 21

Day 13—Kawaguchiko

Fuji-san awaits. Today you leave Hakone for Kawaguchiko and the Fuji Five Lakes. One of the iconic sights of the world, Mount Fuji is a must-see for any visitor. Before tomorrow's hike, we invite you to enjoy an evening of sake tasting. Kanpai!

"Where's my phone?" Mom asks. We're downstairs getting breakfast. Or Mom is. I wasn't hungry, although she insisted I eat the melon she put in front of me.

"I don't know." I do actually know. It's under her bag. But I got another lecture on manners this morning, a continuation of the one from last night, so I'm not willing to give her a hand. I might have been rude, but she refuses to acknowledge that she promised we'd eat alone. Zero accountability.

"Stay here while I check upstairs."

I wait, listening to Tom and Lisa debate hitting the dungeon onsen before we leave Hakone. "It seems strange to bathe first thing in the morning," Lisa says. "I feel I haven't earned that level of relaxation yet."

"We're on vacation," says Tom. "The world is our oyster. Also, we talked about this. You don't need to earn rest, Lisa. You're allowed to simply have it."

"Easy for you, you're retired. Try telling that to my boss."

"You're not at work right now, and your boss is a miserable, dead-eyed, twice-divorced workaholic whose kids hate him. Are you going to listen to him or me, your brilliant, insightful, and, may I say, handsome husband?"

"I'll go for a quick walk, then take a fast soak," Lisa says. She's pleased with this compromise, and Tom rolls his eyes.

"You're such an embodiment of the Protestant work ethic," he says, pouring more tea as she blows him a kiss. His own plan is to read as he waits for his wife, and he settles down with a battered paperback pulled from the multilingual stash of books left by previous visitors.

Mom comes back down. "I can't find it. I'm going to look again."

"I'm going for a walk," I say.

Mom snorts. "No, you're going to stay here so I don't have to track you down before we leave."

"Oh my God. Can't I get any privacy?" I demand. Out of the corner of my eye, I see Tom bury his face deeper in his book. "I'm not the one who misses everything or loses their phone. I'm *responsible*."

"Do as I say, Ivy. I don't want a repeat of leaving for Osaka, thank you very much. Making us all late once is enough for this trip." She goes back up the stairs.

I wait until she's gone and leave. I don't go far, just to the edge of the ryokan garden, but it's enough to give me the break I crave. There's not much to it besides a stone lantern and some benches around a small tree. I don't know what kind it is. It has green leaves.

In my bag is my crochet hook and the yarn from home. I've decided to try to make one of the feelings amigurumi I've been thinking about, a blob with wide legs that's the feeling you get after sitting all day. I thought of it while on the bus. I always start with a magic ring, and I wrap the yarn around my fingers and cross it over to begin.

I've done this often, but for some reason, I'm over-thinking each step and it's messing me up. Do I wrap twice or three times? The yarn keeps slipping off my hook, and it doesn't take long for me to put it down. I should have known better than to try.

I don't know how long I've been staring at nothing when I hear my name being called from down the street. Shouted is more accurate. It's Mom, and when I come out from the side of the hotel, I can tell she's furious.

"Where the hell have you been?" she asks. "I told you to stay put."

"I only went to the garden."

Her mouth works, but she glances at some of the other Adventurers as they come out with their bags. "Come upstairs and help me with the luggage."

My heart is hammering, but she can't possibly be mad because I went three steps out of the hotel. I'm not a prisoner. Or maybe I am, because she turns on me the second we get in the room.

"How dare you disobey me like that?"

I stare at her. "I wanted fresh air, and I went outside. It's no big deal."

"No big deal? I had no idea where you were, and you weren't answering your phone. Again."

I check it to find six missed calls and a text from Mom. "My ringer was off."

"I don't know what is the matter with you lately, Ivy, but I want it to stop. You've been sulky and rude. You're ruining this trip with your attitude."

"I'm ruining this trip. Me. Great. Sure, Mom." I get a red spike through my chest. I knew she would hate it the second I stopped being the old perfect, happy Ivy.

"This is exactly what I'm talking about. I know what's going on. You're pouting because you were told to act like an adult and not a child at dinner last night."

"I'm not pouting. I just wanted a break from people, okay?"

Mom looks like she's going to breathe fire. "Be that way, then. Have your break."

She takes her bag and walks out without looking. I want to yell after her, but I don't know what to say. Grabbing my own bag, I go down the stairs, mind feverishly running through the argument and all the things I could have said until it's a jumble of words in my head.

As we wait for the bus, me far away from Mom, Keith goes up to talk to her about sharing their photos. Matteo and I exchange a look before he blurts out, "Tom loves photos!"

"Nice," I whisper, glad to see him despite the fight with Mom.

"I panicked."

At least that gets Tom to join the conversation, which turns into a discussion of how to start a photo share group. The debate on various photo platforms continues as we board, and Tom and Keith sit together as Mom compares notes about how to tie a scarf with Lisa. That's all good, but it was a close call.

I'm still steaming about Mom when Kimiko starts telling us what to expect for tomorrow's climb up Mount Fuji. "It's strenuous and you shouldn't do the climb if you have doubts. There is no shame in admiring the mountain with plum wine or tea like the poets and painters. It will be a very full and tiring day, mentally and physically."

"Are you going?" Matteo asks.

"Yes." I'm not big on hikes in general, but this is different. It's Mount Fuji. The only problem is having to do it with Mom. "You?"

He sighs. "Mom said she wanted to climb Fuji before she died, but it was a joke, right? Obviously she wasn't going to die before we could get to Japan." Matteo's jaw twitches, like he's trying not to show a lot of emotion. The same with his voice, which he keeps steady. "She and Dad were going to race to the top. Now Dad wants to go and beat some timing record they were looking at. Dom dared him."

"Let him."

"He wants me to race him."

"Do you want to?"

"I want to take my time and enjoy it, but do you think I have a choice?"

He takes out his phone and starts scrolling in an aggressive way that indicates the discussion is over.

That's horrible. Keith definitely isn't a good match for Mom, even if I am mad at her. She'll need to figure that out, with some help from me.

I only wish there was something I could do for Matteo as well.

We arrive in Kawaguchiko, and when I get out of the bus, Mount Fuji is right there, rising in an almost perfectly symmetrical cone that's been flattened on the top. I stare. The mountain is entirely brown, although I thought it would be snow-capped, even if it is July and the temperature is a thousand degrees. It's . . . a bit of a letdown? I could never, ever tell anyone this, because I would sound like such an ignorant and entitled jerk. But I've seen it so often on TV and posters with cherry blossoms and a pagoda in the foreground that the real thing is almost disappointing.

There's another amigurumi. The gap between expectation and reality.

Paulette, however, has far outdistanced my embarrassing lack of enthusiasm. She summons her final handmaiden to her side. "Look at that, Gretchen!" she says. "It's smaller than I thought. Kimmy, is that it? We saw the Colosseum on my group tour to Rome, and let me tell you, it was something special."

We ignore her and head into the hotel. I look through my bags and realize I left my amigurumi and the hook back on the bench at the ryokan garden. For a moment, I'm upset, but that fades into nothing. Who cares. It wasn't working anyway.

"It's a free afternoon," Mom says, kneeling as she pulls clothes out from her bag. "Keith and I were thinking of going to a café he heard about with a nice view of the mountain." Her voice is cold, and she's not looking at me.

I'm on high alert. "When did you decide that?"

"He texted me."

They were texting? We should have anticipated that, but Mom hates texting. She calls. I wait until her back is turned and report this new finding to Matteo.

Dad hates texting. I haven't seen him text.

What if they're hiding it from us? What else are they hiding?

Come to the café and let's implement Plan Perfume and Sock Sandals, a sub-plan of Project Omega.

I'm not particularly thrilled about spending more time than I have to with Mom, but I'll have to suck it up. Normally, I'd be more upset she's mad at me, but right now, I'm just irritated. She's such a hypocrite. It's fine for her to be frustrated when things go wrong and take it out on me, but the second I do the same thing, I'm a brat spoiling the trip.

"Did you want to come to the café or relax here?" Mom asks. "Have some of your precious alone time."

I grit my teeth at how immature she's being. She's *fifty*. "I'm coming."

She says nothing, and I text Matteo. Get ready.

It takes a few minutes to decide the most casual way to douse Mom with perfume, but I manage it right before we go. As she comes out of the washroom, I frantically spray half of one of the sample bottles she brings when traveling on the back of her shirt. She wrinkles her nose.

"Is that my Tom Ford?" she asks.

I wave my wrist as if I put it on myself. "I wanted to try it."

"God, be careful. I only use it for nights out. It's strong."

Is it ever. My eyes water when she walks by, and she coughs. "Go wash your arm," she tells me, disgusted. "We're going to choke on the fumes."

After I do, she decides it must be the lingering scent in the room and we need to go. As usual, she leaves on the lights, and I slam my hand against the switch so hard the bang reverberates through the room.

"Do you have a problem, Ivy?" Mom has her hands on her hips.

"Why can't you ever turn off the lights?"

"Because I didn't notice."

"It's not hard."

Mom rolls her eyes. "Or important, so deal with it."

We head over to the café, me doing my best to keep my temper, because realistically, it's only lights. But it feels like more, somehow. Tom Ford and his Black Orchid accompany us in a huge fragrant cloud down the street, but fortunately someone is burning incense, and that covers the perfume so she doesn't realize the smell is almost all her. We sit at the café, which is an homage to the beauty of Mount Fuji, with a huge mural painted on the wall and cushions covered with miniature Mount Fujis. She leans over and sniffs at me. "It's like you've bathed in it."

Matteo and Keith arrive, and Mom's eyes instantly shoot down to the navy sport socks Keith has pulled up halfway to his calves, and the black sandals. She says nothing, but stares as they come closer.

When they reach the table, Keith's nose screws up like a rabbit. Matteo gives me an approving glance, which I return. Those socks would make anyone cringe, and the perfume is powerful enough to fill a stadium.

Mom raises her eyebrows. "Good look."

"Thought I'd try cosplaying as a German tourist." Keith sniffs at the air. "Holy smokes, Lill, that perfume is something."

"It smells better when it's not impersonating mustard gas." It's nice of her to cover for me, although she shoots me a look.

Then they're laughing? Matteo and I gape at them. This was supposed to be a death spike for any positive feelings. They were supposed to be disgusted and grossed out, then ideally avoid each other until we left.

I squint at Mom as they talk about the sesame latte on the menu, but she seems fine with the socks. Maybe she's decided Keith can take her as she is or not, and she'll do the same. A lot of the tension she used to have around Dad is gone, and she seems more like herself. It doesn't make sense. How could you be married to someone you can't be natural around?

Maybe getting Mom and Dad back together isn't . . .

No. Of course Mom is relaxed; she's on vacation. She's only been apart from Dad for a few months. Keith is totally not the answer.

That night, we're going for a food and sake pairing. "It's more snacks than food," clarifies Kimiko. "If you're hungry, you're welcome to go to dinner at your leisure."

This, I know by now, is tour group code for "on your own and paid by you." She takes us to an izakaya, which is more of a bar than a restaurant and has red lanterns out front that Paulette slaps with her hand to make them swing. We're greeted at the door with a hearty "Irasshaimase!" as we file in.

"You and Matteo will sit here, please," says Kimiko, pointing to a table to the side. "It will help the staff in serving everyone, since you have vegetarian snacks and no alcohol."

We sit down. Kimiko had mentioned this was a good location for Westerners as we could sit on chairs instead of low tables.

"Now what?" I say. "Look, they're together."

"Well, it's not like we can go over and barge in."

We're whispering over the table, which is a small one that only fits two. The adults surround the L-shaped bar, which is narrow and made of polished wood, seated on high-top stools. It's been set with rows of shot glasses, four per person. There are long platters along the counter, filled with the nuts and rice crackers that are also in front of me and Matteo, plus tiny dried silver fish, complete with eyes and fins. Paulette, that fearless traveler, is making faces at the fish and asking how people can eat such things. No one answers, but everyone makes a point of taking some and commenting on how good it is.

The bartender gives a short talk about the history of sake and drinking etiquette before Kimiko drops off wooden platters with four small glasses, one in front of each of us, as the bartenders start pouring the sake.

"I had them choose a selection of drinks you might not have tried before." She points at a thick, white drink in a wider bowl. "That's amazake, their specialty. It's made from fermented rice, and is sweet and creamy."

We try the amazake—I would say it's an acquired taste—and I do a test sip from the rest while reading the guide.

"The cold yuzu tea is nice and light," I say.

"Yeah, but the Calpis tastes sort of like yogurt."

We compare drinks and snacks until the adults finish up. It's nice to be with him and not thinking about the fight with Mom. We talk about school—he likes history, I like math—and what Mount Fuji will be like. Then all sorts of other things, because he's super easy to talk to. I like to make him laugh. Not once do I feel like I've said something dumb, and I never feel like the responsibility is on me to keep the conversation going. I pause with my drink in the air, when I realize how much more relaxed I feel with Matteo after what happened in Hakone. I thought I would be nervous, monitoring him for reactions and trying to guess what he's thinking, but it's just fun.

Also he looks crazy good in the dim light of the izakaya.

Matteo pushes over the bowl of snacks. "Here," he says. I reach out, and our fingers touch for a second. Matteo freezes, and when he glances at me, whatever he sees in my face makes him smile.

"Let's go, Ivy." Mom comes up, and I pull my hand away. "Time for dinner."

We get out and let the others go ahead to a meat place. Mom sighs and gives me a hug. "I'm sorry for saying you're wrecking the trip," she says, breathing sake in my face. "That was wrong of me. I was upset and worried when you weren't there, and I overreacted."

Yeah, you did. But I know what I'm supposed to say. "I'm sorry I left without telling you."

"You have been in a bad mood lately, though," Mom says. "Is it me?"

"You?"

"You said you needed space."

I shrug, not wanting to get into it when I'm still feeling a bit raw despite the apology. "There's a lot of people all the time," I say.

Mom nods. "I get it." She brightens. "At least they're nice. Or most of them. Matteo, Yvonne." She pauses. "Keith."

I give her a look, but she's pushing open the door to a ramen restaurant and waving at the server, who comes forward to seat us.

Keith. He'd better only be a friend.

Because, I'm realizing, Matteo might be something more.

Chapter 22

Day 14—Mount Fuji

Our penultimate day in Japan will be spent doing the ultimate bucket-list item—summitting Mount Fuji and admiring the views from the crater.* Those who wish for a less active day are welcome to enjoy the natural beauty of Lake Kawaguchiko and its many teashops, boutiques, and hiking trails.

*Adventure Group takes no responsibility for injuries sustained during the climb as per our personal health waivers.

I couldn't sleep when we got back to the hotel. That's not unusual, but last night it seemed especially bad. I scrolled on my phone for hours, getting progressively more tired and then upset that despite being tired, I couldn't sleep. The room was too cold with the air-conditioning vent blowing right on me, and I wanted to be at home, in my own bed. It must have been early morning when I drifted off to the sounds of early chirping. The friendly noise made me feel worse, like my body knew it wasn't supposed to be awake to greet the birds.

When Mom shakes me, my head feels like the sandbag Dad once had in the garden to stop some flooding. I want to cry, but that takes too much effort.

Also, what do I have to cry about? My mom took me on vacation to Japan, boohoo. No one's going to feel sorry for poor, ungrateful me. I certainly wouldn't.

"It's mountain climbing day!" Mom's voice seems particularly loud.

"I know."

"What's the matter?"

"Nothing." I roll over and face the wall. Everything feels like it's come to a head. "Can you go without me? I can stay in the room."

She frowns. "Are you sick? Is it your stomach? I brought some Imodium and can get some ginger ale."

She thinks any sickness can be healed with ginger ale. I shake my head.

Mom sighs. "If you're tired, you can nap in the bus. It's about an hour's drive to the start point."

"Mom, I don't want to go."

"What?" She sounds shocked. "Why? It's Mount Fuji."

"I'm tired." That's the easiest way to describe how I feel. Then I try again. "Like a blanket is choking me."

"Stop exaggerating. We're not even on the mountain yet. There's no altitude to affect you."

"I don't think I can do it."

"Right. Great. Not this again." She pulls off her shoes and throws them in the corner. "I thought we came to an agreement last night that you were going to smarten up."

"It's not my fault!"

"No? You're always too worn out, unless it's something you want to do. Have you considered maybe I'm sick of being held hostage to your moods?" Her voice is rising.

"It's not a mood, okay?" I glare at her.

"This isn't like you."

She's wrong, though. This is exactly like me. The real me.

"Sorry I'm not perfect like you want me to be." Then the words are out before I think them through. "Dad would understand."

Her eyes narrow. "Sure. Let's see how that works for you. Go ahead and call him."

"I will."

She folds her arms and stares at me as if it's a dare. I pick up my phone, hoping international calls aren't covered and she has to pay a thousand dollars when the bill comes in. Two thousand dollars. Ten thousand.

Dad answers in a second. "Ivy? Are you okay?"

"Mom is making me hike up Mount Fuji."

There's a long silence. "She's what?"

"She's making me hike up the mountain, and I don't want to."

His sigh is heavy. "Ivy. This is between you and your mother."

"But . . ."

"Come on, what do you expect me to say? You'll regret it if you don't go. It's Fuji."

I don't look at Mom and lower my voice. "Can't you talk to her?"

"You can do that yourself. How is the trip going otherwise?"

"Okay." There's no other answer to give because it's all he'll want to hear.

"Good. Keep sending me photos, and I'll see you when you get back. I found a great brownie recipe for us to try."

I mutter a goodbye and stare at my bed. The feeling of wishing you had no feelings—there's another amigurumi.

"Even your father thinks you're being too much," Mom says.

It's how she says it, like it's a fact, that makes me feel sick. And she's right. I'm being too much because I am too much. Yet I can't understand how I can be too much and still feel like I'm not enough.

I manage to keep my voice level, although my chest is so tight it aches. "I can stay here alone while you go."

"You can't." She doesn't give a reason, which means she wants to be a martyr, and she's doing it to punish me. "Now, are you going to come and enjoy this once-in-a-lifetime experience, or are we going to have to sit in a hotel room all day?"

If I make Mom miss this, she'll be furious and I'll never hear the end of it. I have no choice. "Fine."

She nods, but her face says she's too mad to enjoy her win. "Then get ready. You're going to make us late."

We're the last people to arrive, and this time, Mom points at me and calls out, "Not my fault! Ivy had a case of the blahs this morning." She gives a fake laugh that makes my shoulders hunch.

Most people turn to me with muttered expressions of concern, but Keith claps his hands, loud enough to make me wince. "I bet she was scared an old man like me would beat her to the top. Dom and I are going to race you all."

He doesn't seem to notice he said Dom and not Matteo, but Matteo sure does. His face falls as he turns away from his father. I wish I had something I could say to take away the sting, but I'd probably only make it worse.

I'm tired of people staring at me while I'm on the edge of tears. Anything could set me off, thanks to my head being so thick with thoughts. Dad. This shitty fucking climb. Mom calling me selfish. I don't pay attention to where we're going once the bus starts, and keep my eyes closed and my earbuds in so I don't have to talk to anyone.

The general commotion of arrival causes me to open my eyes, and I wonder if I can hide here until everyone comes back. Mom pauses at my seat. "Ivy. Get up, get off this bus, and put a smile on your face," she says in a low voice. "Am I understood? I've put up with enough from you, and I'm sick of it. I won't let you ruin this day for everyone."

I don't bother to answer. If I'm lucky, I can walk in silence. That might be doable, and maybe exercise will help in the way Mom insists it does. Around me, people exchange boring, typical comments about what a perfect day it is for a hike, until I want to hit the next person who says the word *idyllic*. The sky is blue and the air is cool. I should be thankful for the change from the usual suffocating heat, but I can't bring myself to care. Kimiko gives some last-minute instructions that I don't bother listening to, and we start.

The station where we begin is crowded, and there's a steady flow of people climbing the path. It's not bad. I'm wearing sneakers, but some people are fully kitted out in technical gear and carrying trekking poles. I'd expected more of a nature trail, but stare down at wide steps edged with wood and filled with dirt. Mom is up ahead and doesn't bother to check to see if I'm following the group. I am, though, close to the rear. Matteo is a few people in front of me, nodding through Gary's monologue about some ball game, and ignoring his father's yells to hurry up and get a move on. He's looked back a couple times, with a face that would have made me feel better on a normal day, but doesn't affect me at all right now.

"Mind if I walk with you for a bit?" It's Tom, with his camera around his neck as well as a jaunty red bandana. "It's nice back here away from everyone. Kind of peaceful."

I shrug and he takes that as a yes. To my surprise, it's

comforting to have Tom beside me, although neither of us speak. We keep pace with each other, waiting when he takes a photo or I stop to get a rock out of my shoe. Around us people point at the landscape with *oohs* and *aahs*. We keep walking. Paulette complains about her feet. We keep walking. To one side is the edge of the mountain, and to the other is a smooth concrete wall with some greenery. From behind come about twenty hikers in technical vests that will make Hank die with envy. At least half of them hold poles they plant in unison as they walk, giving the appearance of a military operation. In the chaos of trying to give them enough space, Tom and I get separated from the rest of the group.

We're the last to arrive at the next station, and most have gone ahead. Mom is there, with her stupid new best friend, Yvonne. I collapse on a rock, face tense from trying to keep back my tears, and feeling completely used up. Tom pats me on the shoulder and leaves to murmur something to Mom. He goes to join Lisa after Mom waves him ahead.

"I was waiting," says Mom, her voice annoyed. "We're halfway there."

That means halfway more to go and then all the way down. Suddenly, I can't do it. I can't. My legs are too heavy to take another step.

"Can I meet you at the bus?" I ask. "I can wait here for you to come back, or I can go down by myself."

Mom stares at me. "Are you joking? You can't stop in the middle of Mount Fuji."

"They did." I point to a family that has taken some photos, then turned around to head back down.

"That's different. Get on your feet."

Yvonne looks uncomfortable and steps away to give us some privacy. Matteo, who has been behind us, speaks up. "I'll stay with Ivy," he says.

Mom keeps her eyes on me. "Your father said he wanted you to catch up to him."

"I know."

Before this can go further, Keith himself appears from around the corner of the trail, an avenging god in a light Patagonia jacket. "Where the hell have you been?" he calls to Matteo. "Do you know how much time I lost doubling back? Think of Dom's bet."

"Ivy doesn't feel well, and I said I'd stay with her," says Matteo.

"What?" Keith turns to Mom. "Lill? What's going on?"

"Don't ask me. I only heard it myself right before you got here." Mom sounds fed up.

Keith stares at Matteo. "Dom is going to be disappointed."

Matteo's hands ball into fists. "Then Dom should have come instead of me!"

Keith's jaw clenches, and although he doesn't say it, it's clear he's wishing the same thing. He checks his watch and shakes his head. "I'm going to keep my promise. You can be the one to tell him you couldn't be bothered to put a flower for your mother at the top of the mountain after the race she wanted to do."

Just then, Joanne and Susan come back. "We thought we were in better shape than we are," says Joanne, puffing. "We're going to meet everyone where we were dropped off. There's a café."

Susan smiles at Mom. "We can watch the kids if they're not up to climbing," she says. She must have heard us. "It's not a problem, and Kimiko said the risk of altitude sickness gets worse as you go."

They wave and leave. I look at Mom. "See? There will be people there. It's a single path down. I can't get lost."

"Jesus Christ, I've had enough." Mom finally snaps. "You're sixteen, and if you want to be miserable, go be miserable. I can't force you to have a good time."

And she's gone with Yvonne and Keith, no doubt talking about what an ungrateful and horrible person I am. I should feel bad. I know I should feel bad. Instead, I gaze at the gorgeous patchwork vista below, like looking down from a plane, and feel nothing. No, not nothing. A bit of relief I'm finally alone.

Or would be, except Matteo is next to me, making a face. "At least they let us be."

"You didn't have to stay."

"So you said, but I was done with Dad telling me

what Dom would think about the hike, and how fast Dom would have gone and how I was slow because I quit training."

My bad feeling for Matteo momentarily overrides my own issues. "I'm sorry."

He shrugs. "Kind of used to it, to be honest. I want to sit and sketch for a bit anyway, if you don't mind."

I nod for him to go ahead, and he asks me to watch his bag. In a few minutes, he comes back from the station lodge. "No strawberry tea," he says as he hands me a bottle of water and some snacks. "Here."

"I'm not hungry."

"Put them in your bag for later." He sits beside me on the bench, and we stare at the view. He doesn't talk, and from behind us come bits and pieces of languages from around the world. Japanese, German, French. Mandarin and Thai. There are a few I don't recognize, and I let the tones of peoples' voices float by without bothering to snatch them up for further investigation.

"I can't believe they left," says Matteo. His notepad is still closed on his lap. He's part laughing, part shocked.

"It's not like anything is going to happen to us. We only have to walk down and wait."

"I guess, but it's the principle. Aren't parents supposed to make sure you're safe?"

"I'm safe, and I'd rather Mom not be here. At least this way I don't have to hear about how I wrecked her only chance to climb Mount Fuji," I say. "It doesn't matter. She's still going to be mad at me."

Matteo makes a sort of *mmm* noise, like he's listening. "You didn't trip or get hurt or anything, did you? To make you want to go back down?"

"No. It's nothing. I don't know." I talk to the endless expanse of blue sky. "I'm exhausted all the time, and I don't want to do anything, and everything pisses me off. She says I need to snap out of it."

"You can't?" he asks.

"I tried. I tried going for walks and joining the yearbook club and all sorts of stuff, but I stopped. I didn't have the energy."

"Have you talked to anyone? Your dad?"

"No one, and Dad's worse than she is." I tug at the hem of my shirt. "Maybe Mom's right and everyone feels like this."

He turns around and waits until I meet his gaze. "I don't think they do, Ivy."

"What?"

"I don't think they do. Not like what you're saying."

His voice is soft, and for once, for maybe the first time, I feel like someone hears me. I can't help the tears that start up. They spill out and Matteo grabs me. "Hey."

"Sorry," I manage to gasp, but I can't stop.

"It's okay," he says. "I'm here."

I bend my head further so he can't see my face all twisted

up, and he pulls me close until I'm tucked in his shoulder. I don't know how long I cry. It's like all this sludge from deep inside that has been collecting has to be released in some way. I might have screamed if I'd had more energy, but crying will have to do. His shirt is getting all wet, but he doesn't seem to care, and his arms tighten around me.

It seems like hours later that the tears lessen, and eventually I pull away, staring at the dark patch on his shoulder. Matteo keeps a hand on my arm while he passes me some water. "Here."

I drink it and then sit back on the bench and stare at nothing. My mind is empty, but in a kind of good way. Lighter. My eyes, however, are swollen and delicate.

"Sorry," I mumble.

"Don't be. Do you want to talk?"

I shake my head. "Not sure what to say."

Matteo pulls out his sketchbook again. "Sometimes when I get like that, I can draw it better than say it. Kind of like I'm able to draw the meaning?" He taps his pencil. "That sounds weird. Sorry."

"Hazel does the same things with her poems," I say, after I hiccup. The tears are over, but I'm having a bit of trouble catching my breath. "I'm not an artist."

"Your amigurumi are cool."

I laugh for the first time today, and it feels rough but not wrong. "Because a crocheted toad is a great communication device."

"Maybe a crocodile would work better. Or an elephant."

"Why an elephant?"

He shrugs. "The ears?"

We lapse into silence again, and he flips idly through his sketchpad. "You can work if you want," I say. "It's okay."

"Are you sure?"

I nod, not wanting him to go away but needing some quiet time to think. Or just be. "I want to sit here for a minute. What are you drawing?"

He opens to show me a page split into two jagged triangles. "I've been thinking about the next chapter for my book."

"I thought you gave it up."

Matteo shrugs. "I changed my mind."

I lean my shoulder against his in a show of support, and he presses back. He draws and I sit and slowly start to come back to myself. An older couple strides by, their arms working in unison, and a guy my age trudges up with his hands stuffed in his pockets. There's a family with a baby in a pack on the dad's back. I look at people's faces, wondering if their expressions reflect what they're thinking. Are others sad behind their smiles, or is it only me?

Matteo messes around in his bag and pulls out a flower that he unwraps. It's pretty, white with small, tight buds along the stem. He looks at it for a moment.

"Is that for your mom?" I ask.

He nods. "Do you think it's bad if I leave it here? We

promised Dom they'd be at the top."

I point to a rock near the edge that has a crack in it. It's beautiful, worn into an almost friendly round shape from the rain and wind. "There would be perfect."

He gets up and I look away to give him some privacy. A few minutes later, he returns, his eyes red, sniffing a bit. I hand him one of my tissues. In the rock, the stem stands straight and tall, the shape emphasized by the sky behind.

After a while, we decide to go down. Matteo tells me about his book—it's a dystopian world where people outsource their memories and personalities to robotic pets that follow them around—and I tell him about how to crochet. It's a peaceful conversation, and after an hour, I feel calmer. The sadness has turned to a tired quiet that, while heavy, isn't oppressive. I can live with this.

I can—but do I have to? Maybe Matteo is right and this isn't a normal kind of angsty-teenager, lots-going-on, hormonal sadness. Like, not the kind that can be worked out with thick eyeliner and sad songs and wearing black. Is it possible this veil will never lift? I tried being positive, and getting exercise, and trying new things. What else can I do?

At the monkey park, Tom said something needed to change, and he did it by talking to someone. It felt good to talk to Matteo, and I wonder if it would feel better to talk to other people. But how? A woman in a white jacket passes, her face serious as she scans the path ahead of her. It reminds me of a lab coat. Mom might not be into therapy for herself, but I'm not her. It might work for me, if I can get up the courage to say something.

I don't know, but I'm not doing great on my own. That could be another amigurumi. The realization you can't do everything by yourself.

This is all going around in my head when we reach the station where we're meeting the bus, and we go inside to pass the time. On the souvenir shelves are candies, and shirts, and snow globes I avoid looking at too closely. I browse the aisles, picking things up and putting them down without really looking. Matteo stops at a miniature Christmas tree covered in ornaments and pulls one out to show me. It's a transparent ball and inside is a cat, sitting on some sushi, holding a miniature mountain in its paw, glorious in its tackiness.

He puts it back and I grab it. The ornament might make a good present for someone. As I go to pay, I pass another display, this one of amigurumi. They're all-in-one craft kits to make penguins and ducks and other animals. A whale catches my eye. It's a lovely blue, brighter than the bluebird I'd been working on, and the exact shade I had in mind for the tentacle creature Matteo drew. I think of that abandoned hook and yarn in the garden and pick up the whale, which has a soulful, wide-eyed look and, weirdly, embroidered stripes across its forehead. At the front, the salesman bags my purchases up with beautiful folded paper.

We walk in silence to get something to eat. Joanne and

Susan are visible through the window, posing for pictures.

Matteo goes off and comes back with some cream puffs. "They had strawberry as well, so I got you one."

We split one cream puff, then another, and by the time we split two more, I don't feel like crying anymore. At least for now.

Chapter 23

Day 15—Tokyo

It's time to bid "sayonara" to the Land of the Rising Sun. On your last day in Tokyo, you'll have a free afternoon for shopping and souvenirs, and have dinner at your leisure. Unescorted transport to Narita International Airport will be provided tomorrow depending on your flight time.* Please visit us again in beautiful Japan!

*Guests staying past the tour duration are responsible for their own room, and intracity and airport transport.

The evening is quiet as the group wavers between wired and exhausted from the climb. Since dinner is on our own, we join Tom and Lisa and some others at a pub. Keith and Matteo aren't there, and Matteo sends me a photo of some sushi. I guess his father wants to yell at him in private for letting down the family. I'm grateful to Matteo, but also feel bad, even though he insists he preferred staying with me to racing up the mountain. I hope he's telling the truth; otherwise I'd feel worse.

Luckily, Mom is so tired she nearly falls asleep in the crispy noodles they served as an appetizer. Like, uncooked seasoned spaghetti noodles out of the pack and into the deep fryer that I eat despite my lack of appetite. Double luckily, it means she doesn't get into what happened on Mount Fuji. In fact, she doesn't talk to me about the climb at all, although she's happy enough to relive it with the others.

Unluckily, it means she's still stewing the next day when she wakes up. That's fine though, because so am I. Why was it Matteo and not her who stayed with me? She wanted to do Mount Fuji, and she was going to do it, regardless of what happened. I bet if I'd broken my leg, she'd have told me to walk it off and keep going.

Mom sits up in bed and rubs her feet. "About what happened yesterday."

I shrug, matching her tone. "What about it?"

She looks at me for a moment. "Never mind, Ivy. Just know that was unacceptable behavior. It was embarrassing, and you inconvenienced everyone. Kimiko was worried when you went off on your own."

"I didn't ask anyone to worry."

"That's beside the point. You knew Mount Fuji was something I was looking forward to, and I didn't appreciate you sabotaging it, or dragging Matteo into your drama."

Good to know that while I was freaking out, all she could

think about was how she looked to others and what she wanted. "Really? Because I didn't appreciate you leaving me there. I bet everyone was impressed with that class-A parenting." This feels good to say. It feels *good* to say what I think out loud to her.

She only stares at me, and I know she's mad because I'm right. "Get packed."

We don't talk much as we get ready. When we get on the bus, I don't look at her before I sit beside Matteo.

"Was Keith upset last night?" I whisper.

He shrugs. "Got told I was a disappointment a few times, and he tried to get my brother to text me, but Dom just told me to ignore Dad and send more photos. At least there was a work crisis before I could get Dad's usual lecture on living up to expectations and how Dom would do better."

We lapse into silence as the bus fills and Kimiko counts us up.

As we leave the town, I search in my bag for my earbuds and see the amigurumi kit I bought yesterday. I open the box and run my fingers over the yarn. Right now it's enough to think about what I could make. I like that because it takes my mind off my current worry, namely what will happen when this trip is over. It's been almost like a petri dish and we're bacteria, cut off from everything but specific stimuli and left to grow (thanks, Ms. Brar). I'm going to have to deal with Mom, and Mom and Dad. At least Mom and Keith seem to have stagnated, although my motivations regarding that whole thing have changed. I want them apart but not because of Dad.

It's because of Matteo.

Despite growing closer, we haven't talked about what will happen when we go home. We live in the same city, but that doesn't mean anything. I live in the same city as my own father, and only see him two days a week, if that. Will Matteo want to see me? He has to, doesn't he? After how sweet he was on Fuji? And what might have happened in Hakone by the lake?

He's deep in concentration as he draws a fight scene between my tentacle monster and Godzilla, except it's Toronto and not Tokyo. Godzilla is ripping out the CN Tower to use as a spear, while the other is rising out of Lake Ontario, a ferry in hand to throw.

I give him a sidelong glance, liking how his hair waves when he takes his hat off. He sees me looking and smiles.

I melt. Like, my innards actually twist and then feel like they're disintegrating. It's the strangest feeling and makes my heart pound. Before I know it, I'm smiling back, because he's reached under the hoodie lying between us to take my hand.

We don't say anything but look out the window, making nothing comments on what we see just to talk. I feel . . . happy? No, not quite, but better. I'm not going to jump around doing cartwheels, but I don't feel like I did yesterday, or at least not as much. The edges of that Ivy remain, but a new Ivy might be ready to come out. Not soon, but eventually.

It doesn't take long to get to Tokyo. Kimiko said we're staying in a different neighborhood to give us more experience of the city. The bus takes a special route to show us the Shibuya Scramble, where people cross the intersection from every which way, and LED billboards overlook the chaos. Matteo drops my hand as he leans over so we can gawk out of the window.

"So many people," says Matteo. "I want to come back here."

"Me too. I bet it's amazing at night."

We make our way through the city and pull up to Sensoji, a huge temple with what looks like an outdoor shopping district in front of it. It's crowded and hot, and I end up telling Mom I'm going to take a break in the shade. She looks suspicious, but Tom comes up, his face red and sweating through the brim of his khaki hat, and mentions he's heading to a bench in the small garden.

"Ivy can sit with me if she wants a breather," he says. "Lisa's getting some souvenirs, but I think we have enough cat stuff to last several lifetimes."

Mom agrees, and I follow Tom to a bench. My mind is empty, and I simply soak it all in, breathing the hot air and listening to the sounds of the people behind me.

Tom stretches his legs and yanks out his water. He doesn't bother to drink but pours it down the inside of his shirt. "God, I won't miss the heat, that's for sure. You know Hank has his own personal water mister? It attaches to his hat. Have you had a good trip?"

I nod, wondering if Tom is someone I can talk to. Will he get nervous or uncomfortable to have me unload on him? What if he tells Mom?

However, Tom seems happy to be who he is. I want some of that so badly for myself it forces me to take the risk and speak.

"Tom?"

"Yes?"

I don't say anything, and he glances over, his eyes kind. "Looks like you've got some thoughts, Ivy. Big ones?"

Being asked a question I can answer makes this easier. I nod.

"Sometimes the first words are the hardest," he says gently. "You can just say them."

I take a deep breath, then I speak. "Do you remember the monkeys?"

"I do."

"And you told me about how you got bored of stuff? Like it didn't really matter anymore?"

"Sure." He folds in his legs and looks at me seriously. "What about it?"

I flop back on the bench and yelp when the shrub jabs me in the spine. "What happened?"

Tom is quiet for a while. Behind us is the continuous

heavy hum of people going around the temple. Matteo is there. I could be with him eating ice cream, but for some reason I'm talking to a man I barely know and fighting back tears. God, and I thought I'd cried them all out yesterday. I must have a fountain where some internal organ should be, like an appendix.

"After my dad died, it was rough," says Tom finally. "I felt as if there was a dark cloud over me. I couldn't outrun it. It hung there."

"Mine feels like a veil." I say it without thinking, and when he nods in understanding, I get braver. "You said you needed to talk to someone. When did you start?"

"Well, I didn't, not for a long time," he admits. "It wasn't good."

We laugh, but it's not funny.

"I talked to Lisa," he says. "Maybe you can talk to your mom."

"I tried. She doesn't get it."

"Neither did Lisa, not at first."

I look down, my voice catching. "What if you can't? What if it's too hard and no one listens and you don't even know *how* to talk about it?"

He wrinkles his nose. "Sucks, huh? Like you're trying hard to be heard and the other person just doesn't get it. Like it didn't matter. So what was the point of opening your mouth."

I nod, thankful he put it into words for me.

"Lisa told me I needed to cheer up and do stuff I enjoyed." Tom fiddles with his camera strap. "I barely had enough in the tank to get to work and not rip someone's head off. If I could have laid in bed and stared at a wall for days, I probably would have."

I'm focusing on my shoes. "Did she ever believe you?"

"She did but I had to tell her outright. The problem was, I'd been hoping she would magically get it, or know how to drag it out of me, because I didn't know how to do it myself. When she didn't, that made me more upset, so it was a nasty cycle. Once she understood, she felt terrible for not being supportive. She insisted I talk to a professional."

"Did you?"

Tom kicks at the gravel. "Eventually."

We laugh again, and he looks at me. "Whatever you're going through is tough, plus sixteen is a hard age," he says. "I know because I was sixteen once. Like your mom was. We probably had much worse hair than your generation, though."

I've seen the pictures from Mom's photo album, and this is true. "You think I should talk to her? Try again?"

"Don't you? She might not understand all of it, but she loves you. She can get you help, if that's what you need. The only thing is she might need to be told straight in clear words, without hints or beating around the bush, the same way I had to talk to Lisa."

I guess I should, but . . . "Shouldn't she know? She's my mother."

He winces. "Don't tell her I said this, because it's probably against some parenthood code, but your mother is also a person. Being an adult doesn't mean problems go away, unfortunately. It also doesn't mean we get better at dealing with them."

"Tom?" Lisa's voice comes from the other side of the shrub. "Tom, we're leaving!"

We jump up and Tom gives me a quick one-armed hug but says nothing to Lisa as we come out of the garden. She waves cheerfully at me as she hands her husband a cold bottle of water. "There you are, Ivy. I told your mom I'd grab you. Should we all get one more fortune before we go?"

I say no thanks, and they head off, hand in hand, toward the boxes to shake out a stick with the fortune number.

I'm thinking about what Tom said, but there's no chance to talk to Mom before getting onto the bus. I want to get my thoughts in order anyway, because although what he said makes sense, I'm still upset about Mount Fuji. I don't know if I *want* to talk to her after that.

I don't know if I trust her enough.

I stare at the passing traffic. It's not only what happened yesterday. Tom said it was a nasty cycle. I think of all the times I tried to talk to Mom. I was scared because I didn't know what to say, and I didn't want to disappoint her, or add to her burden. But she didn't want to hear it either.

Mom once told me when she was growing up, she was told to decline a gift three times before accepting. It's like we both stopped at the first offer. I said no to talking, and she took back the gift of hearing me.

Tom made me realize I need to push through, but so does she. How do I tell her that?

Matteo sits beside me, and that pulse thrums through me again. I wish I could put my head on his shoulder and rest instead of thinking about this.

"Should we do one last sing-along?" asks Paulette as she comes on board.

"No," says most of the bus in unison.

She pouts, muttering to Gretchen, who, for the first time, looks done with her. The bus goes down some side streets and then more side streets until we get to the hotel. Kimiko stands at the front and bows.

"This is our last moment together," she says. "I hope you enjoyed our tour of some of the many highlights of Japan. There is much more to see in this beautiful country, so please come back and visit us again."

She goes through what she calls housekeeping—some people will be leaving tomorrow and taking the bus, while others will be staying another day and getting to the airport by themselves.

"When are you going?" Matteo whispers.

"Tomorrow, you?"

"Same."

There's a commotion when we get off as people grab their bags, make final plans, and thank the driver and Kimiko as they hand over tips with various degrees of comfort. Mom gives Kimiko a big hug and the box of fancy chocolates she picked up before we take our bags to our room. It's plain, but Mom nods with approval.

"We won't be here much anyway," she says. "There's a lot to do before we go." Mom looks at me carefully. "Do you need a break?"

"I'm good." It's like we've both decided to be on good behavior for our last day, so as to not mess it up. Maybe I can talk to her today. I feel almost sick at the thought of it.

Mom checks her phone. "Some of the others are going to Shimokitazawa, the vintage shopping district. Want to do that, then we can go to the huge stationery store in Ginza and some other spots?"

I nod, and she turns off the lights before we go down to the lobby to collect Keith, Matteo, and Yvonne.

We take the metro to Shimokitazawa and poke around narrow streets lined with the best vintage shops I've seen. Matteo takes photos of almost everything he passes. There are bomber jackets and 1980s sequined jumpsuits, blouses and shoes. Mom picks up a purse patterned with cherries and buys it for me without asking. She rarely apologizes with words, but she'll make cookies, or cut me fruit, or do my laundry instead. This could be a peace offering, and I politely tell her I love it.

I follow Matteo up a narrow flight of steps to a room filled with old kimono that have been turned into modern clothes. A fan swings lazily in the corner, giving us short bursts of coolish but not cool air. "I wish we had places like this at home," he says.

"Me too." Here's my chance to ask if he wants to hang out back in Toronto, but I feel shy about it. What if he says no? Also, why hasn't he asked me? He held my hand. That definitely felt like the start to something instead of the end.

Mom's voice comes from the stairs, right before she and Yvonne come in.

We split up about an hour later, with Yvonne, Matteo, and Keith heading to another temple while Mom and I go to Harajuku. We step into a street that's a heaving mass of people taking photos of their elaborate ice cream drinks and going into shops. We soon find ourselves in a mall that's like nothing I've seen, filled with pop-ups selling a mix of gothic Lolita milkmaid dominatrix clothes. Mom stares with wide eyes.

"Obviously I'm never going to dress like that these days," she says, waving toward an outfit that looks like a frothy pink prom dress as envisioned by a vampire. "However, this was my dream outfit when I was your age."

I can't picture it. "Really?"

"For years, much to your pohpoh's dismay. I was wearing a tulle crinoline when I met your dad," she says. "I paired it with a secondhand bubble cardigan that smelled like mothballs."

"Dad liked it?" Dad is great, but not what you'd call fashion forward.

Mom picks up a jacket covered in zippers. "When we met, your dad was wearing a vest with a pocket watch and used combat boots. I thought he was so interesting."

I'd heard the story. "You had a boyfriend."

She made a face. "John was a dud. When I met your dad, we laughed all night."

"Then you dumped John."

"The next day, and it felt like a weight was off my shoulders." She sighs and pulls out a tartan jacket. "I always felt like I had to be perfect around John. Your dad let me be me."

I'm listening so close my ears hurt. "Then why are you getting a divorce?" My heart has finally caught up to my brain in recognizing it for what it is. It's a divorce. Not a break.

Mom puts the jacket back and pulls out another one, this one of lace. "Your father is a good man," she says slowly. "We love you very much."

"I know."

"The problem is I wanted him to be the man I met, the one who had fun and didn't care if I dropped clothes on the ground. The one who said yes when I suggested we take the night bus to New York, stay the day, and come back the next night."

She's speaking to me like I imagine she talks with her friends, and while it's uncomfortable, it's like she's treating me like an adult. Do I like it? That's another amigurumi, the feeling of not being sure you want something once you get it.

"He changed?" I ask.

"We changed," she corrects me. "Because we met over twenty years ago, and that's what happens. Perhaps if we'd allowed each other to grow and let ourselves love the new person, then things would be different. The problem was we couldn't get past what we'd had, and we couldn't appreciate who we'd become. We stopped seeing each other as we are now, a mix of that past person and a new one."

This is it. This is my opportunity. She's talking about how people change. I can tell her I've changed, but not for the better, and I need help.

"Why didn't you go see someone?" I ask, putting it off a bit longer. "To talk, someone who could help?"

She snorts. "Like a therapist? We saw a counselor, and it was useless. A total waste of time and money."

Well, there goes any thought of asking her if I can see one. Better change the topic. "Is that why you like Keith? He appreciates the you that you are now?"

She shrugs. "It was nice to laugh again. I haven't in a while." She checks the time. "We should go if we want to hit the stationery store."

We head to Itoya and stock up on paper goods and stamps, but pass on the ten-thousand-dollar pen on display. It's calm between us, but the rest of the day yields no more confidences from Mom. That's fine. I have a lot on my mind already.

Chapter 24

We have dinner as a group for the last time at an izakaya Kimiko recommended. It's hot and loud and fun, with people yelling across the room and cheers rising every few minutes. Tom and Lisa tell us they saw Paulette and Gretchen eating at a chain sushi place near the hotel.

"Poor Gretchen looked so upset. I have no idea why she puts up with that behavior, even if they are childhood friends." Lisa waves at Joanne and Susan as they come in, loaded down with shopping bags. "What did you get?"

The two women show us the souvenirs they'd bought for everyone from grandchildren to the pro at the golf course (a Hello Kitty golf tee) and photos of them in kimono they took at a special studio. I'm sitting across from Matteo, which is the perfect way to get my fill of looking at him as we eat plate after plate of snacks. His face is flushed in the heat, which has made his hair curlier. He sees me and smiles, the dimple on the left peeking out, as he pushes the nori fries over to me and refills my water.

The night ends early, and we go back to the hotel in a

group. Matteo lingers to walk with me and pulls something out of his bag.

"Here," he says.

It's a stuffed Eevee, and I run my hand over the soft fur. "Did you get this from a claw machine?"

"We passed a place, and I couldn't resist trying to get you one."

I want to hug him right here in the street. "Thank you."

He hands me a Bulbasaur and a Pikachu. "I had a few misses," he admits.

I'm still smiling when he comes close enough that our arms brush, making my skin feel alive. I want him closer, though, with his arm tight around me like he never wants to let me go, or holding my hand and raising it to press against his lips like an old-school prince. I want to tug him down for a kiss that would feel so perfectly right because it's him and it's me and it's us.

I want an *us*.

"I wish we could wander around at night," he says.

I shake off my daydream. "Me too. Did you end up at Shibuya Crossing?" He'd texted earlier about maybe going.

He shakes his head. "No time. I guess that's like the Glico man in Osaka, another reason to come back."

Then that's it. Everyone says goodbye in a happy but tired group and that we'll see each other tomorrow for the plane. Paulette reminds everyone to be on time, while staring at me and Mom. She gets roundly ignored, which starts her grumbling, and I celebrate never having to see her again. Her poor grandchildren. She bought them "My grandma went to Tokyo and all I got was this lousy T-shirt" shirts as gifts, which she showed us proudly. I always thought those were a joke, not actual products you could buy. Or would buy, for that matter.

Matteo waves to me, but Gary has caught him to talk about football again. His suffering expression is the last thing I see as the elevator doors close on us. It's all very anticlimatic. I follow Mom up to our room, hands shoved in my pockets. It's the last night. I want to do something memorable.

Mom makes minor conversation about packing and what time we need to get up, and it's mostly brisk and polite. Not a great end to the trip here either, but it is what it is. Apart from the moment when we were shopping in Harajuku, today we mostly existed near each other rather than enjoying each other's company.

Soon, she's dead to the world, helped along by some extra strong melatonin and the beer at dinner. I take a big breath, feeling the atmosphere lift a bit in the room. I try to read a book, then get up and twitch aside the curtain to look out the window. I've brought over my amigurumi whale kit, and although the hook is shorter than is comfortable for my hand, I manage to get a good magic ring. My fingers work on their own, muscle memory taking over, but after a few rows, it's not looking like how I want. I put it down, my new Eevee looking at me with its big dark eyes.

The faint glow of Tokyo reaches where I am in the hotel and I sigh. I'm tired of being suffocated by this veil. I don't want to be like this anymore.

Grabbing my phone, I text Matteo. Are you asleep?

The reply comes so fast he must have already been looking at his phone.

If I was, I wouldn't be texting back.

Funny.

Dad's asleep but I'm drawing.

Are you tired?

No, why?

I have a suggestion, and you should feel free to say no.

Your last suggestion was that we fake date to keep our parents apart.

My cheeks go warm. Why did he bring that up now? I decide to keep it light. Yeah, and look how good that turned out! I'm a genius.

He sends a GIF of a laughing otter.

What's the idea?

Mom's asleep but I want to see Shibuya.

There's a pause.

You want to sneak out?

Sneak sounds sneaky but yeah.

You're not going to tell her?

No.

Okay, I'm in.

We decide to meet in the lobby. This makes me feel alive, and the adrenaline drives back the remnants of that gray veil until I can barely sense it. Mom will be furious if she discovers I've gone out, and I don't care. It's not like she was there for me when I needed her anyway.

I'm only kind of a terrible daughter, so I leave a note saying where I'm going and I have my phone. That's fair. I've stayed out later at home, and it's not like she'd be thrilled if I woke her up. She hates that, because she can never get back to sleep. I'm doing her a favor, if you think about it.

I grab my shoes, then open the door to our hotel room with excruciating slowness. Keeping the handle turned down, I close it to let the lock click gently in place. After a breathless moment waiting outside to see if I woke Mom up, I put on my shoes and run down to the lobby. I feel exhilarated, like my feet are flying over the floor, and I don't know if it's because I'm about to see Matteo or because I feel light and free for the first time in ages.

Matteo is waiting, and he gives me a wicked smile when I show up. We push open the lobby doors and head out. The streets around the hotel are crowded, and I obsessively check the faces of everyone we pass while keeping my own down in case any Adventure Group people are doing some last-minute exploration.

We turn the corner and are waiting at the light when Matteo grabs my hand and shorts out my brain. "You okay?" he asks.

"Only worried someone might see us." Mom will be upset if she finds out. On the other hand, my goal is for that to never happen. Even if she does, she's already not happy with me, so what does it matter if she's more unhappy?

"Hey," he says. "Remember, we can turn back anytime." He squeezes my hand, and it's like he squishes my heart at the same time.

"True." I squeeze back, and he smiles. "I want to explore, though."

We get turned around within minutes, and after a brief disagreement about which way the map is telling us to go, we get on the right track and hop on the Ginza line. It's a long trip to Shibuya, because it's basically on the other side of the city, but the time goes by quickly. Although it's late on a weekday, the subway is busy with tourists and tired workers in rumpled business clothes holding bags and laptop cases.

The second we arrive, I decide it's worth it. Leaving the subway through one of its thousand exits, we plunge into the confusion. There's something about being alone with Matteo in a foreign city with the lights gleaming around us that makes me feel alive. People are eating street food. The crossing is surrounded by brightly lit billboards and stores, and the crowds and cars and smells combine into an experience that hits every one of my senses.

"Did you bring your sketchpad?" I ask.

Matteo looks around with an almost hungry expression, like he's trying to absorb each second. "No. I want to remember this, you know? I want to remember the feeling it gives me."

We stand and wait for the signal to change, and cross the huge intersection, stopping in the middle, like almost every other tourist and none of the poor Tokyoites. We take some selfies before running the rest of the way, laughing as we get to the other side.

"Should we do it again?" he asks.

"Of course."

We end up crossing twice more, going back and forth from different angles until we end up near a small alley that leads to a neighborhood near the subway, with more gachapon shops, restaurants, and stores.

"Hey, congratulations," I say. "We did it."

"Did what?"

"Kept Mom and Keith apart."

"They might stay in touch when we get home," he points out. "We should delete their numbers from their phones."

"I'm not worried," I say. "If anything was going to happen, it was going to be a vacation thing. When we arrive in Toronto, it will be back to real life."

"I get that." He pauses. "You think they'll get back together? Your parents?"

I shake my head, and it feels official.

"I'm sorry." He makes a face.

"I'm not going to think about it tonight. Are you hungry?" A group of people wait at a stand with red lanterns as the vendor turns frying balls in a pan with his chopsticks. The steam rises from the counter as he hands over containers of takoyaki with toothpicks.

"I'm not hungry, but I want to eat," he says.

"Me too. What should we try?"

We spend a few minutes wandering around to look at what's available. There's a lot of seafood, and tons of deep fry that makes my mouth water until I see a Cremia stand.

The night is warm, and ice cream is the only way to go.

Cones in hand, we search for a place to sit.

"There!" Matteo spies a small bench, and we run over before someone grabs it, tumbling down beside each other. I can barely concentrate because Matteo is tucked in so close we're touching. I can't tell if it's because he wants to, or if he has to because the bench is small. I don't care either way. Here in Shibuya, the lights play in his eyes and I get lost for a second.

"Ivy?" He's looking at me quizzically. "You okay?"

If I keep sitting here, I'm going to lean in and kiss him, and I don't know what that will do to the night. I nod and turn away with my ice cream.

When we're done, we go up an escalator that brings us to a hall overlooking the crossing. People flow in and out, waves moving around those who stop for photos or to dance in the middle of the street.

Matteo lays his hand on the rail by the window. "I love that the world exists with all these people going about their business. Like, when I get back I'll be volunteering for the rest of the summer, but someone will be standing here watching the crowds."

I look at the lights reflecting on the people. I've never been to Times Square, but I imagine this is what it's like. "Some of them could end up standing here thinking the same thing about us."

"They could."

I like how Matteo listens, and sometimes when I speak, he asks more questions, as if he really wants to understand. It would be nice to have a boyfriend like Matteo. I want to see him again after this, but he still hasn't said anything. Maybe if I hint a bit.

"Then we go back to Toronto, and nothing changes," I say. "We're the same people but with some cool stories and souvenirs."

"We could go back with more," he says.

"Like what?"

He thinks. "Let's make a promise to each other. Something we're each going to do so we can be different. A big thing."

I chicken out from saying we could be different together. "Like dying my hair red?"

"Bigger."

"What do you have in mind?"

Matteo points at me. "I'm going to finish my graphic novel. The one I sent in to that contest."

"That's a good one," I say.

He looks out over Shibuya. "I'm also going to talk to Dad about cross-country."

This is a bit surprising. "What do you mean?"

"I've been thinking about it a lot. I do love running, and I want to start again. I only quit to get Dad off my case." He sighs. "And to piss him off."

"How are you going to do that?"

"I'm going to tell him I'm trying out for the team, but he's not allowed to give feedback. That's my coach's job, not his."

"Will he listen?"

Matteo shrugs. "I won't know until I talk to him, but it will be worth it."

I give him a hug, and it feels good when he returns it. "That's an amazing idea."

"I hope so." He takes a breath. "And I'm going to tell him to stop comparing me to Dom."

I blink. "Wow."

He rubs his nose. "I don't think it's going to be a fun discussion."

"But probably necessary."

"I wish it wasn't, but I've let Dad's feelings run my life for long enough. How about you?"

"Me?"

"You."

I think of the amigurumi I put aside on the windowsill. "I'm going to start working on my amigurumi again. Or try to."

"Trying is good." He leans on the rail. "Anything else?"

Matteo is going to do a big thing, talking to his dad. It makes me feel brave. "I haven't felt right for a long time," I say. "I tried to tell Mom, or sort of tried. I have to make her listen. Both her and Dad."

He puts his arm around me. "Are you scared?"

"Yeah. You?"

"God, yes. I also don't want to live like this anymore."

"Me neither."

"You know what else I want?" Matteo is looking at me intently, and I feel my face going red.

"What?"

"Karaoke." He gives me a challenging look. "You in?"

Chapter 25

What was I expecting? Well, him to kiss me, but he's close and smiling, and it makes me happy instead of feeling disappointed. I'm having fun, which is so incredible I feel nothing will bring me down in this moment. I want it to last forever.

The spirit of this amigurumi would be bright orange and shaped like an explosion.

"Bring it on," I say.

He points to a sign behind us. "Do you think they have English songs? My Japanese repertoire is slim."

"Oh, your *repertoire,* Monsieur Fancy Words. My dad was into some song about Mr. Roboto."

"I don't think that's Japanese."

We debate this as we take the escalator down and walk through the brightly lit streets to the karaoke place, easily identified, thanks to the huge singing cat on the sign. The narrow staircase is lined with LED rainbow lights and has a painting of a cat on each step. Pompoms hang from the ceiling, with inflatable cats ready to pounce. Matteo looks from the walls—painted with cartoon cats—to the closed door ahead of us, which is, you guessed it, painted with a cat.

"I'm sensing a theme," he says.

"Is it cats?"

"It's totally cats."

We open the door and stand there. In front of us is an empty corridor, which is pink and white with more painted cats and neon lights. Twelve closed doors line the walls.

"What do we do?" Matteo whispers.

"Try a room?" I twist a knob tentatively, but it's locked. "Are there instructions?"

Matteo trains his phone on a poster to translate it. "We need to buy a special keycard from the machine here to get access to one of the karaoke rooms. It looks like it's not staffed."

It takes a few tries, but we pool our money—luckily it takes yen as well as credit cards—and a small pink card falls out of the slot, printed with a cat holding a number three.

I lead the way down the hall and we tap the door for entry. The first thing we see is a cat on the wall, pointing to a camera with a speech bubble. This time I take out my translator app. "It says the rooms are monitored," I report, shielding my eyes from the spotlight trained on the disco ball. The room has two white leather love seats, a hot pink zebra rug and zebra stripes on the walls. Paulette would love it.

Matteo is already flipping through song options. "Do you know 'Plastic Love'?"

"No."

"How are you with the discography of Kenshi Yonezu?"

"Not great."

"How about . . ."

"Probably not."

He makes a face. "'My Heart Will Go On'?"

Mom loves that song. "Queen Celine? Amazing."

We jab at some buttons on the remote before a synth version of the song starts to blare through. It has a backing track, and I grab the mic and belt out the song, although I am the worst singer.

I don't care. Matteo is laughing—not at me, but like he's enjoying me having a good time. I screech my way to the end, hamming it up a bit to make him laugh harder, not to cover my insecurities. Then I pass the mic to him.

He's chosen another powerhouse, Adele's "Rolling in the Deep," and does shockingly well. "You can sing?" I ask. I'm kind of starry-eyed at how good he is.

"My mother used to sing in choirs and took me when I was a kid," he says. "Dom's better."

"That doesn't matter," I say. "You're amazing."

He stares at the screen for a moment, then looks at me and smiles. "Thanks."

Despite our concerns, there are tons of English songs, although many are at least twenty years old and are only familiar once we hear the track. We start one of the Japanese songs and pull up the phonetic lyrics to give it a shot.

We're not that bad, and it's fun to sing together.

After a while, we put some coins into the drink machine and pull out two bottles of Pocari Sweat, which is the only drink they have. I guess you need to replenish your electrolytes after some intense karaoke. Then our half hour is up.

"When do you think the last train is?" Matteo asks.

I check and then check again. "Umm, ten minutes, and if we don't get it, we've got an expensive cab ride or three-hour walk across the city."

He grabs my hand. "Let's go!"

We sprint out of the karaoke place and down the steps, yelling at each other to go faster. This time we don't linger at the crossing, but run through (on the diagonal, always fun) and dash into the station. The crowds haven't gone down at all while we've been out. If anything, they've gotten bigger, and Matteo keeps me close as we weave through. Should I say anything about all this hand-holding? What would I say? I could ask if he wants to hang out when we're back in Toronto. It's only—I mentally count—eleven words. The worst he can do is say no. Actually, the worst would be that he recoils in horror and runs away, leaving me alone in the city. No, worse worst would be if he does that but has my phone in his pocket. Or worster worst would be all of that but then he runs into the arms of Addison, who has magically transported to the other side of the world to mess with me again.

Although she did me a favor by helping to cure me of Connor. I probably owe her one.

We come into a small clearing in the crowd as we reach the train, and I take a deep breath, trying to get the courage to ask. Not only ask, but ask in the right tone of voice that says it's not a big deal in case any of those aforementioned scenarios occur. A crowded platform is not the best place, but I'm in my own head and need to get this out.

"Do you want to see each other when we get back home?" That was twelve words. Not sure which one I added.

Matteo's eyes skate over me, and I feel myself shrinking before I decide he probably didn't hear me. He's looking straight ahead as if trying to find a gap in the crowd we can go through. I lose my nerve and decide one attempt was enough. The idea of him rejecting me is too much.

"There." Matteo points with his unoccupied hand and tugs me forward. "Ready?"

"Ready."

We fall into the crowd and maneuver our way through until we jump on the train. It's the last one, and we high-five. He's acting the same. I'm sure it was because he didn't hear me.

However, he hasn't mentioned anything about hanging out when we get back home, either.

The train ride back is too crowded to talk, and when we get to Asakusa, it's almost one in the morning. The station area is busy, but thins out as we leave the main streets. There are enough people that I don't feel worried or unsafe, and we make it back with no problems.

"How should we do this?" Matteo asks as we turn into the street with our hotel after a brief fight about whether to go left or right. We've gone on stealth mode, scanning for tour group operatives as we approach the doors. This seems like the riskiest part of the whole adventure.

"Why are you whispering?" I ask. We examine the lobby through the door to make sure no one's out for a late drink or a walk.

"I don't know. I feel I should."

"Okay. Do you want to go in together or separate?"

"Ah, fuck it." He shrugs. "Let's go. No one knows we're not supposed to be out."

Although I can almost see Mom waiting impatiently in the lobby, the fact I have no messages on my phone means she's asleep. Still, it's hard not to get freaked out, and I scuttle past the lobby seating to wait breathlessly by the elevators. Matteo catches up to me.

"Safe," he says, touching the elevator door like he's playing a game of tag as I punch the Up button. The doors open, and thank God the light is a flattering dim sepia instead of those harsh fluorescents that make everyone look dead. Matteo looks at me so intently it's like he's going to kiss me. Please let him kiss me.

He smiles and tucks a bit of hair behind my ear. "I had a great time, Ivy. That was the best night of my life."

He did the *hair tuck*. He definitely has to kiss me, doesn't he?

The elevator dings at my floor and the doors open. No kiss.

"Well, good night," I say as I step out.

To my surprise, Matteo comes out with me. "Let me make sure you get to your door," he says. "It's pretty late."

"Then who's going to make sure you get to yours?"

"We can't keep going back and forth. How about I'll text you when I get in."

"Fair."

He doesn't kiss me at my door either and in fact stays a few steps away, which leaves me deflated. "I'll text," he says.

I watch as Matteo goes to the elevator and until he gets back on. He gives me a small wave and disappears.

That's it.

I stand at the door, feeling my pulse hammer through my body. I'm disappointed because he didn't kiss me or say he wanted to be with me. But I didn't, either.

I think about all those times I tried to talk to Mom and gave up. I don't want to keep doing that. I didn't have the guts to ask if he wants to hang out back home again, and to make sure I got an answer, but I can fix that. I feel everything I want to be, the new Ivy who was just starting to emerge, is right here and now. This is the real turning point, not whatever I thought I wanted from Connor. I take my hand off the door handle and dash for the elevator before I lose my nerve.

When the doors open, Matteo is standing right there.

"What are you doing here?" I blurt out.

The doors start to close, and he bangs the button to keep it open. I reach in and tug him out. "I didn't feel like going in yet," he says.

"Me neither."

His smile is enough to make me think I've got nothing to worry about, but I freeze when a door clicks down the hall. We run around to an alcove, trying not to laugh but failing. The more we try, the harder it gets.

Then, when I'm not expecting it, he kisses me.

It's only quick at first, as if he's gauging my reaction, and I shut up. Immediately. I can feel how wide my eyes are, and my smile is almost hurting my cheeks. His hands reach for mine—I love how he does that—and he leans in again.

And look. I'm not going to compare kisses, but what happens with Matteo is so much better than with anyone else that I can't believe it. His hand moves to the small of my back, and I bring my arms up around his neck. I don't feel as if I have to monitor my every movement, like I'm being rated or judged. It's him and me and the kiss I've been thinking about.

"Ivy," he says. Then he laughs. "I've wanted to do that for ages."

"Me too."

He leans me back against the wall, one hand beside my head, before he kisses my nose, then my lips again, before burying his face in my neck to kiss me there, too. When he kisses my ear, my whole body shivers.

"Matteo?"

He's so close he speaks against my lips. "Yes?"

"What's the first thing we should do when we get back to Toronto?" I ask, turning my head so I can press against the corner of his mouth. It's exciting to think we can do anything we want, and all the things we can do together. He closes his eyes when my lips touch his skin.

He doesn't answer.

"Matteo?"

"Uh, yeah." He tries to kiss me again, but my senses shift from being alert in a good way to a bad one. Is this like Connor all over?

"What's the first thing we should do when we get back?" I repeat.

"When we get back?" He frowns. "I can't, Ivy. I told you I was volunteering, right? It's at a camp up north, so I won't be around."

What? It's like he's punched me in the gut, and all I can think of is that text from Connor. *Sure, if I don't have anything else going on*. I'm good enough to make out with, but not to hang out with. I step away, and he reaches for me.

"Come back, Ivy."

"Don't you want to see me in Toronto?"

"Sure, sure," he says. "We can figure it out later."

I think about Connor's messy bed, and the way I'd felt when I got Addison's text. How it was always me waiting for him. I thought Matteo was *different*, but why would he be when I'm the same old Ivy? Too messy to deal with once I let me be me. Figures. It *figures*. Everything comes crashing down, and I step farther back. I thought this was going to be my new beginning, and it's only more of the same. I can't stand it.

"What's going on?" he asks.

"I get it."

"Get what?"

"You don't want to hang out." I won't let him treat me the way Connor did. "Fine. I don't want to hang out with you either." Why is my mouth saying this stuff? It's like my feelings are coming out before my brain can stop them, but my head is a whirlpool of anger and shame. All I want to do is protect myself from more hurt.

"Ivy." Matteo drops his hands, his eyes going wide. "I never said I don't want to see you."

"Really? You said you were too busy."

"Because I'm volunteering! It has nothing to do with you. And I never said *too* busy."

I can barely hold back my tears, but there's no way I'm going to let him see me cry. Not after I told him all that stuff about me. Stupid, stupid Ivy. This is why I should have kept my mouth shut. I thought that kiss was special. I thought I could finally talk to someone and be myself. Now he's using *volunteering* as an excuse. He's not even trying.

Then suddenly, the red anger disappears. All the ups and downs and further downs that have been yanking me around for this whole trip, and longer—it all goes away. I feel almost cold. Numb. Like I'm watching it all unfold but it's not happening to me and I'm only an onlooker, not a participant. My mouth opens and words come out. "Look, it's vacation. We had fun. I get it."

"What's going on with you?" He shakes his head. "This is so not cool."

"You know what's not cool? Your dad was right. You are a quitter."

I know I've gone way too far, but I'm unable to walk it back, even if I wanted to.

He runs his hand over his face. "God. I can't believe this. You are seriously messed up, Ivy."

He's right. I am. He couldn't have said anything more calculated to bring back the anger, but before I can reply, he turns around and leaves, not even waiting for the elevator. He takes the stairs.

Exhaustion hits me, and I nearly stagger back. I want to chase after him and yell all sorts of mean things that will have him feeling the same way I do. I want everyone to feel like this so I'm not alone in it anymore.

I can't, though, because the hall is empty. Going back to the room, I close the door quickly before the light comes in the room to disturb Mom. The last thing I need is for her to wake up and catch me.

She's asleep, snoring gently into her pillow. Safe, I take out my phone and block Matteo. I have nothing to say to him.

It only takes seconds to kick off my shoes and jump into the bathroom with my pajamas. If Mom wakes up now, I have a reasonable excuse.

I don't even care if she does, though. I rub my chest, the muscles so tense I can barely move my arms. Across the room I see the stuffed Eevee looking at me from the window, and I go over and toss it in the trash.

Chapter 26

Day It's All Over

After your chance at love gets demolished (again), get ready for an international flight with the boy who totally broke your heart! Don't forget to add in the potential of emotionally crushing meetings in one of the many last-minute souvenir boutiques at Narita Airport.

I only feel a little guilty the next morning when Mom asks how I slept and I tell her fine. She doesn't suspect a thing about me sneaking out with Matteo, and somehow this makes me feel worse. Not enough to tell her the truth, though.

I lie in bed, going over what happened last night for the thousandth time, as Mom fusses with her last-minute packing and swears at her bag.

I'm still mad.

In a way, it's nice to be mad. I roll this around in my mind for a bit, a small marble of condensed flame that lights up the memory of our fight and everything he said. He was going to be too busy. We could talk about it later. I was messed up. The last was true, and because it was, it lit the flame brighter.

I need to keep being mad at Matteo, because lurking underneath is a horrible sick feeling that maybe I didn't handle things as well as I could have.

"Oh, Ivy, your stuffed animal fell in the garbage." Mom glances over to see me staring at nothing. "You look like you're thinking hard," she says. "Want to share?"

I sit up in bed. "Does growing up mean you're better able to deal with things?"

"Like, you gain resilience?" She considers this. "I think so," she says finally.

"Why?"

"Because as you age, you have more experience to draw on. A situation might be new, but often the feelings it creates are not."

"I have no idea what that means."

She puts the Eevee in my bag, beside the other two stuffed animals I forgot to throw away, and sits beside me on the bed. "Here's an example. This stuff with your father is something I've never done before."

"Okay?"

"Yet the feelings that come with it are ones I've experienced with other breakups and changes. It's not the same, but the DNA is similar. That helps me cope."

"Are you saying you get numb to having the same feelings?"

"Not numb," she says. "It's familiar, which helps with acceptance. I know each day will get a bit better." She gives me a hug. "We've had a rough couple of days, but I'm here to talk, if you want, Ivy-mine."

Like that's going to happen. I get out of bed. I don't want to think about feelings and coping. I want to . . . I don't know what I want. Something. Nothing.

We drag our luggage downstairs, Mom worrying her bag is overweight, thanks to the amount of stuff she bought. Everyone is in the lobby waiting for the airport bus, and I immediately look for Matteo so I can be where he isn't. My heart lurches when I see him look away. So that's how he wants to play it, like he's the victim.

"Well, don't you look well rested after your adventures," calls Paulette over the crowd. She's looking straight at me, but I glance over my shoulder to confirm it's me she's addressing.

It is, because then she turns to Matteo. "You lovebirds, wandering off at night. I can't believe your parents agreed to it, but who am I to say? All this modern parenting is beyond me."

Mom watches with a baffled frown as Keith looks between Paulette, me, and Matteo. Matteo is frozen in place, but I can tell he's trying to figure out the best thing to say. Deny? Ignore? Tell her for once to keep her nose in her own business where it belongs? Everyone watches uncomfortably, except for Tom, who is fiddling with his camera and doesn't seem to notice. I don't know what to do either. Of course I should have known we'd get caught. What was I thinking? The anger shatters into fear. I'm going to be in so much trouble.

It's Mom who breaks the silence. "If you have something to say, Paulette, you should say it."

"Well, Gretchen here told me when she was out last night after we'd all gone to bed, who did she see walking along but these two?" She points at us. "Young love. So sweet."

She's speaking in a honeyed tone that doesn't fool me. I can tell how much she enjoys being the center of attention. I want to say all sorts of terrible things to make her feel the way I know she loves making me feel right now. Small and scared and regretful.

Gretchen's shocked gasp rises over the crowd. "Paulette! I told you that in private and said I would mention it to Lillian and Keith myself. What are you doing?"

"Oh, you're too softhearted," scoffed Paulette. "I knew you wouldn't. What else do you think those two were getting up to this whole trip? And probably in the back of the bus when none of us were looking."

My jaw drops, and Mom blows out her breath as she steps in front of me. Before she can speak, Hank's deep voice booms out from the back of the crowd, and this time, to the group's collective shock, he says more than a word. "Paulette, you are a disgusting woman with a nasty mind to be thinking about two children like that. What is the matter with you?"

If I wasn't icy with horror, I'd cheer.

Paulette's face goes purple as she scans the crowd before landing on Mom. Mom shakes her head. "I'm so grateful I will never have to see you again," she says in a quiet voice that is more serious than if she'd yelled. "I've had enough of you trying to sow discord, you unhappy, insecure piece of work."

Keith speaks up. "Keep your sick thoughts about my son to yourself."

Paulette sticks her chin out. "If this is the response for looking out for you, that's fine. At least I can rest easy knowing I did the right thing. Gretchen, let's go. The bus is here."

Gretchen shakes her head, slowly but deliberately. "I can't believe you," she says. "Sixty-six years old and still a bully. I don't know how I ever thought otherwise. I can't believe I wasted this trip dealing with you. I've had enough. This is the last time I let you pull something like this, Paulette. The last time."

"Gretchen!" Paulette sounds like she's scolding, and Gretchen must hear it as well because she simply gets on the bus without answering.

Paulette stares after her, then defiantly pushes her way through as people turn away. It's like a mass alert has gone out, and all the adults are acting with a polite distance that stops short of acknowledging her. It's a bit eerie.

Mom stands beside me, her mouth working as she stares into the distance. I avoid Matteo's eye. Obviously, we're going to get in trouble.

Keith turns to Mom. "I'll deal with Matteo," he says. "Boys will be boys, huh, Lill?" He seems to be taking it as a big joke, which I can tell Mom doesn't appreciate.

They get on board and Mom doesn't look at me. "Get on the bus," she says in a low voice. "I'll talk with you when we're alone."

I know better than to think this means she's okay with what happened. I do as she says, and Tom gives me a sympathetic grimace as I pass. Mom takes the seat behind me, so I sit alone with my thoughts. There's silence apart from one moment when Paulette starts to complain about the flight time.

"Paulette," says Gretchen. She's sitting nearby and raises her voice to be heard.

"What?"

"For once, shut your mouth."

"Well, I never thought—"

"I said *shut it, you stupid cow.*"

Paulette subsides into an angry kind of muttering designed to show she can't be told what to do, and everyone ignores her. When we get to the terminal, people scatter. I follow Mom without paying attention, not even caring when they confiscate my amigurumi at security, shaking their heads at the hook, like somehow it's more dangerous than the pen they left in my bag.

Mom waits until we get through security to pull me aside to an empty sitting area near the boutiques. I'm already feeling battered, and my head pounds as I try to keep back tears.

"I'm not angry with you," she says. "Well, I am, but what hurts most is how you broke my trust. I didn't think I had to tell you things like don't sneak out at night when I'm asleep. I trusted you."

Mom's right, but I don't care. She can be right about this and wrong about everything else. A couple of weeks ago, Mom telling me I broke her trust would have devastated me. Now all I can think about is that she broke a bigger trust with me. She's my mother. She's supposed to help me, not make things worse. The fact that she's acting like this is all on me makes everything boil over. Sure, I snuck out, but how about the way she's been acting this whole trip? Longer, even.

"So I'm never allowed to do anything on my own? I'm basically an adult!" I don't know why I picked this to fight about when there's so much more going on, but it's enough to get me started. Tom is right. Sometimes the first words are the hardest, but these could open the door to everything I want to say.

"Sneaking out is what a child does. Not an adult."

"This is so unfair." I glare at her. "As if you act like an adult."

"What are you talking about?"

"Who do you think has to keep things organized with Dad gone? Not you, that's for sure. You forget everything. Do you think that's fun for me? You never even turn off the fucking lights in the room, and you know it drives me nuts."

"That's hardly fair or true." She's loud enough that a family glances in our direction. "Watch your language and stop changing the subject. We're talking about your lack of judgment and lying last night, not light switches."

I ignore this, words rising up as if they've finally been released. "It is true and it's stressful and I hate it. I hate doing all that when it's your job. I hate the way you don't think anything through and I'm stuck dealing with the result."

"Ivy!"

But I can't stop. "I know I'm a huge fucking mess, okay? I know you don't want to be with me and I ruined the trip. The second I stopped acting like I was perfect, you got mad. I know you want me to be the good Ivy you're so proud of, but I'm not. I'm sorry that's such a bother for you." My neck is hot and my voice wobbly as it all pours out.

Mom just stares at me, shaking her head. "I have no idea why you're acting like this."

This makes me madder, because she should have noticed. She should have been paying attention. "You would if you ever listened to me! You're selfish! You think just because something works for you, it works for me, and it never does. You know why? Because I'm not you. I'm *not* and I know you hate it but that's too fucking bad. I hate it too. I hate *you*."

Once this cascade is out, she steps back like I've slapped her. I don't care. I've shoved us off the cliff where we were standing and there's no way to go back, and no path to follow. I can barely breathe, like the words dragged the air from my lungs as they rushed out.

Mom turns slightly away, and her hand goes up to her face. When it lowers, there's a slight shine on her knuckles. They're wet. Tears. I made her cry, and she's trying to hide it. The fight drains out of me, and horror and remorse take over. What have I done?

"Go sit down" is all she says. I do, suddenly scared at what's happened, and what will happen next.

She doesn't join me for a few minutes, but when she does, she sits two seats over and doesn't look at me.

I stare at nothing, my muscles knotting enough to make me shake. Matteo and his father aren't at the gate, and I assume they're having their own discussion, if Keith even cared that Matteo snuck out. Yvonne decided to go on to Seoul for a week, so she's not there to keep Mom occupied. Then it's time to board, and Mom hands me my ticket without a word. Tom and Lisa wave as they pass, and I spend a few minutes watching everyone in the hopes of seeing Matteo one last time. I catch a glimpse of him way up at the front.

To say the flight is long is an understatement. Mom falls asleep, or at least shuts her eyes. I've messed up the entire trip, and maybe more.

No surprise, really.

Chapter 27

Hazel sits on my bed, her hand in the chip bowl, where it's been for the last three minutes. I texted her some of what happened, but this is the first time she's hearing the full story.

"Wow," she says when I finish. "You said you hated her?"

I stare at the duvet, littered with crumbs. "Yeah."

"Eomma would have disowned me."

"I think Mom was just sad." The guilt is a lot.

Hazel winces. "Have you talked about it?"

"She's acting like nothing happened, although she won't talk about Japan at all." This isn't like Mom, who likes to relive a vacation for months after. "I'm grounded, though."

"Because of the fight or the sneaking out?"

"Sneaking out."

"What happened with Matteo and his dad when they got home?"

"Don't know. I blocked him."

"Yikes." She finally eats some more Doritos, having turned up her nose at the wasabi-flavored chips. "Poor guy."

I glare at her. "Poor me, you mean."

"Sure, but . . ." She picks up the fan printed with jellyfish I bought her. "Do you think you might have overreacted? A bit?"

"Are you taking his side?" I demand as I squeeze the cover under my hand. Because the feeling I had back in Tokyo, that I might have possibly handled this better, hasn't gone away.

She gives me a look. "Ivy."

"What?" It only comes out as a mumble.

"Ivy."

I groan and throw myself on the pillow so hard my head bounces back up. "I did. I totally messed it up. I don't know what happened to me."

Hazel holds up a chip. "I don't know either. It's not like you to freak out like that, with Matteo or your mom."

I roll over and stare at the ceiling for a while. "What if it is?"

"What, like you usually snap on boys in hotel hallways, then yell at your mom in international airports?"

Her joke lessens my tension, and I toss a pillow at her. "What if I needed to get it all out?"

"Oh, a catharsis? Like when I had three exams in two days and had a meltdown in the stairwell?"

"Yeah, like that."

She nods. "It makes sense, although it seems like yours had way more collateral damage. Do you feel better?"

I think about it. "Yes?" I think some more. "No? Yes and

no. I said a bunch of stuff I've been thinking about for a while, and I needed to say, but . . ." I can't help but remember the tears on the back of Mom's hand, and Matteo's expression. "I could have been less mean. I *should* have been less hurtful." I sigh. "At least I won't have to see Keith again."

"I don't know why you disliked him more than that Paulette woman."

I open my mouth and close it. Hazel knows my parents are separated, but she never knew how desperately I wanted to believe it was only temporary. I felt saying it out loud would jinx it, the same way saying you did well on a test or great in team tryouts curses it to failure. It would doom me to a life of two Christmases, when all I wanted was a single big family one.

This time I'm honest about what I'm thinking. "I thought my parents would get back together," I say. "And Keith was getting in the way."

"Oh." She looks sorry for me.

"That's not going to happen, though. They're over."

I don't have a family anymore. I have families, and I have since Dad packed his things and left, although I refused to accept it. I glance at my desk, where I have the ornament for Mom instead of a snow globe. Even though we're not really talking, I decided it was time for me to start creating my own traditions with each parent.

"That truly sucks, about your folks," Hazel says.

"I know." It does suck. I've been trying to hide it and

pretend it's okay, but it does absolutely suck. I pick up my current amigurumi that's in progress and put in a few stitches with coral yarn. There's nothing more to say about Mom and Dad.

Hazel sprawls over the bed to watch me. "Are you working on more amigurumi?" she asks curiously, spying my yarn piles.

I thought making them would be a good distraction, but since it reminds me of Matteo, it's not quite working out the way I'd hoped. I've stuck with it, though. I remember the promise we made in Shibuya, and I want to keep it.

I hand over the three that passed my quality control. Hazel lets out a slow, low wheeze because she can't whistle. "These are sick," she says, examining the spirit of the urge to write on a blank chalkboard. "What are they?"

I tell her about Billiken and the idea of the feelings behind the amigurumi spirit series. "I was thinking you could write poems for them," I say. "Describing their personalities."

"A collab?" She lies back on the bed and considers it. "That sounds fun. I'm not going to do it, though."

"Why not?" I ask, hurt.

Hazel rolls over and takes some more strawberry Pocky, which she waves at me like a conductor's wand. "Because we were talking about catharsis, and that's what poetry is. You should do it yourself," she says. "In my writing group the other day, someone said poetry is a way to work through what you need to work through."

I grab some Pocky for myself. "Like therapy?" I've been thinking more and more about what it would be like to have someone to talk to regularly.

"Exactly like therapy. You've been through a lot, Ivy, and you try to pretend everything's okay when it's not. Look at this."

A piece of paper comes floating to land beside me. It's the scrap sheet I was using to sketch out my spirits and their areas of expertise, along with some thoughts on what the amigurumi could look like and their color palette. "What am I looking at in particular?" I say.

She leans over and pokes at it. "None of these are happy," she says. "At best they describe a neutral or curious experience. There are no joyful ones. Zero."

"Sure there are." I snatch up the paper and scan through them. "Look, there's the feeling of pulling off your tights at the end of the day."

"That's relief."

"Finding something you thought was lost."

"Also relief. As is sitting down when you're queasy. The closest you get is a cat coming to lie beside you and starting to purr."

I put the paper down. "What are you saying?"

"I'm saying this doesn't scream *I'm a happy person.* I don't want to see you get sad the way you were before."

I blink at her. "I wasn't . . ."

"You were, and you know it." She shrugs, looking down. "I didn't know how to ask you, because you never wanted to talk about it."

"It was hard."

"I know."

Her voice is gentle, and I look away. Hazel noticed. All that time I thought I was alone, she was waiting for me to say something. She was with me, and even knowing this now makes a difference. I take a deep breath. I feel better talking to her, but I need more.

"I'm going to talk to Mom about seeing someone. A therapist." Because the veil is still there. I'm only grateful this mess with Matteo and Mom hasn't kickstarted it back into full darkness.

She looks pleased. "That's a good idea."

"Do you think—" I hesitate, and say it. "What if it doesn't go away?"

"Then it doesn't, and we help you when you need it," she says simply. She gives me a tap on the arm because she hates hugs. "But it'll be easier if you talk to people. Like me. And others."

I nod. "I'll try."

She must understand I feel uncomfortable, because she starts telling me about her upcoming shifts at the taco truck and runs through all the food truck gossip I missed when I was away. Her aunt has a feud with the other taco truck, a Chinese one that makes theirs using fried rice paper and bao. The churro guy and the fancy coffee guy have started doing joint offers, and are also possibly falling in love. The flavored water people gave up on their pumpkin spice drink, which was apparently disgusting.

When she leaves, I do a few more rows on my amigurumi, then toss it aside, feeling restless. I have too many thoughts to focus, mostly about how I screwed things up with Matteo. A text comes.

wyd

What you doing. It's Connor, and all I feel is irritation. I stare at it, debating whether or not to reply before deciding I want some closure for myself.

Sorry, I write. I've got something else going on.

I block him and pick up one of my spirit amigurumi, a vivid purple bulb to symbolize the feeling of doing the right thing. It needs a name.

Bonsat. That's perfect.

It doesn't take me long to lose myself in what I'm doing.

There was an emergency job vacancy at Granite Lake for the rest of August, and my parents agreed to let me work as long as I come home straight after. I don't mind. Addison is away at the overnight wilderness camp her parents send her to each year, and Connor isn't there. Some of my friends from last year are working, and it's fun to hang out.

One of them knows Matteo, and I can't help but casually mention I met him in Japan.

"He's cool," Lenny says. "I was about to fail art—like, how embarrassing is that—but he showed me how to make perspective work. Saved my ass."

"He said he runs cross-country." It's a rush to be able to talk about Matteo.

Lenny rolls their eyes. "Yeah, he's one of the best in the province. Too bad he quit the team after last season. I heard the coach freaked out."

I promised myself not to creep on Matteo on social media, and I've held to that promise. When I get home from Granite Lake one Friday, I think I deserve a treat. My phone is in my hand before I hesitate, wondering what I'll find and what I'm hoping for. I could unblock him and ask if he wants to talk, but what if he's blocked me? I don't think I could deal with that.

I sigh and toss my phone away. It lands on my latest amigurumi, Delly, a yellow canary-like being that is the spirit of looking forward to yummy food. Sometimes I wish Tom was around to talk to about this stuff. I want someone who's not Mom or Dad, but I haven't been able to ask them about getting a professional. That's something for when we're getting along, which definitely has not been the last little while, especially with Dad. Our visits have been tense, because I feel the need to defend Mom from the unspoken accusation she failed somehow. It's hard to escape the fact that while she hadn't always been at her best, Mom had been the one to take off work and bring me to Japan, and Dad had not. Mom at least noticed something was off, although she didn't listen when I tried to tell her how I felt.

I also didn't do very well at explaining.

I pick up the amigurumi and, after examining it, decide to change stitches, humming to myself as I work. Amigurumi is usually done with single crochet and uses a few other stitches for shaping, depending mostly on the design and color to give visual interest. It only occurred to me the other day that I could try different stitches to add texture if I wanted. I could make things the way I liked.

This pleased me, which is as close as I get to happiness lately.

The front door opens, and as usual, into the bowl go the keys, down goes the bag, and off go Mom's shoes. "Ivy?" she calls.

"Here."

She hovers at my door for a second before she sighs and sits down on my bed. "Can we talk?"

"What about?" I don't take my eyes off my amigurumi, but my fingers have gone a little numb.

"What happened at the end of Japan."

"Okay," I whisper. I don't want to talk about this, but I can't avoid it any longer. I know I need to apologize for some of what I said, but deep down, I also think it's the truth.

"First, I talked to your dad, and you're no longer grounded. We think you learned your lesson."

It seems weird to thank her for not punishing me anymore, so I shrug and continue working. I can't look at her because I know what's coming.

She's silent, like she's trying to figure out what to say. "What happened at the airport," she says. "A lot of things were said. Important things."

I drop my hook. When I bend down, I catch sight of one of my amigurumi on the floor, where I left it last night. I haven't named it, but it's the spirit of the words that disappear when you need them. I messed up the proportions, so it's almost jagged instead of the smooth squash shape I imagined. I pick it up, soft and fuzzy in my hand, close my eyes, and let my little amigurumi help me.

"Okay," I say.

"You said I wouldn't be proud of you if you weren't perfect. Where did you get that idea?"

Now I stare at her. "From you? You're always talking about how you never have to worry about me, and how good I am, and how well I do in school. Then the second things started not working for me, you got mad."

"No, I didn't."

Mom's instant denial infuriates me. "On Mount Fuji, when I didn't want to go? You weren't mad then? All the times I was upset and you told me to look on the bright side, or stop being selfish? You never got frustrated when your pep talks didn't work? Seriously?"

Mom's eyes lower until she's staring at her fingers as they pick a thread on my duvet, and when she speaks, it's to the bed, not me. "I didn't mean to make you feel like you couldn't be yourself."

"Well, you did." I don't want to say this, but I have to. I told Matteo I would come back from Japan different, and I'm going to keep my promise. That means being honest. "You shouldn't have left me on the mountain and gone on ahead."

Now she looks up. "Ivy . . ."

"I know you wanted to get to the top, but I was having a hard time. Like, super hard. I needed you to help me, and you left because it was too much for you to deal with. I was too much, just like you said after we called Dad."

There's a long silence. "I should have stayed with you. I'm sorry. I've been thinking about it, too. It was wrong of me to leave you like that, and I feel terrible." Mom sighs. "I just . . . there's no excuse, actually. I was being selfish and stubborn. And you're not too much, ever. I love how you are. I would never change you. I shouldn't have said so."

That's good to hear, and something releases in my chest. But this is only the start of what I need to say. I look at the amigurumi. "I said it didn't matter, but I didn't like it when you wanted to hang out with Yvonne and Keith instead of me. You said this was a trip for us, and you spent your time trying to get away from me."

She shakes her head. "It was to give you space. I didn't think you wanted to be with your mom all the time."

"Yeah, but things like meander days are supposed to be for us. They always have been, and you invited Yvonne. With Dad gone . . ." I shrug. "It's like, I don't know."

"It felt like everything we did as a family was disappearing?" she asks.

I nod. "Especially with you and Keith getting together."

"What?" Mom looks shocked. "Never. I haven't talked to him since we got home. Keith was someone to spend time with, like Yvonne. Nothing more." Mom shakes her head. "I should have been more sensitive about what you were feeling. I'm sorry."

I shrug again, not knowing what to say. Apologies are kind of bizarre, because the feelings still linger. The worst is knowing it's my turn now, and the hurt I caused won't immediately disappear either. An apology isn't an eraser.

"I'm sorry for what I said at the airport when we left." I can't look up because I feel ashamed, and instead focus on the kintsugi bowl from Nara I put on my desk. "I don't hate you."

"I know, sweetie. You were right. I was used to your father picking up my slack, and I didn't realize I was doing the same to you." She sighs. "I've been trying to improve."

I think back and realize that's true. Mom has been stepping up, with timers and lists and a new, huge whiteboard on the wall where she has a calendar and makes notes for herself. I saw it, but didn't register it was her making an effort.

Mom looks at me closely. "Ivy, what do you mean you were having a hard time?"

It's time for the big, big stuff.

"It's been hard for ages, and you never listen."

"I listen."

"No, you don't," I say, my voice louder. "You decide what's bothering me and tell me instead of listening. You say I don't get enough sleep or it's stress or whatever you decide. You tell me I need to cheer up, like that's something I can just do. I can't."

"Every time I ask, you say you're tired."

"I am, but that's not the right word."

"Then what is?"

"I don't know, okay?" I sigh. "I don't feel the way I used to before all this happened. You and Dad, and everything."

"It is a lot," she says. "I'm not surprised you're having trouble."

"It's more than that."

"Like what?" She doesn't sound angry this time, but kind of desperate. "You need to describe it for me."

"I can't," I say. "I need help to find the words." I force out the next sentence. "I want to talk to someone."

Her head whips in my direction. "A therapist."

I shrug, then nod. "I know you think it's weak." This is where she won't listen. Again. I wait for her to tell me it's part of being a teenager and I'll grow out of it. To hang in there, and why don't I go for a walk or have a shower or do one of a dozen things that won't help me solve the problem.

"I don't think it's weak," she protests.

"I heard you talk to Yvonne about it, and then you said you and Dad tried and it was a waste."

She sighs. "I was probably applying my own experience to you. I shouldn't have."

I don't say anything.

Mom frowns as she chews her lip. "These feelings you've been having. Being tired. Not feeling like yourself. They've been going on for a while?"

I nod, not looking at her.

"On Mount Fuji, was it very bad?"

I nod again.

There's a long, long silence. Then she says, "Ivy, do you think you're depressed?"

The word hangs between us. "Depressed?" I echo. It sounds strange when I say it out loud.

"Not only depressed," she says softly. "That you have depression."

"I don't know." I stare at the amigurumi. "Maybe."

I wait for her to tell me it's all in my head, but her arms wrap around me. "Ivy-mine. Yes, yes, of course. I'm so sorry, sweetie. I didn't realize how bad it was."

I wait for Mom to start in on how this is all her fault or

she should have known, something that would mean I need to reassure her. She doesn't. All she says is, "It was wrong of me to leave you, even if I didn't understand. I'm sorry. I should have listened to you, really listened. I'm sorry for that, too. I'll find you someone. I'll talk to your dad. We'll get you help. You can trust me."

Then she stays holding me. I don't cry, but I feel a bit of warmth return as I bury my face in her shoulder, her quick breath ruffling my hair, and the misshapen amigurumi clutched in my hand.

Chapter 28

School starts, and my classes aren't too hard. I've started working on my amigurumi on the ride from school to the apartment, which makes those extra two hundred minutes a week feel less wasted.

I talked to my therapist about how nice it was to enjoy crafting again. I've also started to keep in some of my stitching errors, instead of ripping it all out and starting over to make it perfect, and asked if that was wabi-sabi. She's biracial like me, but white and Japanese, and she had some good insight.

"A lot of the time we use concepts like that to guide how we should approach the world," she said. "It sounds like embracing imperfection is something that's helping you."

Talking to her is a release. I was lucky Mom found someone almost right away, so I've seen her a few times already. She's helped me find more words for some of the feelings I've been struggling with, which is good. She's also suggested medication. Mom and Dad agreed, but I've only been taking it for three weeks. Not long enough to make a difference, but knowing things might improve helps a lot.

Today, I get home to find Mom already there. She's shifted her schedule to reduce her commute as well and now works from home two days a week.

I can tell from her face she's about to lose it, though, because she's staring between her phone and her laptop, looking like she wants to toss both out of the window. "What's up?" I ask.

"I'm trying to upload my photos from Japan to the album site Tom set up," she says, waving her phone around. "It's impossible. I've tried everything."

As the one to set up the router in the apartment when we moved, and to show her how to change the brightness settings on her phone, I find it hard to believe she's tried everything. "Want me to do it?"

"Yes." She vacates the seat and goes to cut up some apples as I sit down.

"Do you want all the Japan photos up, or just a few?" I ask.

"I put hearts next to the ones I want to share." She puts the apples next to me and kisses my head. "Thanks, sweetie."

I don't mind. I haven't looked through my own photos since I got home, not wanting to see Matteo and remind myself of how I screwed up. But Mom's are different. I double-check to make sure there are no embarrassing ones of me, then upload them. The whole process takes less than ten minutes.

Almost everyone has put up at least a few photos, even Paulette, although they're all of herself. Tom has. Joanne has. Yvonne. Keith.

Matteo hasn't.

I've been thinking a lot about how things ended in Tokyo. I went over what happened with my therapist—it was one of the first things I wanted to talk about—and it led to a discussion on how sometimes things aren't our fault, but they are our responsibility.

"Your feelings were overwhelming, and you acted out," she said. "But they had an impact and consequences."

I still have Matteo blocked, but it's not up to him to reach out to me anyway. I was the one who screwed up. I need to fix it.

The thing is, I'm not entirely sure how. I still don't have the courage to contact him, not without knowing I wouldn't be at least a bit welcome.

In front of me on Mom's screen is a summary of the two weeks that changed my life. Monkeys, and gardens, and mountains, and someone sleeping on the bus. I open my phone to look at my own photos.

Mixed in with the ones I took are the photos Matteo sent me. The whole conversation we had without speaking, sharing our days from the first photo I sent of the Fushimi Inari Shrine, to the final temple Matteo saw in Tokyo. I smile as I go through them, remembering how I felt when each arrived. Maybe these were good memories for him, too. Good enough that he'd be willing to hear me out.

I hesitate, and upload all the ones I sent him.

Then I add one more, of a finished amigurumi. It's blue with long tentacle arms, and I hope he recognizes it.

It's hard for me not to check the album for a response every few minutes, but I do before I go to bed. No change. No new photos.

There's nothing the next day, either.

Or the next.

Every time I see there are no uploads from Matteo, I lose a bit of hope. Luckily, my amigurumi are there to keep me occupied.

A few days later, I'm waiting for Hazel to finish cross-country practice after school. She joined the team with her crush, Petra, a girl who transferred from a school in Manitoba. I ended up doing micro-amigurumi good luck charms for the two of them, and eventually the whole team. It's fun.

Hazel comes up to the picnic table I'm sitting at as I'm packing my yarn away. It's the last practice before their meet on the weekend, and she sits down and nudges me. "What's that one?"

I twist the amigurumi I was about to put away around in my fingers. "Abazus. Spirit of the satisfaction of cracking a bit of new ice with the heel of your boot."

"Nice. I like the silvery color." She leans over. "I have news for you."

"What?"

"Remember the girl in my acting class who saw my amigurumi charm and wanted one?"

"I made her a squirrel." I was only doing real animals in the micros. The spirit feelings series were about the size of my hand.

"So, turns out a guy in her math class saw it on her pencil case."

"Does he want one too? What animal?" They're fun to make, so I don't mind.

"It's Matteo."

My heart thumps, and I stare at her. "What?"

Hazel nods. "He wanted to know where she got it."

"Did she tell him?" My heart is banging so hard I can barely get the words out.

"She told him she got it from a friend of a friend." She pauses. "She said he seemed really interested."

"In a good way or bad way?" I can't believe I have to drag this out of her.

"Good, because he offered to buy it from her."

"Are you serious about this right now? Like *serious* serious? No joke?"

"I am, and he's going to be at the cross-country meet tomorrow. By the way, Ms. Delaine says we need volunteers."

I'm not listening anymore, because I'm too busy looking at the photo album, where there's something I hadn't noticed before.

A heart on my amigurumi picture. Someone has liked it. I hadn't noticed because I was focused on looking for new photos.

"I need to sign up." I jump to my feet, my entire body buzzing and causing my hands to shake. "Where's Ms. Delaine?"

"Gone home." She holds up a hand. "Which is why I forged your signature and signed you up before she left."

"You did what?"

Hazel shrugs. "You were going to support me anyway, weren't you?" She stands up and dusts off the back of her coat. "Also, come on, Ivy. Give me some credit. You want to see him."

She's right. "I do."

She sighs and pretends to smooth her hair back. "I know."

I can't sleep that night. At four in the morning, I give up and begin sorting through my amigurumi looking for the perfect one before deciding none will do. I'm still crocheting as we meet at the school to get on the bus at seven. The team and volunteers stand around, our breath puffing out in the crisp fall air and my fingers freezing as I work.

"What's that?" asks Hazel curiously as I cram in stuffing.

I don't tell her. It's a secret for Matteo.

My anxiety grows as we travel to the conservation area where the race is taking place. I'd debated unblocking and texting him last night before deciding I wanted to see him in person. The second we arrive in the parking lot, I start searching for Matteo. There must be hundreds of people milling around in sporty-looking clothes, and rows of school buses. Music and cheers fill the lot as people do warm-ups or drink from thermoses and pin labels with their number onto their jerseys. A woman with a megaphone keeps calling out race times and instructions. The wind has picked up and brought in the clouds.

I can't see Matteo, or anyone from his school at all.

"Ivy!" It's Ms. Delaine, looking calm and warm, bundled up in a winter coat and high boots. "You're on cheering duty near the finish. Energize our team to get over that line!"

She sends me off to find the marker for the last hundred meters and tells me good luck, like I'm the one racing. Hazel is doing warm-ups, and I blow kisses to her and Petra before I hurry off.

It's cold standing there on the edges, and I end up cheering for each person as they run by because they all deserve a bit of encouragement after doing six kilometers on a Saturday. Also, it's getting frosty, and the cheering warms me up. There's a lull that tells me it's between races. I shift my weight back and forth, cold from standing but ready to do my job. To my astonishment, I'm having a good time. Despite the worry about seeing Matteo—which is more like hopeful anticipation, honestly—I feel good. I stretch out my arms toward the sun and feel it on my face.

My therapist told me to watch for these moments, which she calls glimmers. The small blips that make me feel I'm where I should be, doing what I want to do.

Then two boys come bursting out of the trees in a dead sprint. Neither of them are from my school, but I begin cheering anyway, because they're going fast. They get closer.

One of them is dressed in Roseton Collegiate's burgundy and has a shock of dark hair and a familiar profile. It's Matteo.

I stop mid-clap, my hands held apart and my mouth open. He glances over and then stares, his step faltering.

"Go, go!" I yell at him, suddenly realizing that maybe this was a bad idea. If Matteo loses because of me, then I've really blown it. But he shakes his head, smiles, and suddenly zooms by the other guy.

I don't wait, but run toward the finish line, which Matteo reaches way before I do, despite him running, and winning, an entire race and me only going about sixty meters.

He's getting congratulated by a bunch of people. Then I blink, because Keith is there too, clapping for Matteo and wrapping him in a big hug before passing him over to a guy who's an older version of Matteo and a younger version of Keith. This must be Dom. I've missed something in the last couple months, I see, but it makes me glad that they've made up and Matteo is getting the support from his dad he deserves. Keith looks over and sees me.

To my relief, he gives me a thumbs-up and a big smile.

I wait on the sidelines until Matteo looks around. When he turns in my direction, I wave, and he jogs my way. Where he gets the energy, I have no idea, but I run to meet him. His hair is a bit longer, and his face is red from running, but he looks as incredible as I remember.

Then we're face-to-face, staring at each other. "You're on the cross-country team," I say, as if this is a normal way to start a conversation for people who had a huge fight then didn't talk for two months. The thing is, it's always been easy to talk to Matteo.

"I did what we promised." He nods to Keith. "I talked to Dad, too. It's better."

"I'm glad." I take a breath. "I talked to Mom."

"Good."

"I'm doing my amigurumi again, too."

Matteo kicks at the ground. "I saw. A girl in my class has one." He grinned. "They're kind of collectibles at my school. She wouldn't sell it to me."

"I can make you as many as you want." I hesitate. "You went on the online photo album."

He laughed. "Dad didn't know how to add more photos, so I did it for him. At first, I couldn't figure out why they were so familiar and then I realized what you'd done." He hesitates and gives me a quick look before looking away. "I thought maybe you wanted to talk."

"I do." I reach in my pocket and grab the amigurumi I

made for him. "This is Novit." I swallow hard. "I made it for you." Novit is yellow with all sorts of arms, as if reaching out for opportunities. Matteo reads the bio I tied onto its foot with matching yarn.

Novit of the Second Chances:
Appears when someone is very
sorry for what they said and
hopes they can be forgiven. When
someone promises to do better.

"I really screwed up," I say softly. "I'm sorry. I hope you can forgive me, but I was so mean and rude I understand if you don't. I needed to apologize, no matter what. You didn't deserve to be treated like that."

"I don't get what happened," he says. "We were doing so well and then you just sort of changed."

"It's . . ." I make a face. "I thought you were rejecting me."

"After I kissed you."

"Yeah. After that."

He nods. "Okay. Why?"

"Because you hesitated when I asked what we should do together when we got back home, and then you didn't seem like you wanted to hang out."

He frowns. "All I said was that I'd be busy volunteering for a bit. Because I was going to be *out of town*."

I wince. "I know, but that's not what I heard. It was

like Connor again, someone who didn't want to be with me. I was already kind of a mess from a bunch of other stuff, and I freaked out. I was out of line, totally and completely."

"Ivy."

"What?"

"I hesitated because I was so excited at all the things we could do. I was making a list of them in my head and trying to figure out if I could come back on weekends to see you."

"Oh." I blink. "Wow, did I blow *that*."

"I tried to text you, but you blocked me."

"I'm sorry."

"Then the Paulette stuff happened."

Here we both roll our eyes. Paulette.

"I wanted to text you as well," I admit. "When I got home. But I was scared you'd be mad at me. I deserved it."

"How did you figure this out?" Matteo asks. "It's a lot."

"I talked about it with my therapist."

He looks at me, his brown eyes almost hazel in the light. "You got one?"

"I did what we promised. I talked to Mom. I'm not great, but I'm learning to manage it better." I shrug. "I'm not perfect, though. I think that's okay."

Matteo leans in, his face intense. "It's definitely okay. I don't need perfection, but I also don't want to be guessing what will set you off and having to tiptoe around you."

"I'm starting to recognize when I need to chill out," I say. "I have a code word with Mom that says I need space but it has nothing to do with her. I can do that with you too. If you want to."

The wind kicks up, and he peels off his long-sleeved shirt and wraps it around me. The cold makes my face flush, which is good because I can feel it about to go up in flames as I wait for Matteo to answer.

"I want to," he says. "I accept your apology. Thank you. I missed hanging out with you." Matteo's hair is blowing; it's gotten longer, and I want to run my fingers through it. He takes my hands in his. "Yonge-Dundas has a scramble crossing, which is basically like Shibuya, except tiny and not as cool," he says. "And I know a great ramen place nearby. If you want to hang out."

I feel like dancing, I'm so light. "I want to. Then can we do karaoke?"

"Absolutely karaoke." With every word, his face has come nearer to mine. I move in to close the tiny space between us so I can kiss him the way I want, my arms tight around him and so close I can feel his heart. Mine is about to float away from me.

"How about we go on a hunt to find that amazing soft bread? The sweet kind?" I ask. "We can get onigiri."

"Where?"

"I don't know. We'll find it."

He kisses me again. "I love the amigurumi."

"I'll make you more."

He grins and tucks my hair back. The hair tuck, *again*. I love it. "Can you do one for the feeling of being happy it all worked out?"

I nod, then kiss him until we're breathless. I know exactly how to do that amigurumi for Matteo. It's going to look like a heart, lit by the golden sun of an autumn morning.

And I'll do a matching one for me.

Acknowledgments

The idea for Ivy came to me on a plane to Tokyo, where I spent the next two weeks exploring Japan, and jotting down details about everything Ivy could have done. However, it's a long road from the Notes app to an actual book, and many people helped along the way.

Thank you to my agent, Carrie Pestritto, who encouraged me to step into the world of young adult romance after I sent her my idea.

A huge thanks to Jennifer Ung, my editor at Quill Tree Books/HarperCollins, whose insights strengthened every aspect of this book.

I owe a big debt to my friend and writer Farah Heron, who read over an early draft and provided very welcome feedback.

And to Nyla and Elliott, my favorite travel companions.

